TALES OF WITCHES AND WYVERNS COPY

S RAMSEY

Contents

AFFLALON

PROLOGUE: BURIED SECRETS

Nine Years Ago

SHE AWOKE WITH HEART pounding, not sure where she was. The old nightmare had returned. In it, her mother was as still as death.

Enid rubbed at the tears streaming down her cheeks. Her body relaxed when she saw the sun had finally risen. She rose and crossed to her window to view the garden. *Who are all those people?* Something uncomfortable fluttered in her stomach, and she thought, *Where is Dadi?*

After throwing on some clothes, she left to investigate. Enid stepped out of her house to a chaotic scene.

She found her father standing out front with hands on his hips and a face etched with worry. Rowland Davies' scruffy outfit of an old sweatshirt and jeans was spattered with droplets of mud as he inspected the fallen remains of a once mighty yew, brought down in the previous night's raging storm.

The Blaney brothers stood nearby, their faces grim, while a strange car sat parked near the curb.

Enid's eyes widened as she took in the sight before her - the roots of the centuries-old yew had been ripped from the ground, leaving a gaping hole that led deep into the earth. A shiver ran down Enid's spine as she half-remembered her dreams.

An unfamiliar man and a boy about her age stood beside her father. The boy had curly hair and amber eyes that seemed to be filled with fear and anticipation at the same time. She caught herself wondering what he would look like if he smiled. *I wonder if we can be friends*, she thought, but reluctantly dismissed it. The boy glanced up at her, and for a moment their gazes locked.

The small crowd gathered around the gaping pit in the ground, huddled together in a half-moon shape. Her father's rough hand squeezed hers in affection as he spoke with a tall gentleman dressed in a natty vest. Without interrupting the conversation, her father scooped Enid up in his powerful arms, giving her a quick hug.

"This is my daughter, Enid Davies. Enid, this is Mr. Nigel Roberts and his son, Dylan. They have moved from London into the old manor house and are our new neighbors." The boy stood still behind his dad's legs, watching but not speaking.

Just then, the elder Blaney, Owen, shouted from the hole. "There is something strange here at the opening!" Everyone crowded around to see what caught his attention.

Mr. Davies—wearing his work boots—jumped down into the crevice and disappeared for a few moments. Dirt scattered everywhere as he and the Blaney brothers frantically dug through the earth. Her father finally climbed out. In his arms, he carried an old wooden box.

Enid's father laid the chest on a musty horse blanket and brushed debris from his shirt as he sat back to survey it. The seals were unbroken and had the appearance of coiled snakes. Her father removed his wire-rimmed glasses and polished them against a shirttail before placing them back on his nose. Reaching for a set of tools retrieved from their garden shed, he crouched over the lock and manipulated it.

The onlookers hushed as the seals gave way with a gentle creak. The lid opened. Jasper Blaney, eager for any photo opportunity, took out his cell phone and captured each moment with a series of clicks. Enid and Dylan wriggled through the ring of spectators until they could see inside the box. The children scrunched up their faces at the sight of cups, some dirty old coins, and an unremarkable plate rotting away to nothingness. *What was so special about that?*

At the bottom of the chest, something caught Enid's father's eye - a leather-wrapped object, which he pulled free and opened to reveal a stunning silver ring with an unusual stone flashing like the Northern Lights in the winter sky. *Finally, there was something worth all this fuss.*

THE FOLLOWING DAY WAS Monday, and Enid headed back to school. She made it to the bus stop early and was trying to stay hidden until it arrived. She climbed a nearby pine tree to wait. She got the idea from one of her dad's many stories about ancient Celtic battle tactics.

She was tired of being picked on for being different. Her mother, Lillian, was murdered three years prior. The neighboring families had kept their distance ever since, and the other children decided Lillian Davies must have been a witch, making Enid an easy target.

Enid's current strategy was working so far. She arrived long before the other kids, and no one had spotted her yet. *This might be the solution.*

But then Tommy Brighton, her chief antagonist, glanced up and his gaze met hers. His eyes widened with recognition and surprise at finding her in such a precarious situation. "Guys," he called out, pointing his finger at her before adding, "It's the witch's brat."

Every drop of saliva went dry in her mouth as those kids collected stones. When they started tossing them, relief rushed through her when the first few flew far off their mark. However, the reprieve was short-lived.

Each throw became more accurate, and sharp stings ran down Enid's arms in response. With increasing dread, the size of their projectiles had grown too - now stings became more like punishing punches with every strike.

To her dismay, the new kid, Dylan, arrived in time to witness it all. *Will he join them?*

Her head snapped up when Dylan said something extraordinary. "Hey, stop throwing stuff at her."

"Oh, you're the new kid. Haven't you heard? Her mom was a witch, and her family is cursed," Tommy said.

A wave of heat burned her cheeks at those words.

"Don't be daft. And if you don't stop, I'll make sure you're the one who is cursed." Dylan's eyes narrowed.

"Go away, new kid. This is none of your business." Tommy gestured wildly with his hands full of pebbles and made to throw another projectile.

Dylan shoved Tommy away from the tree. The bully fell hard and skidded across the wet grass. One of Tommy's friends swung at Dylan, but he still knocked the rocks out of the other kid's hands.

An unfamiliar buoyancy traveled through Enid's veins, filling her with a bubbling hope she hadn't experienced since her mother's death.

Chapter 1

REFLECTIONS

Present Day

THE BRIGHT AUGUST SUN burned overhead, nine years after the infamous bus stop incident. Dylan Roberts arrived early at the Davies' cottage. Now that school was out for the summer, he and his best friend, Enid Davies, were taking full advantage of the fine weather.

"It would be a great day for a picnic, don't you think?" Dylan asked. As Enid absently nodded her agreement, a rumbling sound emanated from Dylan's stomach. After a moment of silence, both teens burst into laughter.

"It's as if your folks don't feed you, but we both know that's *not* true." Enid's eyes twinkled as she teased him. Dylan had changed from the shy boy who got his nose bloodied defending her from the neighborhood bullies.

Dylan had shot up and filled out with muscle since then. *He is attractive,* Enid decided.

"My mom claimed that since the school's been on break that we never have any milk," Dylan said, while getting a glass from the cupboard.

Dylan was almost a year older than Enid, but that didn't affect their friendship. Since that long ago day at the bus stop, Enid's world had permanently altered by making a friend. They walked to catch the bus together and were almost inseparable.

Enid laughed at Dylan's comment. He then asked, "Is your dad going prospecting this afternoon?"

"Yes, I believe that was his plan. Discovering one Celtic treasure hoard should be enough for a lifetime, but I guess he's an over-achiever." Enid shook her head, recalling that long-ago day. From then on, her father, an amateur archeologist, was like a man possessed.

"Just think, if those moldy old riches hadn't been found, we might never have met," Dylan said and then frowned a little, as if he found that thought upsetting.

"Oh, I'm not so sure about that. We are neighbors after all, and you would've shown up here to raid our fridge if nothing else." Enid's giggle brought Dylan's grin back, as intended.

She preferred for her friend to smile. He deserved to smile more, after all the heartache he'd experienced. Dylan was the adopted son of the Roberts, who doted on him. Both of his birth parents perished in a motorcar accident when he was four, but he had somehow miraculously survived.

Enid empathized with Dylan's situation, as she had no clear memories of her mother, killed when she was just a toddler. She had only vague recollections and became acquainted through photos and the many stories her dad would share.

They bonded over their misfortunes and the infamous bus stop incident. Dylan was very protective of Enid.

"You mean I can raid your fridge like a pirate?" her friend asked in a hopeful tone.

"I haven't forgotten about your weird pirate obsession," Enid said and laughed again.

"So, you keep saying, Davies—constantly," Dylan said while rolling his eyes. He leaned towards Enid to muss up her hair. She swatted him away half-heartedly.

Enid's father entering the kitchen interrupted their banter. "If you two plan to hike, don't stray too far, and be sure to stay together. I've heard reports of an enormous animal spotted in the woods. I'd hate to see either of you get hurt, since the authorities aren't sure what it is."

"Yes, Mr. Davies. My dad gave me the same warning before I left the house. I'll make sure Enid stays safe." Dylan always seemed a little intimidated by Enid's father.

"Hey. I can take care of myself." Enid protested.

"Both of you, just watch out for each other." Mr. Davies said and headed off in search of lost relics.

"You be careful too," Enid called after her dad.

"I'm bored," Enid said, turning back to her friend. "Let's spend the day exploring like we used to. Should we wait on Zoe?" Zoe Floyd was the third member of their group, who became friends shortly after Dylan's arrival.

Enid had been more than happy to share a lunch period with not one but two friends. Zoe had befriended Dylan over shared crayons and someday planned to become a scientist. Enid adored her. In school, the trio often hung out together at lunch and during free periods.

"Yup. She should get here soon," Dylan said, glancing at his cell phone.

Enid placed warm apple tarts, still steaming in their wax paper wraps, into the well-worn wicker basket. Her eyes met Dylan's, and they shared a smile at the memories of all the summer days that had been spent exploring the countryside together. Zoe still hadn't arrived, but Enid knew she would get there soon enough.

As they waited, Enid couldn't help but reminisce about their childhood adventures. They used to spend hours exploring every inch of the woods, chasing butterflies, and catching frogs in the nearby pond. But things had changed since then. They were older now and their explorations had become more mature, riskier. Enid couldn't help but wonder what kind of adventure awaited them today.

Just as she was lost in thought, a car pulled up outside her house and Zoe hopped out, pulling her bike down from the bike rack. She waved at Enid and Dylan as she hurried towards them. "Sorry I'm late!" she called out.

Enid grinned and greeted her with a hug. "No worries," Enid said. "Are you ready for some exploring?"

"Absolutely!" Zoe said, grinning from ear to ear.

With that, the trio set off towards the lake near the manor — it was one of their favorite places to relax and enjoy some swim-ming. As they went, Enid felt a surge of excitement knowing they would spend one last day together. The sun was high in the sky and the birds chirped all around them as they walked. Enid felt a wave of nostalgia wash over her. It seemed like only yesterday they were chasing each other through these same woods.

But something was different today. As they biked deeper into the woods, Enid could feel a sense of unease growing within her. She thought about how everything would be so different once Dylan left for London. In the back of her mind was always the fear of becoming an outsider again, but Enid willed herself not to dwell too much on it as she pedaled faster to keep up.

When they arrived at the lake, they left their bikes on the grass and walked to the water's edge to skip rocks. The surface of the lake appeared calm today, a deep blue. The only ripples were from the friends' stones.

Soon, they sprawled on a checked horse blanket, munching on apple tarts.

"Do you think things will change between us when you're at school?" Enid asked Dylan as she stared up at the sky.

"Of course not," Dylan said. "Why would they?"

"Everything is changing so fast, and I'm not sure I like it," Enid said with a slight frown.

Dylan fell quiet for a moment before he spoke. "Nothing will change for us, Enid," he said. "You, me, and Zoe will always be friends."

Enid smiled at Dylan, and her fears receded a little.

"Maybe you could study for your A-levels a little closer to home? Can't you tell your parents that you want to stay?" Zoe said, because she did not want Dylan to leave either.

"I think it's probably too late to change plans now," he said, frowning.

"You'll be so far away. You won't be able to visit often." Enid blinked to stop the tears from forming.

"You know my dad has always planned that I attend his old school," Dylan reminded them both.

"Do you want to go?" Zoe asked. "Did your dad even ask what you wanted?"

"I can't disappoint him. He and Mom have done so much for me. I'm sure I'll learn to like it, but I will miss you guys a lot," Dylan said.

Enid sighed because she didn't want Dylan to leave, but she could do nothing about it. Enid would miss Dylan but decided not to make it any worse. "I guess you're right, but don't forget about us, okay?"

"How could I forget my best friends?" Dylan asked. Both girls laughed.

The trio got ready for their swim. Zoe had her usual bikini with a bright floral print, and Enid suddenly felt a bit self-conscious in her one-piece tangerine swimming suit. Dylan wore just swim trunks and had a deep tan from days spent in the sun.

Enid remembered Zoe had once confessed to her she had a crush on Dylan. "Dylan is so cute and funny. I think he could be the most popular boy in school if he tried. But I like that he is not obsessed with all that."

Enid agreed Dylan was crush-worthy, but she never confessed it to Zoe. Enid didn't want anyone to guess her feelings, especially Dylan. She realized he thought of her just as a friend and nothing else. Enid never viewed herself as interesting or smart as Zoe. Dylan already knew all Enid's secrets, except how she felt about him. *Would Dylan consider dating Zoe?* If that happened, Enid would have to be happy for them, no matter how her heart ached. Enid shrugged off her worries, and the three of them raced to the lake, laughing.

Zoe and Dylan jumped into the cool water right away, but Enid hesitated a bit. She sensed eyes on her. Enid was still so painfully aware of how she looked compared to her friends. She slowly waded in until the water was waist high before submerging herself to her shoulders.

The cool water was refreshing against Enid's skin. The friends splashed around for a bit before Zoe challenged Dylan to a race. Enid didn't bother to compete with the two best swimmers in school, so she busied herself diving to look for any fish.

Enid dove for a while but had seen nothing. She had decided she might need to dive deeper when she saw it, a glimmer of gold below. It dazzled against the murky pond water and reminded her of a goldfish. *How odd.* She followed the bright color further down below the surface.

Though the lake was shallow, Enid looked back up at the dim sunlight. It made her think about how far away the surface appeared, and her heart raced as a sense of dread crept up in her chest.

Reacting to that instinct, Enid forgot the glimpse of gold and made to swim toward the surface. The weeds at the pond's bottom were too many, and something wrapped itself around her ankle. She struggled to break free. With every second that passed, Enid became a little more powerless.

Her friends' legs were kicking in the water just above her. Zoe and Dylan seemed so far away, and Enid knew they wouldn't be able to help her in time. Her lungs screamed for air as Enid thrashed around, trying to escape the pond's grasp. Her heartbeat thundered in her ears.

She was running out of strength. How was she going to escape? *Think!* She had to focus on freeing herself from the weeds before it was too late. She had no time to lose. Enid reached down and pulled at the weeds with all her might.

Their grip on her did not budge. Enid tried swimming towards the surface again, desperate to free herself from the slimy grasp, but she was held in place near the bottom of the pond.

After what seemed an eternity, Dylan appeared beside Enid, swimming like a fish, and loosened the grip of the weeds around her body. He then pulled her towards the surface.

Enid burst through with a deep gasp of air. Zoe had seen Enid struggling and raced over to help her swim back to shore. Enid accepted their help, and together the trio made it out of the water.

The friends were relieved that Enid was okay. "You had me scared half to death!" Dylan ran a trembling hand through his dripping hair, before giving his friend a suffocating hug.

"What happened to you, Enid?" Zoe asked.

"I saw something in the water," Enid said, still a little winded.

"What?" Dylan asked.

"I'm not sure. It looked like some kind of weird fish... a giant goldfish." Enid shook her head, a little confused, and Dylan's gaze snapped back toward the water's edge.

"Oh, it couldn't have been a goldfish. They would not survive when the lake grew cold and froze over." Zoe said.

"Whatever you were following, you've got to be more careful. You scared me." Dylan said and gave Enid another hug. The friends all fell silent, thinking about how their picnic might have ended in tragedy.

Chapter 2

THE FAIRY HOUND

As THEY DRIED OFF, Enid noted the shore around the lake felt deserted. Even the bird song sounded muted, which was odd given the trees and dense foliage surrounding the place.

Getting bored, the friends hiked around the lake. Dylan scouted ahead, but Enid and Zoe took a more leisurely pace. Several times, Dylan circled and snuck back to give the girls a jump scare. Their mingled laughter rang out in the stillness. Enid, Zoe, and Dylan might have been the only humans left on the planet today.

Enid's trainers kept her footsteps silent as she crept from tree to tree. She tugged on her jeans when they snagged on a blackberry bush. *Where might Dylan and Zoe be hiding now?* It was almost time to leave.

The silence caught Enid's attention again. She glanced around and realized the light under the trees was fading. In the eerie silence, Enid became certain there was something in the trees watching her.

She meant to call out to her friends, but their names froze in her throat when she heard something moving in the bushes, something big, something that made the hairs on her neck stand up.

She stood still under the trees and held her breath. Just then, a cracked twig sounded like a gunshot. Enid's heart skipped a beat as she focused her eyes on the dark shadows where she heard the noise.

She moved as quietly as she dared to take shelter under the pine-scented canopy of a giant tree whose lower branches drooped to the ground and obscured her from view.

Enid hugged the trunk of the ancient conifer, heedless of rough bark. Her head pounded with tension, and she wished she had listened to her dad and stayed closer to home. *Oh, where was Dylan? And where was Zoe?* This was like a scene from one of her nightmares.

Enid's eyes acclimated to the surrounding gloom. She sensed a presence in the forest, and tried to conceal herself more, but with each quiet breath, she imagined she was shouting her position.

In the unnatural stillness, she noted a menacing shape gliding through the trees. The giant figure moved on all fours, fast and deadly, like a wolf. The dark shadow paused near Enid's tree. Enid's pulse thrummed in terror. She hoped her friends had spotted the animal's shadow in the trees. She hoped they had the sense to hide until the potential danger passed.

Another sound came from a snapping twig. The dark shadow got distracted and slid away from Enid's position. Enid held her breath until it moved away.

A vicious snarl snapped the silence. Enid peered through the tree branches and made out the outline of Dylan's bright red, ringer T-shirt, and a flash of Zoe's turquoise top. The loud snapping sound synced in time with her friends' movements as they stepped away from the tree. Enid's gaze widened as the inky silhouette moved closer to her friends. The menacing growl rumbled from the creature's throat.

The creature might kill them because of Enid's reckless insistence on exploring the woods far from the safety of their homes.

What should I do? She was torn and her instincts told her to remain hidden. But what about her friends? Would they get hurt, or worse? Could she just hide?

What would Dylan do if our positions were reversed? Suddenly, she had her answer.

No one had spotted her yet, and she searched for a weapon. Out of the corner of her eye, she located a sturdy tree branch. Enid was unsure how to defend them against a ravenous beast with only a stick, but she had to try.

She stepped out of her hiding place, brandishing the tree branch. The beast had Dylan and Zoe cornered. Its fangs bared. Enid glimpsed the largest, most ferocious wolf hound she had ever seen. The growling canine had a midnight coat, and the only gleam came from the beast's enormous fangs. She swallowed past the sudden dryness in her throat.

"What are you doing? I had this under control." Dylan sounded frantic as she placed herself between them and harm.

"I-It will take all of us to get away." She kept her eye on the hound and tried to make herself appear larger and more menacing, which was difficult being slightly over five feet tall.

Dylan and Zoe scrounged quickly for branches of their own. The teens faced off with the creature pressed shoulder to shoulder. The terrifying beast circled them at a distance and bared his fangs. While the dog snarled, Enid noted the raised body hair and tense posture of the canine.

They shouted and swung their branches at their tormentor, but the beast stayed outside their reach. The hound circled, and it stopped occasionally, and scented the air while growling. The barking became almost continuous, and Enid was certain someone would die. "I can hold him off while you go for help. You both run so much faster than I do," she said.

"I'm not leaving you behind. We're getting out of this together," Zoe said, sounding offended by Enid's suggestion.

"Don't be daft. We aren't leaving you," Dylan echoed.

The teens stopped turning in a circle and stood shoulder to shoulder, facing their adversary with grim faces. The dog continued to scent the air and looked from one to the next as if trying to decide who to eat first.

Enid didn't know where her next impulse came from. It occurred to her that the dog appeared frightened, and she thought back to the many times before friends came into her life when she had run-ins with the neighborhood bullies. Dogs were intelligent animals, and she hoped kindness might work.

Without taking her eyes off the beast, she said, "I'm going to try something. If the dog attacks, get some help. It may be our only chance."

Before the friends realized what Enid planned, she placed her stick on the ground in front of her. She spoke to the beast, "Hi. My name is Enid. Are you lost? We won't hurt you." She gestured between herself and her friends.

The hound stopped snarling and sat staring at them. Enid spoke to it again. "Are you out here all alone? My friends and I could help you if you're in trouble."

The dog lay down on its belly but kept its wary eyes focused on her.

Enid moved forward to be nearer to their tormentor and held out her hand for the dog to sniff. "No, don't." Dylan said. He held his breath, though he remained ready to pounce if the dog made any move to eat her.

The dog inched forward on its belly to meet Enid halfway. Inexplicably, the snarling and growling stopped. Enid imagined a curious expression on the hound's face. The petite teen and the giant dog inched even closer. Enid's hand was within reach. Dylan held his breath. His palms were slick with sweat, and he worried he might drop his only weapon. At that moment, he appeared ready to throw himself between Enid and certain doom.

"You're not as vicious as you would like us to think," Enid spoke with mocking sternness. The hound sniffed her entire hand and then took a quick lick. Both girl and dog eyed each other with suspicion. "Guys, please put down your sticks and slowly come over to make friends."

Dylan was about to object, but then he witnessed Enid reach out to give the big dog a cautious pat on the head. Slowly, he and Zoe laid down their weapons and made their way over to their unpredictable friend. Zoe grinned in relief when the dog allowed pats from her as well. "Do you think he belongs to somebody?" she asked.

"What do you say? Are you lost? Do you belong to somebody?" The dog maneuvered his head to be petted by Enid.

Zoe sensed what that meant. "I think he's trying to tell you he now belongs with you."

"What sort of dog do you think he is?" Enid studied the now friendly hound with a critical eye.

"I'd say he's a fairy hound. He's huge, mean, and he looks like he just escaped from the wild hunt." For once, Dylan beamed because Enid wasn't familiar with the reference.

"A fairy hound? You're not seriously suggesting a fairy king may come to collect him? You know I don't believe in that stuff." Enid's eyes lit with mischief as they patted their new friend.

"This beast might only pretend to be friendly so he can eat you in your sleep." The dog raised his head and huffed as if offended by Dylan's suggestion.

"Ha. Once I take him home, I'll ask him to stay as my new friend—fairy hound or no fairy hound," Enid said.

"What's a proper name for him?" Zoe studied the dog with a critical eye.

"Let's see if he comes home first, but I want to call him Bendith," Enid said. "Do you like it?" She addressed the last remark to the hound, who gave a happy yip in response.

"A blessing, huh? I would have called him Bezerker or Fangs." Laughing with Enid after all that tension was a relief for Dylan. "I guess we'll soon learn if finding him in the haunted forest was good fortune or ill."

When the trio arrived back at the cottage with the enormous hound trailing behind them, Enid's dad greeted them. Enid had never seen her father's face so flushed. "Where have you been? I told you to stay in the woods near the house."

The friends and Enid all spoke at once, either to apologize or to defend her friends. Mr. Davies put up both of his hands. "Kids, I know you would protect Enid, and I know she would do the same for you. But, as parents, we can't help but worry about you. I was ready to call the constable. I thought something awful had happened."

Enid realized with a sudden pang that this situation had reminded her father of the trauma of when her mother died, which was a sobering thought. All her excuses and justifications evaporated when she considered how the day might have ended. "I'm so sorry, *Dadi*."

Her father nodded in understanding and gave her a quick hug. "Now, you two, I suggest you head home. Your parents were just as frantic." With a lingering glance toward Enid and a second apology to Mr. Davies, Dylan and Zoe left.

"Now, Enid, I..." but she never got to hear what he was going to say next, because at that moment her dad spied the hulking beast, who, until then, was trying to look inconspicuous, by hiding behind a chair. "What is *that*?" He asked, gesturing towards the canine.

The hound's size shocked Enid's dad, and Enid quickly stepped in. "Dad, this is Bendith. Bendith, this is my father, who is the most wonderful, kind, understanding, and patient man in all of Wales."

Bendith acted as if he realized he was on probation. He slunk forward, sat down at Enid's feet, and cocked his head to the side with his tongue lolling.

The dog then did an amazing thing and raised his giant paw to be shaken by Mr. Davies, who opened and closed his mouth several times, before finally reaching out to take the giant paw and shake it. "How did you... Where did you... This dog is huge and *must* belong to someone."

"I don't think he belongs to anyone. Can he stay here until we find his people... Please?" Enid held her breath, waiting for his response.

"I don't know, Enid. How can you control a dog of this size? What if he misbehaves? He's the size of a pony."

"I'll take full responsibility. He won't be a nuisance. I swear. He's well-behaved and friendly," Enid said.

"Hmm... I take it that Bendith is the large animal that was reported prowling about?" he asked.

"Most likely, but if not, I'd be so much safer with him around." She winced at this statement, but crossed her fingers and hoped it was true. *If I run into trouble without Dylan, Bendith could protect me.*

In the end, Bendith stayed and became part of the family. Her father worried the dog would be challenging to train, but Bendith proved him wrong on that score. The faithful hound was stuck by Enid's side and almost always shared her many adventures following Dylan's departure.

Chapter 3

A SURPRISE GIFT

DEAR DYLAN,

Hi. Your classes sound amazing, and I wouldn't worry about that quiz. I'm sure you aced it.

Everybody here is fine. Dad is always cooking up a storm, and he's working on writing a paper for that fancy archeologist's journal. And before you ask, yes, he is still treasure hunting on the weekends. He calls it his research (ha, ha).

Bendith is the best thing that ever happened to me (well, second best, besides meeting you and Zoe). It's hard to feel lonely with him stuck to me like glue, though I still miss you (don't worry).

Zoe misses you a lot, too. Lunchtime is not as exciting without you around to give us your expert running commentary on the quality of our cafeteria choices... (sigh!)

I've been having some weird dreams since you've been gone. They have me worried. I hope you are taking good care of yourself and staying safe.

These nightmares are gross. Sometimes they are about finding my mom, but mostly they feature wasting bodies and stuff. In them, I am invisible, but it's like I'm there to be a witness to their suffering. The only person who acknowledges me is someone that looks an awful lot like you. I guess I miss you more than I thought, right?

I mean, it's no surprise you're in my dreams because you are my best friend. I just wish I could have pleasant ones like everybody else, at least occasionally. Don't people usually have a mix of good and bad? Why does mine have to be so terrifying?

It's getting so bad that I wonder if there is something wrong with me.

Anyway, don't worry about that last sentence. I'm fine.

Please write back soon, but not about your test schedule, okay? Give me some juicy details about your new friends and adventures, please? I need some distractions.

Your bestie,

Enid

AS THE CHRISTMAS HOLIDAYS drew near, it came time for Enid's sixteenth birthday, which fell on the Winter Solstice.

Her dad planned a small dinner party the following evening but also wanted to mark the occasion with a memorable present, which intrigued Enid. *What did he have planned?* She was hoping for a new laptop.

The morning dawned chilly but full of sunshine. Dylan was due home from London on the evening train.

Enid sat in her bedroom thinking about their strong connection. Enid still didn't know what to make of it, but she was drawn to Dylan in a way she found hard to explain even after all these years.

The sound of her father's voice calling her downstairs pulled Enid out of her thoughts. She grabbed her coat and went to see what he wanted.

"There you are. I suggest we leave for the village soon. Are you ready?" her father asked.

"Yes, I've got everything," Enid said. "No. Not you, silly," she added to Bendith, who almost always accompanied them into town. The enormous hound yawned in reply, unimpressed.

Enid was dressed in her favorite jeans, a chunky white turtle-neck sweater trimmed in primary colors, and a navy-blue corduroy hooded barn jacket. Soon, they left for town.

They planned to do some Christmas shopping and then lunch at a favorite pub, the White Stag. The conversation on the way into town gave no clues about what Enid's birthday present would be. She couldn't wait.

Celliwig had a population of about ten thousand souls. The town catered to tourists who came to view the local Roman ruins. It had some shops, a couple of restaurants, a theater, and several pubs. Everywhere were signs of the upcoming holidays. Greenery and twinkling lights decorated all the shops. A pine tree stood in the town square dressed in red and gold.

As they got closer to their destination, Enid's father spoke up. "Enid, I wanted to give you something special for your sixteenth birthday. I know your mother would be so proud of you. You are growing up so fast, and I wanted to do something memorable."

Enid couldn't contain her curiosity. "Where are we going?"

"Well, I found this fantastic antique shop in the village. The moment I stepped inside, I realized you would find something extraordinary. The shop's name is Albion's Plunder and the gentleman who runs it is a local character. I enjoyed conversing with him. His store is a must-see for tourists and carries quite a variety of items," Enid's father said with a chuckle.

"Albion's Plunder is an odd name for a store. Was Albion a famous pirate?" Enid asked. She thought back to Dylan's long-ago pirate obsession.

"No. He was the son of Neptune, the Roman god of the sea," her father said.

"Wow. That's a weird name to pick," Enid said, now intrigued by the shop despite a lingering disappointment. It didn't surprise her that her father chose an antique shop for her gift, given his love of history. Her hopes for a new laptop were quickly fading.

"Trust me. It's a very unusual shop and owner," her father said. "Here we are." He pulled into a parking spot beside an unassuming storefront. The outside appeared like any other Welsh shop. The blue-striped awning overhead proclaimed "Antiques" in a tall, old-fashioned script. A sign picturing a blue giant wielding a golden trident was the only clue to a tie with Neptune.

The inside of the shop didn't disappoint. It dazzled the eyes and lured the senses. Everywhere Enid looked, vibrant colors assaulted her vision, and scents of pine, orange, and cloves reminded her of the holiday. The owner had crammed every nook and cranny with treasures. The number of things packed into the shop overwhelmed her.

An endless array of carpets completely obscured the wooden flooring. Aside from the usual inventory, the odd treasures were hard to categorize. Lewis Carroll's first-edition children's books sat beside a plague doctor's mask. A medieval executioner's hood hung on a chair near a pile of old comic books. A battle ax stained with what appeared to be dried blood or rust casually leaned against a nearby wall. The front case had antique coins, jewelry, and a crystal ball resting on the back of a golden dragon.

Enid's father directed her toward the front case with instructions to select a favorite jewelry item. His thoughtfulness touched

Enid. But how would she possibly choose? The gems shone with a brilliant light and appeared expensive.

So intent on viewing the contents of the case, Enid almost missed the shop owner.

He was a funny sort of chap—bent with ghost-white hair sticking out in all directions. He had several pairs of spectacles resting on his head. The shopkeeper used an old wooden walking stick to get around, though his movements appeared nimble. His clothes were a hodgepodge of different eras. Purple cowboy boots mixed with khaki pants circa WWI. A brilliant gem-colored paisley silk waistcoat held a bright orange puffy shirt in.

"Young miss, it is always a pleasure to see you. If you need any help, my name is Mr. Ambrose. You will find most items in my shop prefer to choose their new owners and not the other way around." The shop owner chuckled while encouraging her to look. "Your dad mentioned this was for a big occasion."

"Yes, Mr. Ambrose. It's my birthday. It's nice to meet you," Enid responded, confused by the shopkeepers' words. She was positive this was their first meeting, but maybe she had misunderstood.

"Take your time and be sure to view it all." He gestured toward the ring case. "Do you see anything that you like?"

Enid weighed the pros and cons of each selection. There were twelve rings, each elaborate in its way. The artisans made them from solid gold, and each contained a different coat of arms. Garnets, amethysts, or emeralds decorated the rings. Someone had cleverly worked the gems into each design. Enid couldn't decide which one appealed to her the most.

"Not seeing anything that speaks to you?" the proprietor prompted.

Enid didn't want to offend the man. "I like everything I see in your shop. These rings are all beautiful, but I'd hoped for something in silver."

He lifted his finger in the air triumphantly. "Ah. I almost forgot. I have something set aside just for you. It's an unusual case. Now, where did I put it?" Before she objected, the shop owner glanced around and brought down an individual ring box stored high on a shelf. He blew off a thin layer of dust and placed it before her on the counter with a flourish.

Enid reached for the ring box made from polished black stone with an intricate owl design carved into the lid, which seemed oddly familiar. She removed the cover and inside was a bright silver ring. The band had carvings that looked like runes. The small circular stone in the center flashed in all shades of azure, like the heart of a bright star.

"How cool." Enid murmured, tempted to place it on her finger, but waited. What if the ring was too expensive? Her father had finished with the books and made his way to the front counter. He was eager to see what Enid had chosen. She showed him the stone box, which elicited a surprised response from her dad. "W-Where did that box come from?"

"I found it at a yard sale. You might find this of particular interest, Mr. Davies. I believe you found the original. This ring is an actual replica, though it's quite exceptional," Mr. Ambrose explained with a wink.

"A replica?" Her dad peered over Enid's shoulder with a curious expression.

"May I try it on, Mr. Ambrose?" Enid inquired.

"Of course. Please, help yourself." The shopkeeper nodded encouragingly and studied the family for their reaction.

"Oh, wow," her father exclaimed. She removed the ring from the box, immediately recognizing it. "I didn't know they made a replica of that. What a lovely thing to find in your shop," Mr. Davies added.

Enid looked down at the ring, which seemed crafted for her hand. It was a perfect replica of the ring found in their own treasure trove.

"Imagine that. Finding this here in your shop and on such a perfect occasion," her father said, beaming from behind Enid.

Enid had no words. She remembered being six years old and wanting to keep the shiny original. Now here it was, waiting for her. Enid thought she would burst as her dad settled the bill. What a perfect birthday token. She planned to never take it off. She didn't care that it was a replica. She was grateful her dad hadn't opted for the laptop.

Mr. Ambrose expressed delight that they found the perfect gift for Enid. He reminded her that each item picked the owner rather than the other way around. "I'm delighted that you love your ring, young lady. It is an exceptional piece meant for an extraordinary person. Oh, I'm so happy that I believe I'll close early today. I enjoy it when treasures find their perfect home. It's always a cause for celebration."

The shop owner's enthusiasm touched Enid. "It's all because of you, Mr. Ambrose. I've had the best birthday so far."

So distracted by her new treasure, she missed most of the discussion between her father and Mr. Ambrose. Her dad mentioned a recent break-in reported at a London museum. Nothing was stolen, but apparently vandals took issue with the placards for the Dark Ages exhibit and posted their own corrections. "Kids and their pranks…" Enid heard her dad say.

Her full attention snapped back in time to hear her father inviting Mr. Ambrose to her party the following evening. She was glad. Her father needed more friends.

Mr. Ambrose expressed delight at accepting the impromptu invite.

Enid turned to her dad. "I can't imagine it getting any better than this."

"That is so sweet of you to say, but you will have other surprises in store for you. Some of which you may even enjoy as much as that bauble," Mr. Ambrose replied.

What did Mr. Ambrose mean about another surprise, Enid wondered? Had her father told him he arranged something else? This gave Enid much to ponder as they had lunch at the White Stag. The fish and chips with mushy peas tasted glorious. Enid kept stealing glances at her ring.

Chapter 4

CAR TROUBLE

ENID AND HER DAD got into his old mini and Enid sat in silence as her father drove. She was lost in thought, wondering what Dylan would say when they finally reunited that evening.

Enid admitted to herself that butterflies set up permanent residence in her stomach. Several months had elapsed since she last saw Dylan. Would he see the changes in her? Would he notice she was grown into a young woman? *Blasted butterflies.* Why wouldn't they pick on someone else?

Snow dusted the surrounding countryside. The world outside the car window appears as a winter wonderland. The tree branches dripped with icicles and snow painted the pastures and roadways a blinding shade of white. It was like millions of tiny frozen diamonds sparkling in the snow in the sunlight. Enid was unsure how the car would manage the weather, but her father promised her they would be fine.

Partway home, their car experienced a sudden bump as the wheels caught in the snow. The car lurched sideways to a sudden halt. Enid's father revved the engine to no effect. He swore a little under his breath. "Oh, dear. I'm afraid I was being a bit too optimistic."

Mr. Davies tried alternating shifting between drive and reverse, but the car wouldn't gain traction on the icy roadway. They also tried digging out of the snow, but the wheels would not bite on the pavement because of the ice.

Giving Enid blankets from the car's trunk to keep her warm and leaving the radio playing, he left to find help. Luckily, they were near the Roberts' manor. Enid tried to stay positive, but as the minutes ticked by, a tightness in her chest slowly increased.

Enid sat lost in thought about what she would say to Dylan. The letters they exchanged had gotten less personal. Dylan's correspondence focused mainly on his studies and activities. Enid found the information helpful for her studies, but the insight into Dylan's thoughts dimmed.

Before he left for London, Dylan would confess all his innermost hopes and fears. With their time apart, those thoughts had given way to minor personal observations. Was it because she was a girl, and he believed she wouldn't understand? Enid's cheeks burned when she thought about her last letter. What would her friend think about her dreams? She really hoped he wouldn't think she was being too weird. She missed her old confidant.

Enid wasn't sure when she stopped daydreaming and noticed her surroundings again. The breath left her lips as gentle puffs of smoke. The car's closed windows had a layer of condensation on them. Enid realized it was much colder than when her father first left to find help. *How long had it been?* From inside the car, the world outside now appeared frozen and alien. Enid pulled the blankets a little tighter for warmth and wished for her father's swift return.

Enid jumped at the sound of someone knocking on the car window. How did she miss their arrival? Enid glanced up to see a tall figure through the fogged windows. She couldn't make out his features because of the condensation, but he seemed familiar. She wiped the moisture away.

A well-dressed, handsome young man of a similar age stood outside the car, but whispers in her head warned that appearances could be deceiving. Enid checked to ensure the doors remained locked. Without knowing why, she had a strange notion the young man was up to no good.

He knocked again at the window and murmured something. With her thrumming pulse booming in her ears, Enid must have missed his comment.

When she glanced back at the stranger, his gaze held Enid captive. His eyes narrowed and Enid experienced an odd sensation in her head. The pressure seemed to pull her toward the window while Enid fought the invisible tugging with all her strength. She grabbed her forehead as a quick zap of pain shot through her skull. Enid's breath hitched as her heart raced.

After turning the radio volume down and taking a calming breath, she fumbled for the window control. Enid cracked open the window. She shivered as icy cold air displaced the warmer air inside the car. Enid now had a much better view of the young man. He had black hair and frosty blue, piercing eyes. He was almost a full head taller than she was and built solid, like a rugby player.

He was handsome enough, she supposed, but not in a way she found appealing. The set of his mouth was cruel, and his eyes were full of contempt. They were the eyes of a bully. She didn't know why a stranger would be trying to help her unless he was up to no good. He didn't seem the type who would help anyone but himself.

The stranger smiled. "Hello. Let me help you. I can get your vehicle out of the snow and back on the road in no time."

"That's quite all right. I've got this all under control." She replied.

The young man leaned closer. "I beg your pardon, miss, but are you sure?"

"Everything is just fine," Enid repeated, using a confident tone.

The stranger studied the vehicle, its occupant, and the road conditions. With a faint condescending tone, he said, "You appear to be having some difficulty. If you only unlock a door, it will only take a moment."

"It's alright. Help is on the way," Enid said. "You don't have to wait."

"I assure you I mean no harm and would only like to offer my help," he said, lifting his left eyebrow in concern, though part of his upper lip tightened in contempt.

A wave of panic swept over her. She couldn't get the comparison with the neighborhood bullies out of her mind. The stranger's presence was becoming suffocating, and Enid could barely breathe. She had difficulty focusing, as if in a trance-like state. Enid shook her head to shake off the effects of the stranger's words.

Enid couldn't explain her reaction to him. Everything he said sounded polite and well-mannered. Still, that inner voice shouted at her to be cautious. She knew bullies could hide behind fake manners and a handsome face.

She was fighting not to tremble, which would only make her appear more vulnerable. "Thanks for the kind offer, but my dad will be back at any moment. I'll be fine."

The young man nodded and turned to leave. Enid hadn't realized she was holding her breath until she exhaled, but suddenly he was back, looming over the windscreen. His eyes lit with an unnatural inner fire, and she was certain his teeth became impossibly sharp.

Enid screamed, and the blood drained from her face. The stranger held Enid in his menacing gaze. "Listen, human. You will unlock the door and let me in." The young man hissed, as his attractive face twisted into a menacing sneer.

Terror rose inside her as the stranger's voice seemed to invade every cell of her body.

Enid shook uncontrollably and fell back into her seat as a sharp pain surged through her head again. She rubbed at her temples.

Enid experienced dizziness and, with what strength she could muster, shook her head and gasped out, "I'm not unlocking the door." She had to force the words out. Enid's hand strayed to the door lock, but she didn't disengage it.

The stranger's gaze bore into her. Enid grimaced. With another sudden jolt of pain, Enid gritted out, "Please leave."

The young man fell back. He stammered and searched for a suitable reply when Enid experienced a final blinding pain behind her eyes. She put her head in her hands to contain the pressure. Red was suddenly everywhere—on her gloves and the front of her coat.

Blood.

Had her nightmares caught up with her? She heard distant barking and the tinkling of breaking glass before she lost consciousness.

WHEN ENID CAME TO, she lay on a settee in the Roberts' drawing room. She recognized the pale green wallpaper and cream-colored curtains. A cloth containing ice pressed against her cheek.

Bendith was by her side on the pale green and pink oriental carpet and growled when anyone got too close. Enid closed her eyes in embarrassment. *What would the Roberts think of this?* She heard her father's voice, and the sound comforted her. "Her mother sometimes had nose bleeds," Mr. Davies said. He sounded anxious.

"I was unsure what had happened, sir. When I saw the blood, I realized I had to help. I apologize for your car window. I would be happy to pay for the repairs."

That voice! It was that dreadful boy. Bendith growled again. Enid tried to sit up and remembered the delicate pink fabric on the couch, praying she hadn't ruined the furniture or the rug.

"Please, Enid, remain still. You gave us all quite a fright." Mrs. Roberts sat on the other side of Enid and patted her hand.

"I'm so sorry," Enid said. "It was kind of you to bring me here."

"Nonsense, child. I've never seen your father so upset. Don't rush sitting up. You've had a nosebleed and lost a lot of blood. You might feel dizzy upon standing. We've called for Dr. Thompson." Enid thanked Mrs. Roberts and apologized for the disruption. "No apologies are necessary. You're one of the family. It was fortunate that our nephew was out walking. He had to break the car window to get you out, then he brought you here."

Enid opened her mouth to correct Mrs. Roberts, but shut it again. *Nephew? Oh, goodness.* Why did he have to be Dylan's cousin? *What horrible luck.* Maybe no one would believe her story about how oddly he behaved. Enid decided at that moment to keep quiet and be grateful for not bleeding all over the Roberts' settee.

Her father's face grinned down at her. "I can't leave you for a second without you getting into some mischief, eh, *cariad bach*?"

Even at this embarrassing moment, her father's teasing made everything seem all right.

"I'm sorry, *Dadi*. I'm not sure what happened. I've never had a nosebleed before." Enid frowned as she tried to comb through her fledgling memories, distracted when Bendith demanded to be petted. "How did Bendith get here?"

"Don't worry, honey. I'm afraid that nosebleeds run in the family," her father admitted. "I remember your mother used to get them, though it only happened when she became anxious. I'm sorry I left you alone. In hindsight, it probably wasn't the wisest idea." His words reassured her, but his expression hinted at his concern. He reached down to give Bendith a friendly pat. "As for this fellow, he showed up when you arrived unconscious, with that young man." He lowered his voice. "We had a terrible time keeping Bendith from biting him. I'm afraid Bendith does not care for Dylan's cousin."

Enid frowned. "Yes. I didn't know Dylan had a cousin."

"I didn't either, but he seems like a nice enough young man. I can't understand why Bendith acted that way," Mr. Davies said with a nod towards the rude stranger.

Enid tried to get up when her father stopped her. "Enid, I don't think you should move just yet."

"I'm much better. I don't want this to spoil Dylan's homecoming. Has someone gone to meet the train? Can we go home?" Enid looked down at her ruined coat and outfit splattered with her blood.

She privately agreed wholeheartedly with Bendith about not liking the odd young man.

"Oh, goodness," Mrs. Roberts exclaimed. "In all the excitement, I forgot to send someone to fetch him."

Chapter 5

HOMECOMING

AFTER A SHORT TIME, Enid's color returned. She was determined to attend the celebration the following evening because she'd never had a birthday celebration that included all her loved ones.

Mr. Davies lost no time in getting Enid back to their cottage. He also arranged for the doctor to meet them at the house. Enid declared the doctor's visit unnecessary, but her father insisted. Before leaving, Enid begged Mrs. Roberts to not bore Dylan with the gory details of the incident.

Enid overheard her father invite Dylan's odious cousin to the party. Her teeth ground together in annoyance when she overheard him accept the offer.

Her arrival back at the cottage coincided with the appearance of Dr. Thompson, an older gentleman with a slight paunch, gray hair, and a courtly bedside manner. Enid adored him and had been a patient of his since birth. Dr. Thompson gave her a quick examination. After a little gentle prodding, Enid reluctantly mentioned her vivid dreams. Dr. Thompson ultimately found nothing wrong, much to her dad's relief. The doctor attributed the incident to elevated stress levels. "Get some rest, Enid," said Dr. Thompson as he left. "After the holidays, we should schedule a full workup, just in case. Anyway, we look forward to seeing you at the party tomorrow. My wife and I were excited to receive an invitation."

After the doctor's visit, Enid got changed into jeans and a pale-yellow, ruffled blouse.

Instead of resting in her room as the doctor suggested, Enid found herself in her father's study gazing at the picture of her mother. As usual, Bendith was by her side. Enid often found herself drawn to this image. She sometimes played a game trying to guess what her mother had been thinking as they snapped the picture. Today, Enid looked for any similarities between herself and the beautiful phantom in the photograph but found none.

She unconsciously rubbed her ring. Remarkably, it perfectly matched the photos of the real find.

Was it Enid's imagination, or did she hear the faint voice of a woman? For a moment, she let herself believe that her mother spoke to her. It was as if Enid received whispered replies to her many questions. However, Enid quickly came to her senses.

Bendith waited patiently at her side while Enid stared blankly into space and gave a quiet whine of concern. Enid jerked back to awareness and patted the dog reassuringly, and started shelving books that lay on top of his desk.

This was where Dylan found her when he arrived at the cottage. Bendith gave a warm, welcoming bark and demanded Dylan's attention, earning an affectionate pat.

"Oh, Dylan. I'm so happy to see you. Have you been home yet?" Enid's smile lit her face, and she had the urge to throw her arms around him like she used to do. She settled for taking his hands in hers instead. *No one would disapprove of that, would they?*

"I came straight here after I heard what happened. Are you all right? Shouldn't you be resting? What did Dr. Thompson have to say?" Dylan's lips pulled down in a frown of concern. He explained he had stopped at home just long enough to drop off his luggage, greet his mother, and meet his cousin. Afterward, he left immediately for the Davies' cottage, full of concern for his friend. His sharp gaze now traveled over Enid, as if to reassure himself that she was there and in one piece.

Her stomach dropped at the pity in his eyes. "Oh, I didn't want your mom to mention it. Don't worry, though. Dr. Thompson gave me a clean bill of health." Enid's lips pulled into a slight frown. "I'm really okay."

"Mom didn't have time to tell me anything. My father told me all about it on the way back from the station. What on earth happened?" Dylan's eyes blazed with fear, and he squeezed Enid's hands.

She shook her head, flummoxed. "I'm not sure exactly what happened. One minute I argued with your cousin, and the next I got a sharp headache and fainted. I woke up at your house surrounded by my dad and your parents. Dr. Thompson wants me to make a follow-up visit after the holidays." Enid's cheeks became rosy with embarrassment over her admission that she argued with Dylan's cousin.

"Yes, you better listen to the doctor and keep that appointment. As for my cousin... He's not impressed with me at all because I came straight here. He's been in Europe, and I've never met him." Dylan's nose wrinkled in disapproval. Enid wondered if his cousin annoyed Dylan as much as he annoyed her.

Dylan sighed. "I guess family can be difficult sometimes." He looked down at their joined hands and then up into Enid's eyes. "I'm so glad you're all right. I was worried about you." His thumb stroked over the back of her hand in a gentle caress, sending tingles up her arm. Enid stared back at him, mesmerized by his eyes. She was drawn to him as if he were a magnet.

"I'm fine. I'm just glad you're here." Enid's voice was barely a whisper. She couldn't look away from Dylan even if she wanted to. It was as if he had cast a spell over her.

He leaned closer, and Enid's heart quickened in anticipation. She held her breath, waiting for his lips to touch hers. Dylan's eyes flicked to her lips, then back to her eyes, and Enid's cheeks flushed with heat. After all these years, he was finally going to *kiss* her.

Mr. Davies appeared in the study doorway, and Enid and Dylan sprang apart. Her father warmly greeted Dylan and invited him to tea. The three made their way to the kitchen, the true heart of the cottage.

Walls and cabinets where the stone didn't peek through appeared as a pale shade of sky blue. This color contrasted nicely with the thick, wooden butcher-block countertops. A white porcelain farmhouse sink sat below a window, looking out over an herb garden in the back of the property. There was just enough space for a small round cafe table and chairs, where Enid's dad had set out the tea.

He poured the tea into the delicate cobalt-and-white dishes and served some lemon cakes. They discussed Dylan's progress at school. As usual, his mock exams were all top marks. Then Enid's father said, "Dylan, why don't you tell us a little about your cousin?"

Dylan shifted in discomfort. "I don't know much. He's the son of a cousin on my mother's side. His name is Aeddan Hughes. He grew up on the continent. That's all I know."

"So, this is your first meeting? We'd better make sure he has fun tomorrow night. We should try to make up for Enid's frosty greeting." Mr. Davies smiled at Enid to take any sting out of his words.

"It will also give him a chance to make a better impression," Enid grumbled into her teacup.

"Yes, you mentioned something about an argument. I hope he behaved himself." Dylan's eyes narrowed with concern.

"Don't worry, Dylan. I'm sure it was all just a misunderstanding. If I'd realized you were cousins, there might not have been an argument." Enid didn't want to be responsible for the cousins falling out.

"Neither did I. I'm not sure how I feel about it yet," Dylan confessed, staring out of the window.

"It's always good to be surrounded by family." Enid's father insisted.

After tea, Dylan took his leave to return home. "I want no more stories about your fainting. I was concerned." he said. "Please get some rest." Enid nodded.

"I will. And Dylan," she said, looking up at him with a mischievous glint in her eye, "don't be late."

Dylan grinned. "I'll try not to." He leaned down and kissed Enid lightly on the forehead before turning to leave.

After Dylan left, Enid's father asked her to remain longer. "Enid, we need to discuss you two."

"W-What about?" Enid responded. Her cheeks were still rosy after Dylan's affectionate gesture.

"Well, I know how I felt about your mother when I was your age. You and Dylan are both fine young people, but you are getting to an age where it's easy to get carried away. Remember, there is a whole big world that you haven't seen yet. Have fun, and don't be in a hurry to get serious. Now that Dylan's cousin has arrived, that may prevent you two from spending every moment together."

"Quit teasing me." Enid's blush deepened, realizing her dad may have seen more than she thought in the library.

"I'm not kidding. I'm giving you good sound advice." He said, "Did I ever tell you the story about how your mother and I met?"

"Yes, only about a *thousand* times. You said she was running toward you through the forest, and it was love at first sight."

"That's right, but did I ever mention the bit where she was in love with someone else at the time?" He asked.

"N-No. You never said that. Who was it?" Enid asked.

"I'm only mentioning it to you now to show you that life can take some very unexpected turns. It doesn't always turn out like a fairytale," her father said.

"I know that *Dadi*, but who was mom involved with before you?" she had a burning desire to know.

"Let's leave the rest of that story for another day, shall we?" her dad suddenly looked pale and exhausted.

"Alright," Enid took the first opportunity to leave and returned to her room.

Of course, Dylan was aware of her stance on love. Before she settled down, she wanted to have adventures. She wanted to go to university and travel. *Besides, he wasn't interested in me that way, was he?* She hoped she hadn't made a fool of herself over an almost kiss.

THAT NIGHT, ENID HAD another awful nightmare.

At first, Enid wasn't sure what was happening. Tufts of snow and ice sparkled in frozen majesty. She glanced left and right and recognized a hard-packed wall of snow on either side. The floor appeared constructed of thick blue ice. Enid glanced up to view the winter sky, but dark smoke blew over her head like ominous clouds.

She was too short to peer over the tops of the icy works, but the sudden screams chilled her more than the frigid temperature. Enid realized she had company. There were figures everywhere. They dressed strangely, like they were from another century. But which? Some appeared to be sleeping but with no telltale rise and fall of their chests. Were they still breathing? *Alive?*

Enid noted all the figures appeared drained of all vitality. As she investigated further, the entire setting appeared leached of any vibrancy. As she continued to search for a way out, she noted a dark fog in the distance spreading through the trenches.

The closer Enid got to the black tendrils, the more they receded. *Were they aware of me?* Enid quickened her pace and ran towards where she thought freedom might be. All around her were cadaverous figures, and Enid pushed forward, still searching for the way home.

Nearby was a boy, not much older than herself, huddled in a fetal position, his back to Enid. As Enid approached, she noted his curly brown hair, so like Dylan's.

Reaching out to touch his shoulder, Enid got an electric jolt. The boy's body arched, and he let out a blood-curdling scream. Enid looked on in horror as the black tendrils coalesced around him, choking off his breath.

"No," Enid screamed as she tried to push away the dark tendrils as they closed tighter around him. The faster she shoved the tendrils off, the more they multiplied until they enveloped him. Enid let out a pent-up scream of frustration. Her arms were so tired, and she had welts from the tendrils. Worst of all was that the boy was gone.

As she continued to observe, any movement or faint color in the trenches ceased altogether after the dark fog passed through. *Was it killing everything?*

Enid panicked and tried to find her way out of the trench, but the emaciated figures were everywhere. Their faces haunted her.

She reached a point in the trench where the channel widened. One figure grabbed her hand, and she glanced down, startled. It was the boy again. There was something so familiar about his face. "Please help me, Enid."

That voice sounded like Dylan's. Enid tried to jerk away, but the figure held on with a grip of iron. Terror bubbled up inside her. Enid searched around wildly for an escape. The walls closed in on her as the dark fog loomed nearby.

The figure abruptly released Enid, and she scrambled away. She turned for another look, but there was no one. Only mounded snow and dark fog met her panicked gaze. Enid covered her face with her hands and sank to the ground in despair. *What was happening here?*

A distant bark and whine diverted her attention. It sounded like Bendith calling her. Enid closed her eyes and focused on the sound of her dog's barks. *He'll show me the way home,* she thought.

She opened her eyes, and the boy was back. He slumped over and the dark fog enveloped him. Before her eyes, he turned into a solid sculpture of ice, his eyes fixed on something she could not see. Enid's scream echoed through the frozen wasteland.

She experienced a tremendous sense of grief at this sight, so she reached out a shaking hand to touch the boy's shoulder. Just before she made contact, she got jerked away into a whirlwind of color and sound. Enid placed her hands over her ears. Her movement stopped, and she free-fell as if from a great height. She screamed again.

Enid awoke safely in her bed. Bendith had come into her room and was by her bedside. Her pajamas twisted about her legs. The tears streaked down Enid's face. *What was that?* Even being back in her bed didn't dissipate the terror of her nightmare.

Enid tried to get Bendith to lie down, but he wouldn't. He stared at her with his big brown eyes as if he, too, had seen the nightmare. Enid hugged her dog close and rocked back and forth, trying to calm herself.

It was only a dream, Enid told herself repeatedly. But it seemed so real. She still saw the boy's face, frozen in terror. And the way he had called her name... Enid shivered. It was as if he had recognized her.

But that was impossible. Enid had never been to that place before. She was sure of it. It must have been a dream brought on by all the stress of her party. Enid tried to push the nightmare out of her mind, but she couldn't. It was too real, too terrifying. As if mirroring her agitation, Bendith hopped down and would occasionally pace the length of the room.

Bendith stayed by her for the rest of that night, acting as if he guarded her against those terrible images. Bendith would growl low in his throat. He then demanded Enid pet him, as if seeking comfort from her.

Enid obliged and hugged her dog close. Together they faced the nightmares that Enid knew would visit her again.

Chapter 6

CELEBRATIONS

ENID ROSE BEFORE DAWN on the day of her party. After her nightmare, she slept only fitfully and finally gave up because she was too excited. She viewed turning sixteen as a milestone. Enid had been studying diligently to prepare for her O-levels. After that, she would go away for her A-levels and then go off to university. She dreamed of this since she was a little girl. Becoming an archeologist was all she ever wanted. Tonight, would be a significant step toward adulthood.

She became nervous as she glanced at her dress. It was a gorgeous shade of peacock blue. "Wow. It brings out the amber in your eyes," Zoe insisted at the shop. Thin straps held up the simple dress. A skirt embossed with the pattern of peacock feathers fell above her knee. When Enid stepped out of the dressing room, her friend said, "Finally, I've got you into something more fashionable than jeans. Everybody will be in for a surprise."

Bendith noted Enid was awake. Soon the entire house would be up. She let the dog sniff around in her room. Bendith circled her and kept pushing Enid toward the door. His tail wagged the whole way.

"No, silly. It's too early and way too cold to go outside. Can't you tell it snowed again?" Enid asked as she glanced out the window.

But Bendith acted undeterred. His barks would wake the house unless she took him for a walk.

Enid dressed in her warmest clothes and took Bendith out for a quick run. It was freezing. The mammoth dog barked as they made their way around the house. The snow dazzled her eyes, and Enid understood Bendith's excitement. They would make the first prints on the pristine landscape.

Inside, she was excited, though not about the precipitation. Dylan would see her in a stylish grown-up dress. Would he recognize her as a woman rather than a friend?

She thought back to their almost-kiss yesterday, and her chest tightened and her stomach flipped over, like riding a runaway coaster. The more she analyzed what had almost happened, the more nauseated she became. Enid experienced a jumble of conflicting emotions.

She kept replaying what happened. *Did he intend to kiss me?* Did she even want that? She got shivers thinking about how close they came to brushing lips. *What if Dylan just got carried away out of concern for me?* Enid's mood plummeted after that thought.

Bendith didn't let her dwell on her thoughts for too long, however, and gave a quick yap to regain her attention.

Enid and Bendith made their way out of the gate and Enid glanced out over the snow-covered lawn, noticing an odd circular patch of green interrupting the white expanse. Enid approached cautiously. *What was going on there?* The green space spanned about four feet in diameter. She then noted the location where that old yew tree used to stand—curiouser and curiouser.

So intent on the strange green circle, Enid paid little attention to Bendith and almost tripped over him. "Sorry, fella. This is one weird spot of grass." Bendith barked as if in agreement. Through the clouds, a bright shaft of sunlight shone on the green spot.

Enid glanced up at the sky, trying to figure out where the light originated. A hole in the cloud cover, perhaps? There had to be a rational explanation. Bendith barked again in a warning and nipped at her fingers. "Ouch. What's up with you?" Enid asked her friend. He tipped his head in consideration and replied with staccato yips.

After a moment's hesitation, she knelt and scooped up some snow. Bendith eyed Enid with a cocked head and his tongue lolling to the side. Enid started a one-way snowball fight with her four-legged friend. Bendith knocked Enid down several times in retaliation, and soon the odd green spot was forgotten.

LATER THAT EVENING, AS Enid got ready, she danced along to the music from the radio. Enid pictured dancing with Dylan and shook her head. They'd tried to teach each other several times over the years, and the results were always laughable. Neither teen was very coordinated. The thought of dancing close to Dylan made her cheeks blush. Considering her confused feelings and two left feet, she was relieved there would be no dancing.

She fidgeted as she put on her dress, gorgeous but uncomfortable. Her shoulders and neck would be exposed. She found herself second-guessing the choice, but Zoe insisted. Enid preferred jeans and sneakers, but this was her milestone day.

Enid sighed in resignation. She also had to do makeup and hair. By the time she finished, she didn't recognize her reflection in the mirror. She put her new shoes on and stumbled across the room several times for practice. *Oops. Maybe my sixteenth birthday par-*

ty was not the time to learn to walk in heels. Enid chuckled a little at the thought and seriously considered changing into her high tops.

Finally ready, she headed downstairs. Enid's father met her on the landing. He had a small, clear florist's container. "I hope you don't mind, but I got you a corsage for the party." Mr. Davies opened the box and displayed a striking winter wrist corsage made of mistletoe flowers, frosted hawthorn berries, and assorted sparkling greenery.

"You shouldn't have. It's so beautiful." Enid got misty-eyed at the thoughtful gesture.

"Nonsense. I hope it works with your dress. You look pretty, *cariad bach*." Mr. Davies' voice sounded rough with emotion.

Enid ran a hand through her hair when she noted tears in her father's eyes. "Is everything okay?" Enid wanted everything to be perfect.

"Of course. You've grown into such a lovely young lady. You look just like your mother, and I wish with all my heart that she could be here with us to celebrate. I'm sure she would burst with pride at the strong young woman you've become. I've told you that your mom was a seer, and her dreams always seemed to come true. I know for a fact that her favorite one was seeing you healthy and happy at sixteen." Her father wiped away his tears with great effort and brightened. "But tonight isn't about endings, but beginnings. It's an exciting new time in your life. Don't worry if I get a little misty-eyed. They are tears of joy." Her father beamed a genuine smile, and Enid relaxed.

But then she had a horrible thought. "Do you think everyone will show up?" A party with everyone she cared about seemed almost too good to be true.

"Of course, they will. Now, let's go have some fun." He grinned from ear to ear as he escorted his daughter to the party.

Her father had fussed and suffered over the guest list. It wouldn't be a large party, but he had wanted to mark the occasion with people close to the family.

Try as he might, Mr. Davies hadn't been able to find an added guest to round out the group since Aeddan's last-minute invitation, so they would be a party of thirteen. Enid knew thirteen was only a number, and people harbored few superstitions in the twenty-first century.

The Roberts family was attending, and Enid's stomach clenched picturing Dylan. His obnoxious cousin would also be there, and Enid had practiced fake smiling in her mirror that afternoon.

Dr. Thompson and his lovely wife would also make an appearance. Enid couldn't picture a family celebration without them.

Enid's school friend Zoe, her younger brother Zack, and her parents, the Floyds, also made the list. The two girls had enjoyed shopping for their dresses together and were pleased with the results. Zoe planned to wear a gorgeous pink dress with a floral print. She was tanned and had curly auburn hair, and Enid felt a twinge of insecurity with her choice. But then Enid took a deep breath and reminded herself that beauty comes in all shapes and sizes. Besides, she was proud of who she was as a person, and her outfit didn't define her.

To complete the guest list, Mr. Ambrose had called the night before to double-check the details of the party. Enid heard her father's infectious laughter on the other end of the line. It seemed he and Mr. Ambrose had formed a quick bond over their mutual love of history - her father said that he especially enjoyed hearing Mr. Ambrose's long-winded tales.

The Floyds and the Thompsons arrived at almost the same time. Fortunately, it was a clear night, and the roads remained passable. "Oh, I just knew you'd look perfect in that dress," Zoe exclaimed.

The girls complimented each other after loads of giggles and hugs. As predicted, Zoe looked incredible. Zack even wore a suit.

At the first opportunity, Zoe took Enid aside and asked, "Has Dylan arrived yet? It seems like forever since he went away. I haven't heard from him lately and can't wait to catch up."

Enid stammered a little, "I-I saw him yesterday. H-He's not here yet, but I'm sure he's anxious to see you too." Suddenly, a flash of Dylan's lips right before their almost-kiss popped into her head, and Enid's cheeks reddened.

"Are you nervous?" Zoe asked.

Enid nodded in response and felt badly not confessing to her friend the cause of her anxiety.

She felt relief when her dad mentioned that hors d'oeuvres were available in the living room. The distraction saved her from having to elaborate.

With her stomach tangled in knots, Enid could not eat but held a cup of punch for reassurance.

The Roberts arrived fifteen minutes later with the dreaded cousin in tow. The boys were dressed in sharp suits. Enid was hard-pressed to think of a more attractive set of boys, except in the pages of a magazine. Dylan did not disappoint. A navy blue suit set his curly brown hair and amber eyes off to perfection. He was tall, lean, and muscular. *When had he become so handsome?*

Aeddan appeared as the opposite of Dylan, but no less attractive. His ebony hair and piercing blue eyes would have no trouble attracting attention. Annoyingly, he acted aware of that fact. Confidence oozed from every pore. He was similar in height to Dylan and wore an expertly tailored, expensive charcoal pin-striped suit, which set off his features to perfection.

Enid rushed over to greet Dylan and his family. Unlike his jubilant mood the day before, Dylan acted distant. His parents hugged and fussed over her, but he only nodded and murmured a generic birthday greeting. He hardly glanced at her and didn't comment on her dress at all. Enid was crushed. Where was her affectionate friend? Had she completely misread the situation? Or worse yet, did Dylan regret their almost-kiss?

In contrast, Dylan told Zoe how beautiful she looked. He smiled often at Zoe and gave her all his attention. Zoe, a loyal friend, looked a little confused by his behavior excluding Enid, and glanced her way for direction. Enid gave a little shrug and nodded. It wasn't Zoe's fault that Dylan ignored Enid. Enid gritted her teeth, trying hard not to let tears of disappointment fall.

She got unexpected help from the abrasive cousin, who she got stuck entertaining—*Oh, dear.* There was no way she would reveal her pain. Unfortunately, she had only practiced pretending to smile, not small talk. She assumed Dylan would be a buffer between them.

"Hello. Lovely to have a formal introduction at last. You look different when you're upright and conscious," Aeddan said after his uncle introduced them, leaving the two, so they could get acquainted.

Enid fumed but pretended to smile. "Hello, Aeddan. I guess I should thank you for your help yesterday, and for attending my party." Enid thought her teeth would break with the force of her clenched jaw. Aeddan had tried to bait her into making a scene, and she was delighted to disappoint him.

"No need to thank me. You had troubles, as I assumed yesterday. I am always prepared to help the ladies." Aeddan winked at her with teeth bared in a fake smile.

"Yes. Well, thanks. Please excuse me. I should say hi to everybody." Enid escaped and joined the Thompsons and Zack for a lively stroll down memory lane. Out of the corner of her eye, Enid noted Aeddan join Zoe and Dylan at the punch bowl. Zoe appeared to be having the time of her life, and indeed, both boys smiled and laughed a lot. *Hello sixteen,* Enid thought. It didn't surprise her that both boys were drawn to the vivacious Zoe.

Outside, an unusual winter thunder snow began with no warning. The crowd viewed the swirling snowfall and forked lightning through the tall windows. Enid noted Dylan acting apprehensive. Aeddan's smirk had faded, and he appeared uncomfortable as well.

Enid's father worried about Mr. Ambrose, who still hadn't arrived. "I should phone to see if he's left yet," her father suggested and entered the study for privacy to make the call.

Just then, a thunderclap sounded and the cottage floor trembled, rattling the windows in their frames. Lightning flickered like a strobe light on the winter landscape.

"Maybe we should get away from the windows and go into dinner," Enid suggested. Poor Enid ended up paired with Aeddan to escort her. She hoped for a quick word with Dylan to determine if anything was wrong, but he acted maddeningly distant, yet all smiles for Zoe. Was it the near kiss or had she offended Dylan with her words about his cousin? Enid stared at Aeddan, trying to remember what she said.

"Do I have something on my face, or are you now realizing how gorgeous I am?" Aeddan asked. With narrowed eyes and a slight frown, his expression looked horrified at the thought.

Before Enid replied, Bendith appeared in the doorway. Gone was the friendly, playful dog of the morning. In his place was the fierce fairy hound they first met, all teeth and bite. The vicious, throaty growls sounded chilling. Dylan pulled away from the group, and his gaze now burned into Enid.

The room was suddenly thrown into darkness, and Enid's pulse jumped. The power was out. Her father called from his study, "Please remain calm. The electric line must be down. I guess those are the perils of ancient wiring. Stay where you are and I will fetch a torch."

Enid tried to move closer to Bendith. She wanted to intercept him before he bit anyone. Though if he did, she hoped it would be Aeddan. She sensed a firm hand on her arm to keep her in place. "Oh, no you don't, little peahen. You should stick near me until this storm passes," Aeddan said.

As Enid glanced around, she discerned an eerie, unnatural glimmer from three pairs of eyes. Aeddan, Dylan, and Bendith all had eyes that shone with an inner flame. *What is happening?*

Moments later, in the pitch-black void, Enid could just make out a circle of swirling color on the floor. It started so small, almost six inches across, but grew more expansive. "Aeddan, do you see what I see? And what's up with your glowing eyes? Are they a new type of contact lens?" Enid stared at the churning spot which reminded her of pictures she'd seen of the aurora borealis. It glowed with all the colors of a kaleidoscopic rainbow.

A new rumbling noise began. It started like thunder, but the crescendo kept building to an unnatural decibel. Enid tried to place her hands over her ears, but Aeddan gripped her. The sound reminded her of her nightmare. She glanced toward Dylan and tried to call a warning to him, even though he couldn't hear her over the roaring noise.

The colorful circle rose from the floor until it became a cylinder of swirling, iridescent light. The crowd broke out in an uproar and Bendith launched himself at an unseen target. Then, like a shimmering curtain, the incandescent pillar parted, and a dark spectral figure emerged into the room.

Everything stopped.

Chapter 7

STOLEN AWAY

ENID GLANCED ABOUT THE room, realizing that everything appeared frozen in time. Next to her, Aeddan looked as though it caught him mid-snark. There was no movement around her. Indeed, even the flashes of lightning had frozen mid-strike. which threw the familiar room into stark relief. All the party guests were statues. Even Bendith got caught mid-stride. No one glanced about or even breathed, as far as Enid could tell, but she found she had no trouble moving around. *Why was that, and what the heck was happening? Am I dreaming again?*

She settled for a stealthy survey of her surroundings, since she didn't want to catch the attention of whatever emerged from that weird pillar of light. Her heartbeat drummed in her ears. She was certain the creature had heard it.

The shadowy figure glanced in all directions. Enid realized it was only slightly taller than her. This gave her some small sense of comfort. Dark tendrils emanated from the shadow and appeared to probe the room. It was dressed all in black, but as the form glided further, the robes shone with the dark radiance of beetles' wings. Enid realized that, instead of an absence of color, the figure absorbed the entire spectrum. As the shadow drew closer, the temperature of the room dropped. If it got much colder, Enid's breath would show.

Enid moved as much as she dared while working her arm free of Aeddan's grasp. As she worked to get loose, she noted Aeddan didn't react. He didn't glance her way or appear to be aware of what had transpired. *It figures he would have to grab me just before everyone froze.*

Enid was almost free when she heard an angelic voice say, "Where are you? These are all such fascinating humans, but I'm after much bigger fish."

The voice was so compelling that Enid almost responded when a zap of bright pain flew through her skull. She barely kept herself from wincing. The brilliant silver ring on her hand suddenly warmed, and Enid swore the stone pulsed. She slipped free from Aeddan's grasp.

"Come out, my prince. You can no longer hide amongst these weak humans. Please, no more games," the unearthly form said. It sounded so forlorn that Enid almost sympathized. Again, a sharp stinging sensation behind her eyes said differently.

The shape passed by Bendith and paused. Enid's muscles tensed, unsure what to do. "You are an unexpected find, and such power, too. I am on a particular quest, or it would tempt me to take you back with me as well," the angelic voice said, sounding full of disappointment.

Enid recoiled at those words. Her hands clenched at her side. Enid refused to allow anyone to be taken by this creature.

"Oh, there you are, my prince. Let me look at you," the creature said. To Enid's horror and utter confusion, the shadow stopped in front of Dylan, blocking Enid's view.

Why did it refer to him as a prince?

"Hmm, in this form, I suppose you're handsome enough, but maybe a bit too human for my taste. Never mind, I will see your true, magnificent self soon."

The creature circled Dylan and appeared to study him. It completed the circle and stopped again. When the shadow reached up and removed its hood, Enid almost gasped in surprise. She wasn't sure what she expected, but the sight shocked her.

The figure appeared to be a young girl of a similar age, with glowing emerald-green eyes and blood-red lips. Her teeth had a vicious, serrated appearance. Her hair was pure silver and looked alive with a nest of argent snakes. Yet, for all her strangeness, the unknown girl appeared achingly beautiful.

"No response, my prince? No comment on my beauty?" the girl said, her eyes narrowed with fury. A moment later, she lifted her chin and laughed. It sounded like music. "Oh, apologies, I almost forgot how weak you are in this cursed realm." She reached out her hand, dripping with blood-red nails, and touched Dylan. Enid almost screamed.

Dylan jerked as if he had awakened from a nightmare. His eyes widened as he beheld the diminutive force standing in front of him. "Malagant? Why are you here?" His eyes darted wildly about the room, looking for something. His gaze locked on Enid for a split second and then shifted.

"Is that all you have to say to me after all these years? You know why I am here. They pledged us to each other, and I vowed to retrieve my betrothed," Malagant said.

Enid decided this must all be a horrible nightmare.

"Our families made that pact, not us," Dylan said. "When members of your wretched court foully murdered my parents, it rendered any agreement between us void. There is no power on this earth or the next that will compel me to come with you willingly," Dylan spat. His voice held notes of frost, and he stabbed his finger in Malagant's direction as he spoke.

Enid didn't understand what he meant, because his parents were standing right behind her, frozen like everyone else. Did he mean his birth parents?

"I'm not convinced, my prince. There seems to be a room full of hostages to ransom in this place. I would enjoy making each one scream out all the reasons you should reconsider," Malagant threatened as she again glanced around the room and sneered.

"You can't believe that the fate of these humans matters to me. They will all fade and die anyway," Dylan said. His bored tone suggested he was discussing the weather.

Human? What does he mean by a human? Is there another option? Aliens? Dylan's callous attitude and words convinced Enid she was in the throes of a nightmare. One in which her best friend confessed he wasn't human and that the lives of his family and friends were of no consequence.

Enid almost spoke, but she waited to see what other revelations would come.

Malagant sauntered over to Dylan's mother. "If these humans will die, why don't I start with this one? Isn't she the woman who took you in and raised you?"

Tendrils of black smoke flowed from Malagant like a dark moonlit waterfall and inched slowly toward Mrs. Roberts. Enid flinched as she witnessed their aching progress. When the drifting black fog got within a foot of poor Mrs. Roberts and solidified, Enid realized she had to do something. Just as she was about to leap in the way of the deadly fog, hallucination or not, Dylan spoke.

"There's no need for any murder here, Malagant. If I must come with you, I will. But not if you harm any here."

"Very well, my prince. I will spare these wretched beings and leave them to their misery if you make a solemn promise to join me in my realm," the creature said as she withdrew the inky black tendrils and gestured around the room at the still-frozen party guests. Enid almost sagged in relief.

As Malagant neared Dylan, Enid witnessed an unsettling sight, which sent shivers down her spine. Dylan's body lengthened and morphed in appearance.

One minute, Dylan looked like a stretched-out version of himself, and then, after a bright flash, a giant serpent sat where her friend once stood. The serpent had leathery wings with sharp claws, and it covered the body in scales of a light gold color that reflected prisms of different hues. The mouth hid teeth which were the size of steak knives, shiny and deadly. As far as Enid could tell, his legs were gone, absorbed into the serpent's undulating body. Her stomach felt nauseous.

"There you are, my magnificent wyvern. It is so good to see you like this. I was afraid you had remained in this realm for too long. Don't you feel better now?" Malagant asked with a raised brow.

Dylan opened his huge, intimidating mouth to reply, and Enid strained to hear his answer. But instead of words, a molten river of blue flames erupted from his mouth. A solid jet of ice-cold fire enveloped Malagant. The frozen fire didn't touch anyone else or damage anything, but Malagant froze solid, just like the figure in Enid's dreams.

Should she just stay still and remain unseen? But what about her friend? She had to take the risk and find out if he was safe.

With the monster's shift in focus, Enid made her move while everyone stood frozen, snagging a stray carving knife from the roast beef station. Monsters or not, she had to find out what happened to the real Dylan.

The wyvern continued to pour his glacial flame on Malagant while Enid crept closer. The flame lessened in intensity and stopped altogether. Enid was relieved. She stepped out from her hiding place and addressed the wyvern.

"Hey. What have you done with Dylan? Where is he? I want my friend back."

The wyvern had an expressive face, and his surprise was written across his reptilian features. His eyes opened wide, his brows raised, and his terrible mouth hung slack. "Enid? How are you awake? How are you not frozen in time by Malagant's spell?" the wyvern asked. His voice sounded like Dylan's in timber, but the pitch was lower in tone.

"I'm warning you, I'm armed, and I want my friend. Where is he?" Enid held the carving knife in an aggressive stance.

"Enid, it's me, Dylan. This is me. I'm standing right in front of you," the wyvern said. His tail whipped nervously back and forth in agitation.

"Don't try to trick me. Dylan is human, just like me. He's my best friend. If he were a wyvern, whatever that is, I think I would know by now. Wyverns don't exist. This is all some kind of bad dream," Enid declared, her voice full of confidence.

"I was afraid of this. I'm so sorry for lying to you, Enid, but you don't know everything about me. Wyverns exist, and I'm really Dylan," the wyvern said, his head bowed. The wyvern's voice sounded patient and gentle, just like Dylan's.

"If you're Dylan, prove it. Tell me something only he and I would know," Enid challenged. Her nose crinkled in disbelief, but the carving knife never wavered.

"I confessed to you as a kid that I wanted to be a pirate. You called it my pirate obsession and never failed to tease me about it. Do you believe me now?" The wyvern's tail stilled, and he appeared as if bracing for a blow.

The hand clenching the knife faltered. "Dylan? What happened to you?" she gasped. "What's going on here?"

Dylan started to respond when a resounding crack rang throughout the room. The friends' eyes flew to the frozen figure behind Enid just as the thick ice enclosing Malagant blew apart. Malagant was free once more, and Enid caught between the two.

"Impressive try, my prince. Oh... Hello. What do we have here?" the medusa-like creature asked. Her sweet, purring voice sent a shard of pain ricocheting through Enid's skull. Malagant punctuated her question with a tendril of that deadly smoke aimed squarely at Enid.

Enid ducked and swung the carving knife at the same time. The weapon cut through a tendril and it fell to the floor, splattered with an inky blue substance. Her blow had struck home.

"How dare you, human?" Malagant's green eyes glowed with unholy fire, and she bared her sharp teeth. Malagant shot out another tendril, and this time it hit its mark. The tendril attached to Enid's back as she turned toward Dylan. Enid experienced an unbearable freezing pain. She sensed it drawing out her essence. Her soul was being pulled out of her body. Enid cried out in agony.

"Malagant, stop." Dylan pleaded. The wyvern's tail waved with Dylan's agitation.

"Make the promise, my prince, or this human will die screaming in front of you." Malagant's response sounded devoid of compassion. Enid gasped out Dylan's name, trying to give a warning.

"All right, Malagant. Anything you say, just please don't hurt her. You have my promise to accompany you to our realm. Just, please stop." A crystal tear fell from the wyvern's eye and hit the ground, twinkling like a blue diamond, while a green glow encircled the dragon's left claw.

"This human seems to know you well, my prince. What exactly is she to you?" Malagant gestured at Enid and then glanced down at her nails. Malagant showed no inclination to release Enid, who cried out in pain.

"Please release her. You're killing her. I've already promised to go back with you," Dylan said, desperate. He sensed Enid's life draining away with each passing second and held his breath.

A yellow light appeared in the center of the space and flashed warmly in all corners of the room. The center increased in intensity like a small sun, causing both creatures to glance away before they were blinded. A small, bent figure stepped out of the center of light and stood before the nightmarish apparitions with a confident stance. In one hand, the figure held a staff that he pointed at Malagant.

"Be gone," he said in a loud, booming voice. The end of the staff glowed with a white-hot light. A bright, swirling funnel cloud appeared near Malagant and enveloped both Malagant and Dylan. As quickly as she appeared at the party, all traces of Malagant and the wyvern-Dylan vanished.

Chapter 8

A Faraway Isle

Enid focused on her surroundings. It was unnaturally quiet, with none of the typical background noise. She lay on the floor in the dining room. Everything ached. As she stared up at the ceiling, she noted the electricity was out, but a stark light shone through the windows. How on earth had she ended up on the floor?

Dylan. With a sudden jolt, she remembered everything. Enid shot to a seated position. Her head pounded like a kettledrum as she whipped around to take in her surroundings.

Did that happen?

"Oh, good. You've come around at last. How are you doing? That was a nasty business." Mr. Ambrose helped himself to some hors d'oeuvres on the side table. She noted he'd already piled his plate relatively high with prawns and there was a smear of cocktail sauce on his pastel pink floral waistcoat.

"M-Mr. Ambrose? When did you arrive?" Enid glanced around the room and realized everyone stood frozen in place like living statues.

"I only got here twenty minutes ago, but it appears I arrived just in time. I offer my sincerest apologies for running late," Mr. Ambrose said while eating a mouthful of shrimp. "My compliments to your father on the food—delicious."

She shook her head. Certain she must have bumped it when she fell to the floor. "Mr. Ambrose, does everyone in the room look frozen to you?"

"Yes, dear. No one has moved an inch since I arrived—most unusual," Mr. Ambrose said as he glanced around the room.

"Did you spot anything else unusual when you arrived?" Enid's eyes were wide with fear. She glanced around again at her friends and family, all frozen in time.

"No, I saw nothing odd beyond that strange weather," Mr. Ambrose said. After a moment's hesitation, he added, "And I saw a gatecrasher make off with your young friend, Dylan."

She eagerly held onto his words. "Yes, Mr. Ambrose. Did you see where they went? I'm afraid Dylan is in trouble and needs my help." Enid's heart hammered in her chest as she waited for his reply.

"Yes. I know where they are, but I'm not sure you can help. They have gone to a place that is most difficult to travel to, and there is no guarantee of your safe return. But I agree your friend is most definitely in a pickle," Mr. Ambrose said, selecting some gherkins to add to his overflowing plate.

"Please tell me more. I... I'd like to understand. This is a weird situation, and I'd appreciate anything you could tell me." Enid held herself back from shaking the story out of the old man, knowing such behavior wouldn't help Dylan. She had to be patient.

"I'm sure you are aware the Roberts adopted Dylan at a very young age. He comes from a place that is dangerous for people like us. Dylan is from Afallon Isle." Mr. Ambrose took a seat at the table and gestured for Enid to join him. She perched on the edge of her chair, ready to take flight once she got the information.

Mr. Ambrose took a deep breath and began the tale of Dylan's original home and family. "Afallon Isle is a remote place shrouded in mists, not found on any maps."

"Is it an island in the Norwegian Sea or further out in the Atlantic?" Enid's head pounded with this new information.

"Afallon Isle is actually on a different plane of existence," Mr. Ambrose corrected her.

"A different plane of... How is this possible?" She leaned backward in her chair as if distance could improve her perspective.

"There are many layers of reality. Sometimes those planes intersect, as they did tonight. May I continue?" Mr. Ambrose asked and waited for Enid's nod before continuing.

"They divided the island into four separate kingdoms: mountain, sea, valley, and earth. The mountain folk, known as the Gwyllion, have Malagant as their leader. The Gwyllion practice life-force magic, using other beings' powers to fuel their spells. Dylan's people, known as the Annwyn, come from the sea and control all forms of water magic. Valley folk called the Ellyllon, command all forms of nature magic. The inner earth's inhabitants, known as the Coblynau, have their kingdom underground, and they have power over all rock, metal, and fire magic."

Enid couldn't help but interrupt again. "Now I know I must be dreaming. You're saying magic exists on this island?"

"Magic exists amongst all the realms, even this one. But here, magic has fallen out of fashion, so to speak, and science has taken its place. If you look hard enough, though, magic is everywhere and all around us," Mr. Ambrose said. Enid's mouth compressed into a straight line.

She did something quite odd at that moment. She pinched herself, hard. "Ouch."

"I assure you that you are very much awake. Now, where was I? Oh, yes. The four kingdoms of Afallon lived in peace for many years until the mountain folk encroached on other lands. The Gwyllion lived high on their mountain, encircled by both valley and sea. Being cut off caused them great difficulties in obtaining resources, so they attempted to spread their influence over the sea kingdom of Annwyn, which Dylan's family ruled."

"Hold on a minute, please. That creature called Dylan a prince. Are you telling me he is an *actual* prince, as in royalty?" Enid asked.

Mr. Ambrose nodded as he continued his story. "Yes, Dylan is the Prince of Annwyn, whose people are involved in a bloody conflict that has raged for centuries. Finally, the mountain kingdom proposed a truce. To seal the bargain, they suggested their mountain princess, Malagant, become betrothed to the sea kingdom's prince, Dylan."

"B-Betrothed? Dylan is betrothed. But that's impossible. He's only sixteen." Enid's mouth hung slack in shock.

"Yes, dear, but remember, this happened when he was only four years old. Royalty did that kind of thing all the time, you know. On the way to the betrothal ceremony, someone viciously attacked and murdered Dylan's parents. Naturally, the people of the sea kingdom blamed the mountain folk and vice versa. His people spirited Dylan away, hiding him in a land far beyond the Gwyllion's reach until he could come of age. That is how he came to live with the Roberts, who only knew he had a tragic past." Mr. Ambrose fell silent for a moment.

"How awful." Despite her disbelief, tears choked Enid's throat as she thought about all her friend had been through. Losing parents in an accident was a tragedy, but to have them ripped from you by murder was something with which Enid was all too painfully familiar.

"I guess that the Gwyllion princess, now Queen, found out where Dylan was and came to take him back to her mountain kingdom. I'm afraid he may be in terrible danger," Mr. Ambrose surmised as he finished his plate of food.

Dylan was in danger, but what could Enid do to help? It would be safer to just let it be, but this was Dylan. Even if he wasn't who she thought, he was still her best friend.

"Can I get to this island, Afallon? Can I travel there to free Dylan?" Enid reached out a hand and gently placed it on Mr. Ambrose's arm. Her eyes filled with tears for all Dylan had been through.

"Enid, you realize that Dylan and Malagant are not human, don't you? I'm afraid, even if there was a way to Afallon, you would do little to help." Mr. Ambrose patted Enid's hand. "You are only human, after all. You should just leave him to his fate."

"It doesn't sound like he'll have much of one unless someone tries to help him. He's been a loyal friend for as long as I can remember. He protected me when no one else would. I know if I were in trouble, he would try to help me no matter what. I have to do the same for him," Enid insisted.

"I'm not sure leaping into danger will help your friend. The cost you mention could very well be your life. Your father would never forgive me if I allowed something to happen to you. I'd never forgive myself." Mr. Ambrose said, shaking his head.

"Is there a way to unfreeze my father so we can ask? Is there a way to unfreeze everyone?" Enid asked, looking around, her eyes shining with sudden hope.

"I'm afraid this is a powerful time enchantment made by an Unseelie Queen. There is very little I can undo from here." Mr. Ambrose shrugged.

"Help me get to Afallon. Please, Mr. Ambrose. I'm begging you. I know my dad would understand if he could speak. Dylan means the world to both of us. Dylan is family. I don't know how I could live with myself if I sit back and do nothing." Enid's tears, bravely held in until this moment, spilled slowly down her cheeks.

"Oh, dear. Please don't cry." Mr. Ambrose held hands out as if to ward off Enid's tears.

"Please, Mr. Ambrose. I don't want to lose anyone else in my life." Enid choked on the last word as her tears continued to fall.

Mr. Ambrose's shoulder slumped a little. "Very well, Enid. I shall help you get to Afallon. I am forbidden to accompany you because of some... youthful follies, but I believe I can find guides to help you. Why don't you get changed while I work out the details?" Mr. Ambrose suggested.

"Oh, thank you, Mr. Ambrose." Enid wiped her tears and hugged the old man before dashing up the stairs to change, wondering, *what am I getting myself into?*

She rummaged through her closet and came up with the best outfit for these unusual circumstances. She decided she needed blue jeans, as well as sensible walking shoes. Enid layered a long-sleeved rugby polo over her favorite concert tee, then nabbed a dark hooded jacket full of deep pockets and ran back to the dining room.

Hoping vainly that she would return to the room to learn all she'd witnessed was only a terrible nightmare, she stepped into the dining room to find everyone still frozen and Mr. Ambrose studying Aeddan's face. "What's the story with this young man, Enid? I don't recognize him." Mr. Ambrose propped his chin in his right hand and used it to point in Aeddan's direction.

"He's supposed to be Dylan's cousin, which means I'm not sure who or what he is." Enid's nose scrunched in distaste.

"I see he made a good impression on you," Mr. Ambrose said.

Enid's gaze bounced from Aeddan to the rest of the party guests. "Why didn't they move again when Malagant left to go back to Afallon? Are they aware of their surroundings or in any pain?"

"That's an excellent question. I am unsure how widespread this spell is. Time enchantments are exceedingly tricky." Mr. Ambrose tapped a finger on his chin. "Don't worry. They are not aware of what is happening, and I assure you they are not in any discomfort. They are merely frozen in time. If we can get time moving again, it will be as if nothing happened to them. There's not much I can do until everything is set right. However, I may have just enough juice to free your guides to the island. At least I hope I do."

Mr. Ambrose suggested Enid step back as he said the words of an incantation. Enid understood none of it, but his hands took on a greenish cast. Soon, ropes of light stretched out to touch Aeddan and Bendith. It enveloped them in green. Once Mr. Ambrose's voice stilled, both figures jerked forward. They then halted, confused. Enid was bewildered. *Why did Mr. Ambrose choose Aeddan and Bendith?*

"What in the nine realms is going on here?" Aeddan's strident question boomed over the silent room. Aeddan whirled and noted Enid standing with Mr. Ambrose, and his eyes lit with the same molten fire Enid had seen earlier. "You, there. Tell me what has happened." Aeddan started toward them.

Mr. Ambrose whispered another string of words and Aeddan froze again. "Pity, I hoped he had more answers than questions."

Bendith padded over to Enid and the wizened shopkeeper with a slight shake of his head. The dog sat at Enid's feet, tail wagging, and tongue lolling to the side, ready for an adventure. Bendith frequently glanced at the pair. Enid reached down to give him a reassuring pat.

"I can't believe I'm going to ask this, but can you unfreeze Aeddan again? I have a few questions for him," Enid said.

"Of course, dear. He's a churlish young man, isn't he?" Mr. Ambrose asked. He then uttered a strange word, and Aeddan immediately cursed and exclaimed over his predicament.

"A wizard? Really? That's unfair," the boy groused. "Please set me free. I mean no one here any harm. They only sent me here to bring Dylan back to Afallon." Aeddan's eyes flashed fire again, directed at Enid.

"Wait." Enid placed a hand on the shopkeeper's arm. "Mr. Ambrose, are you a wizard, as he says?" She mentally kicked herself for not putting the pieces together on her own.

"Yes, that is one way to describe me. But look here, young man. Were you sent here to cause trouble? Did you bring Malagant here?" Mr. Ambrose's typically friendly smile evaporated as he asked Aeddan. The end of his staff glowed with a menacing light.

"N-No, sir. My name is Prince Aeddan of the Coblynau. My people sent me to bring Dylan back to Afallon. Dylan told me he would come back with me, but only after the human's party." Aeddan spoke in a more respectful tone to Mr. Ambrose.

"Well, Malagant took him by force to the island, and this young lady is determined to see him safely returned." Mr. Ambrose pointed to Enid.

Aeddan scoffed and rolled his eyes. "Surely, sir, you would be more suited to such a dangerous task."

"This is Enid's quest, and I have complete faith that she can prevail if she has the proper aid. Are you willing to help her find your cousin and ensure they come to no harm?" Mr. Ambrose asked.

"I'm not sure she's up to the task, but I would be in your debt if you would free me and send me back through the portal. I will help the human if that repays my debt," Aeddan's mouth turned down in distaste.

"Done, and the bargain is sealed," Mr. Ambrose intoned solemnly. Aeddan glowed with the green light again and moved once more. On his left wrist flashed a swirl of the beautiful bright green script. Enid squinted at it. *Is that something to do with the deal struck between Mr. Ambrose and Aeddan?* She wondered. *Some sort of contract?* She shook her head, frustrated—the tiny writing was impossible to read.

Mr. Ambrose leaned down to Bendith and asked if he also needed a bargain. Bendith barked once in response, his tail swishing back and forth, and leaned into Enid. "No? I thought as much. You're happy to assist her with no further inducement," Mr. Ambrose said. He chuckled and gave the dog a friendly pat on the head.

Mr. Ambrose directed Aeddan to drag a festively colored bag from the far corner of the room. "I have three gifts for you that may prove useful in your journey."

The first object he pulled from the bag was a beautiful wooden bow and a quiver bursting with sharp wooden arrows. Enid reached for them, setting the arrows at her feet, and carefully examining the bow.

She tested its compression and tension, admitting the smoother action when compared to her practice bow. She also noted that someone had painted the bow with a lovely golden script, very similar in appearance to Aeddan's green mark, and added blue gems, like the one in her ring.

"This bow is called Fail-Naught and is made from the wood of a yew tree. It will help you never miss your target. I made the arrows myself from sharpened hawthorn wood, which can purify the tainted." Enid startled and bit her lip in sudden reflection as she thought about the corsage she had left on her dresser, ornamented by frosted hawthorn berries.

Enid reverently set the bow to the side. "Did you call this bow Fail-Naught after Trystan's bow? King Arthur's Trystan? I appreciate the gift. I've had some lessons. This should come in handy."

"Yes, someone called Trystan used to own that bow, but now it is yours. Use the arrows sparingly and with pure intent, and you shall not fail in your quest. The next item I have is a cup, the Horn of Bran. With this cup, you will never know thirst or hunger." Mr. Ambrose handed Enid a beautiful cup made from an ox horn tipped in silver with a sturdy leather strap affixed.

"This can't be the actual cup of Bran. I thought that was just a myth lost to the ages." Enid's brow creased in concern.

"Oops, right? It's a replica, just like the bow and your ring," Mr. Ambrose corrected himself and winked at her.

Enid's eyes flashed like a laser beam at the kindly old man and then at her ring. "Mr. Ambrose…" she said but didn't finish. Enid decided if he pulled Excalibur out of that bag next, she wouldn't be surprised.

"May this always light your way, even when faced with total darkness." Mr. Ambrose fished out a chrome-plated flashlight from the bag with an impressive flourish. Enid accepted this last gift with raised eyebrows. A flashlight was the last thing she expected, considering the history behind the other items. Then a thought occurred to her.

"Mr. Ambrose, how come you have these gifts on hand?" she asked with a suspicious tone. "It's almost as though you knew I'd need them." She wondered anew if this was all a dream.

"Hmm… I can see why you would ask that," he nodded. "But no time to explain now. You'd best be on your way."

Chapter 9

THROUGH THE MAELSTROM

"NOW, THERE ARE SOME customs you must memorize before you travel through any portal. The world of the fae is full of rules that you must not bend, deceptions you must not fall for, and creatures you must not cross if you are to survive," Mr. Ambrose cautioned.

Though his posture suggested Aeddan was bored, Enid noted him leaning forward ever so slightly as he listened to the wizard's words. Bendith ran around the room, his black nose twitching and tail wagging as he inspected each pair of hands with confusion before giving a little whine and dashing off to the next victim.

Mr. Ambrose's list was brief but must be followed at all costs. Enid must not eat or drink anything, except from Bran's horn, while in Afallon. She should never remove her ring under any circumstances. She could not make any bargains or promises with anyone. And she must always be polite and speak the truth.

"The bargaining part is important, Enid," Mr. Ambrose said, his voice serious. He bobbled up the sleeve of his robe and revealed a burn scar in the shape of runes. "If you make a promise to a fae and then break it, there are painful consequences to endure." He gestured to the scar on his wrist with a sad look.

Enid swallowed before continuing. "Mr. Ambrose, is there something different about this ring? It pulsed with some sort of power when Malagant spoke." Enid studied the ring on her finger with a narrowed gaze.

"Yes. It is called the Ring of Dispel. It should protect you from all enchantments. A goddess forged and gifted it for just such a purpose. Do not take it off your finger for even a moment, or you will be lost," Mr. Ambrose warned.

She held the ring in front of her face and whispered, "The Ring of Dispel. You don't mean Sir Lancelot's legendary ring… do you?" Her mouth hung open in awe and wonder at the rare treasure that glinted on her hand.

Mr. Ambrose frowned in irritation. "Lancelot? Who is this Sir Lancelot that everyone keeps nattering on about? I've never heard of the poor fellow. Sounds like a dodgy character, if you ask me. The ring was a gift to Sir Cai, a most valiant knight."

"Not Lancelot's ring?" Enid's shoulders deflated a little but perked up when she realized she had a token from one of her favorite Arthurian knights.

The four figures hunched their shoulders in the biting cold as they ventured out into the frozen wasteland. A thick blanket of silence hung in the air, smothering all life from the landscape.

The snow crunched eerily beneath them as they walked, and Enid shivered as she noted that the wind stopped its howling - not a single branch or blade of grass stirred. She glanced around her, perplexed, wondering where on earth they were heading and how long it would take them to reach the mysterious portal.

The coldness outside burned Enid's ears, and she could see her breath. These details lent support that she wasn't dreaming. Enid pulled up the hood of her jacket and found gloves in her pocket. Oddly, she was the only one experiencing the cold. Aeddan and Mr. Ambrose showed no signs that the weather affected them much.

Mr. Ambrose came to a stop outside the small gate of the cottage, tapping his staff on the ground and pointing its glowing end at the green grass circle formed earlier that day.

The landscape was harshly illuminated by the frozen lightning in the sky, making it hard to make out any of the details from before, as a fresh layer of snow had covered up his own footprints from this morning. The carefree moments with Bendith seemed like a thousand years ago.

"Mr. Ambrose, what is that weird circle of grass? I spotted it this morning," Enid asked.

"That is what the ancients used to call a fairy circle. It is a portal between realms. These realms are distinct realities, all coexisting simultaneously but on separate planes. All over the globe are areas where the walls are paper thin between those realities. At the weak spots, during certain times of the year, a portal can appear. You are fortunate you did not step inside this earlier. There's no telling where you might have landed." Mr. Ambrose walked around the circle several times in a counterclockwise direction and muttered a chant. A Neon green glow lit the edges of the circle.

A wave of nausea washed over her. She took a deep breath, but fear still wriggled through her veins like an electric current. "How will we know if we end up in the correct place, since there are so many realities?"

Mr. Ambrose nodded sagely. "All I can tell you is that some of these portals are more stable than others in connecting different domains. This doorway has existed for an incredibly long time and leads to Afallon Isle. However, in an abundance of caution, I think you should all travel together through the gateway."

Enid, Aeddan, and Bendith lined up around the portal's edge in preparation. Of the three, only Enid appeared uncomfortable. She fidgeted with her bow and repeatedly checked to make sure she still had the flashlight and horn. Aeddan spoke with a hint of irritation. "Human, are you ready to do this, or should I take care of this alone?"

"No, I'm ready. Except I have one last question. How do I find my way back?" Enid asked. Her eyes narrowed, concentrating on Mr. Ambrose's reply.

The shopkeeper smiled. "You must do very well in school. These are all excellent questions. If we set everything back as it should be, time will move forward here, and a portal should open for your return. Otherwise, it would be best to locate a sovereign to cast a portal for you. That's a little trickier because they might send you somewhere nasty out of spite. That's why you must be always polite to whomever you meet." Mr. Ambrose nodded knowingly.

Enid's hands were clammy, as she nervously reached toward Aeddan. He looked down at her outstretched hand with a mix of trepidation and resignation. His eyes widened in surprise when he saw the slight tremor that shook her body as she stood next to him. She could feel his sigh even before it left his lips, and then he grasped her hand. Enid counted for the three companions. "One, two, three..."

As they stepped into the circle, the surrounding air shimmered and a loud hum began. The energy was palpable and the ground beneath their feet vibrated.

The surrounding green light became blinding and swirled all around them with all the colors of the rainbow. The hum built into a roar, and steadily gained in strength until it sounded like a continuous rumble of thunder. It seemed as if she was falling down an endless well. Only the hand she grasped desperately kept her from screaming in complete terror. With a start, Enid realized she'd experienced this sensation before, in her dreams.

Enid's eyes fluttered as the multitude of colors and shapes threatened to overwhelm her vision. The deeper they fell, the dizzier she felt, and her grip on Aeddan's hand tightened involuntarily. She feared the falling sensation would never end. Finally, with a jarring thud, they landed. As soon as she felt solid ground beneath her again, Enid let go of Aeddan's hand.

"Human, you should probably open your eyes now," Aeddan stated with barely concealed laughter.

"I have a name, you know," she grumbled with irritation. Her eyes snapped open, and she turned her head to have a look at the mysterious Afallon Isle.

They landed in a meadow full of wildflowers of all colors, and their fresh fragrances filled the air with hints of citrus and spice. Delicate white moths with azure patterns tattooed on their wings flitted about, drunk on nectar. The sky overhead was dotted by an occasional puffy cloud. Far off in the distance, an imposing snow-capped mountain loomed over the beautiful landscape.

The extreme time and weather change made Enid's head spin. Back home, it had been approaching midnight in the dead of winter. In this new realm, it appeared to be a lovely spring day, just before noon. *The temperature is so much warmer here,* she thought and removed her jacket.

Enid frowned and glanced around again, noticing with a start that her dog wasn't with her. *Bendith must be close,* she thought and called to him. It took a moment as she searched for her furry companion for Enid to notice that Aeddan's appearance changed. She tried hard not to stare, but couldn't help herself.

He appeared taller and more muscular, if possible. His blue eyes were more prominent and further apart, and the color looked even more vibrant than Enid thought possible. His hair shone blue-black like a raven's wing. The charcoal pin-stripe suit had been replaced with dark brown fighting leathers. He was armed with an assortment of knives and a deadly-looking sword. When he shifted his head to look around, Enid noticed his pointed ears.

"Human, you're staring again," Aeddan pointed out. His voice growled in irritation.

"S-Sorry. Did you realize that your appearance has changed?" Enid said. She understood the question might be rude, but she couldn't resist.

Aeddan sighed. "Human, I have many guises, and all of them are stunning. If you stare each time I change, people will think you are besotted."

Enid snorted. "Not a chance..." she muttered under her breath. She called Bendith again. "Aeddan, have you seen where..." Enid didn't get to finish her sentence because, at that moment, a head popped out of a nearby clump of flowers. "Oh." she gasped. Aeddan drew his sword.

"Enid?" the head said.

How does this stranger know my name?

Before Enid formed another question or reached for her bow, Aeddan leaped up with his sword unsheathed, facing off against the stranger. "How did you come by that name? Speak quickly before I use my blade to get the answers."

The stranger didn't appear intimidated. He looked as if he would relish tangling with the formidable Aeddan. He was tall and solidly built, with corded muscles. He wore black leather and was armed with a fearsome sword. The stranger had shaggy brown hair that fell almost to his shoulders, and he had warm, friendly brown eyes. As Enid continued to stare, she recognized those eyes.

But that's impossible. "Bendith?" Enid's tone was a mere whisper.

The stranger, careless of Aeddan's threatening posture, gave a courtly bow in Enid's direction. "Lady Enid, it is a delight to speak with you at long last."

Aeddan cocked his head for a moment and studied the scene before him. A throaty laugh and a genuine smile lit his attractive features. "Human, you are full of surprises. First, the wizard Merlin is a friend, and now I discover you kept a prince of Ellyllon as a lapdog?"

"M-Merlin? A prince?" Enid's mouth opened and closed several times in a perfect imitation of a fish out of water. "W-What are you saying? That Mr. Ambrose is Merlin? And Bendith, my dog, is a prince?"

"You have a gift for restating the obvious, Human. Did you not suspect Mr. Ambrose's identity? I thought Merlin had been imprisoned for all eternity by a vengeful witch, but he was at your party. As for this one, I can understand your shock. I was surprised myself," Aeddan said.

"Just to be clear, I'm no one's pet. I'm a fierce warrior and her protector." Bendith's eyes flashed as he took a menacing step toward Aeddan. "And I don't appreciate a prince of Coblynau trying to beguile my charge."

"You're both princes? Does that mean the same thing here? Dylan is a prince. You two are princes… Does everyone have the title of prince here? And you," — Enid pointed at Bendith — "were you like this all along? Why pretend to be a dog for all these months? Why pretend to be my friend?"

Bendith took a step toward Enid, and Aeddan raised his blade further into a menacing stance. "Enid, I pretended nothing. I'm your loyal friend. Someone cursed me before I traveled through the portal to your realm. I'm a shapeshifter who got trapped in my animal form. When I arrived, I was terrified and confused and couldn't change shape. Then I found you and Dylan, and we became friends. You treated me with love and kindness. I owe you a great debt that I can never repay."

As he spoke, Enid wiped her eyes on her sleeve. By the end of his story, she blushed. "Oh, my. What an awful thing to happen to you. What should I call you, Ben…? Er, what is your actual name?"

"Lady Enid, my name is Prince Rhodri of the Ellyllon. I owe you a great debt and pledge my service to you until I repay it. I am dedicated to your safety and will help you in any way I can." As Rhodri said these words, a bright green light surrounded his left wrist and flashed. When the light faded, there was a circle of gorgeous script encircling Rhodri's wrist, identical to what Enid witnessed on Aeddan.

Did we just make a bargain?

The amber flecks in Enid's brown eyes flashed as she glanced at Aeddan. "What did Rhodri mean when he said you tried to enchant me?"

Chapter 10

BEGINNING OF A JOURNEY

ENID'S BROW FURROWED IN confusion as Aeddan spoke, her mouth drawn into a thin line and fists balled at her sides as she attempted to control the rage boiling inside of her. He had tried to cast a spell on her when they first met.

She was right that he was a bully and couldn't be trusted. She stomped more than necessary as they trekked toward the forbidding mountain, where the princes assumed Dylan was being kept. It was the home of the Gwyllion, Malagant's kingdom.

"Human, are you still angry about our little misunderstanding?" Aeddan glanced back at her, and the smirk on his mouth showed he was anything but sorry.

"Of course not," she said with a saccharine smile. "You merely tried to control me with magic and then everything good in my life blew up right after you arrived. My family is frozen in time and an evil fairy kidnaps my best friend. Why would I possibly be upset?" Enid stomped through some gorgeous flowers. Maybe she should calm down a little.

"I take responsibility for trying to trick you. As for the rest, none of that was my doing. I was not involved with your precious Dylan's troubles until it affected my people." Aeddan's lips tightened in annoyance.

"He's not my precious anything. He is simply Dylan, my friend, who is a giant snake and a prince." Enid almost tripped on a tree root, trying to wrap her brain around it.

"He's not a snake. Dylan is a wyvern, which is rare, even in Afallon." Rhodri spoke up from behind Enid.

At the discovery of Dylan's secret identity as a wyvern, Enid was perplexed and scared. But what troubled her more was the fact that her beloved pet dog was actually a fae prince, cursed to remain in animal form for months on end. She couldn't help but feel guilty for not recognizing the truth sooner.

She slowed her steps, so Rhodri caught up with her, and they walked side by side for a while in silence. Finally, Enid spoke. "Was it awful being trapped as a dog?"

"At first it was painful because I couldn't change. Then it frustrated me because I couldn't speak. Even if I had communicated, I was still trapped in a strange place." Rhodri spoke calmly, but his lips turned down as he remembered that difficult transition period. "But I discovered friends who became dearer to me than anyone, so not all of my experience was bad." His expression brightened, and he ended with a shrug.

"I'm sorry you had to endure any of it. Was it just a coincidence that you and Dylan ended up in the same spot? Are there more of your people in my realm?" Enid said as she gave Rhodri's hand a gentle squeeze. Her eyes tracked Aeddan's movements to check if he listened.

"My people are aware of your realm and have visited many times in the past. We also knew that the wizard, Merlin, lived there because he's infamous in Afallon." Rhodri grinned as if remembering a funny story. "I ended up near Dylan because I needed to find him, just like our friend Aeddan, here. At first, I wasn't aware that I'd been cursed, and Dylan couldn't sense or help me because he hadn't yet come into his powers." The grin faded and Rhodri's eyes narrowed as he recalled the past. "I came through too soon."

"His powers... Dylan has powers?" she asked. "Why is he so important here? He's lived in my realm for many years. Is it so important that he returns?" Enid bit her lip in consternation.

"The Gwyllion influence over all the kingdoms was witnessed years ago, which is why I attempted to bring Dylan home to Afallon. They spread like a blight over the entire land, consuming everyone and everything in their insatiable quest for power. Everyone believed that Prince Dylan was the key to containing the Gwyllion in their mountain home and stopping incursions into the other kingdoms. Dylan may have remained too long in the human realm, acting as one of you. He should have had the power to defeat Malagant instead of being taken by her." Rhodri shook his head, discouraged.

"How was Dylan supposed to know how to defeat her when he'd been banished for so long? I think everyone is expecting a lot from one person. He can't be your only answer." Enid was filled with conflicting emotions as she defended her friend. She wanted to believe that Dylan stood a chance against Malagant and her magic, but Enid had seen the fae queen break through his ice without breaking a sweat. Malagant froze time itself—how could Dylan possibly hope to stand alone against such an adversary? And yet, despite the fear, Enid refused to back down and leave Dylan on his own.

"I agree with the human for once. When I met the prince, he seemed no more and no less human than all the others in that cursed realm. This human displays more fire and courage than he does. If he's our only chance for salvation, then we're doomed to failure." Aeddan tossed this gloomy pronouncement over his shoulder.

Enid exploded. "Dylan does have courage. Besides that, he's loyal, smart, and kind. Dylan is the best friend anyone could ever hope to have. He has a strength of character. If you ask me, this all is a little unfair. You've all pinned your hopes on him for a quick solution." She caught herself stomping again.

"Our people didn't invent these hopes without some basis," Rhodri said. "There is an old prophecy of a dragon prince who will defeat the Gwyllion and trap them in their mountain home. This prophecy has been in place for centuries, and some say it is why the Gwyllion attacked the sea court first."

"A prophecy, huh? Many humans believe in the power to write their destinies. We don't all believe the future is set in stone. What if Dylan isn't the only way to defeat Malagant?" Enid asked what she deemed to be a fair question, but no one responded. The unlikely trio walked on in silence.

The going seemed a little rough in places, but they made good time, and the forbidding mountain inched closer with every step.

Enid marveled at the varied scenery they passed. The sun was still high in the sky when they paused by a beautiful lake with a surface as calm as glass for a brief rest. Enid had her jacket around her waist as the temperature was warm. The air smelled of vegetation, like water mint and meadowsweet. Sounds of buzzing insects and croaking frogs filled the air. This lake was memorable, and not just for the beauty of the crystal-clear waters.

As Enid enjoyed a drink of water from the horn, the surrounding wildlife mesmerized her. Silvery fish often leaped out from the placid surface. These minnows varied in size, and as the fish jumped, rainbow-hued gossamer wings spread from their backs and practically carried them across the length of the lake.

Lily pads dotted the placid surface and lounging idly on a few were frog-like creatures with long, sharp tusks. Instead of a green color, these frogs reminded Enid more of goldfish since they were covered with brilliant orange-gold scales and had golden eyes.

Enid watched in awe as Rhodri and Aeddan bowed their heads slightly to that group of creatures. The way they approached the beasts with caution clarified that they were dangerous, and Enid quickly followed suit.

Sure enough, as soon as the group achieved some distance, Aeddan turned to Enid. "Those are the Afanc. They're territorial and quick to anger. They will eat anything that enters the water without their permission. These are beings who could alter reality if they wished. It would be best not to cross them."

Enid slowly bobbed her head up and down, but her eyes had a far-off look. She was sure she had seen those golden scales before, but where? An inquisitive gleam filled her eyes as she studied the strange creatures before her. Aeddan read her mind. "They are also rumored to grant wishes if captured, but it's not worth angering them to find out, Human."

After that terse warning, the group continued their journey. Enid's mind swirled with images of the Afanc as she slipped into a comfortable silence behind Rhodri and Aeddan. The creatures seemed familiar somehow, but she couldn't remember how and was intrigued by their wish-granting abilities.

The group continued their journey and Enid couldn't stop wondering what it would be like to capture the creature and have her wishes granted. Until today, Enid had put little faith in wishes. They hadn't worked for her so far. But what if she was wrong? *Was it a way to save Dylan?*

The journey took most of the day, but eventually, the sun started its descent. They arrived at a suitable camping site near a stream.

Enid trudged up the path, her face and clothes smudged with mud from an earlier misstep. She was famished — she hadn't eaten since breakfast — and every muscle ached, yet a spark of anticipation lit her eyes as she thought of the day ahead.

They each took turns washing downstream a little way from where they had stopped. For Enid's turn, she plaited her long, dark hair in a single braid to keep it away from her face, then stripped down to her t-shirt and rolled up her jeans.

She stepped into the cool stream, shivering at the sudden change in temperature. It was invigorating though, and Enid quickly splashed water on her face and body, becoming more awake with each passing moment. She tried to clean away as much of the mud as possible.

As Enid finished preparing to return to camp, a movement in the water caught her eye. She peered closer and saw what looked like a large fish swimming lazily downstream. It must have been at least four feet long, with thick scales that glinted gold in the setting sun. Enid took an involuntary step backward because that this was no fish. The thing had legs. Sure enough, webbed feet propelled the creature through the water with ease. Enid stared, transfixed, as an Afanc swam closer.

The Afanc opened its jaws, revealing razor-sharp teeth, and lunged for her. Enid yelped and leaped out of the way, stumbling on the bank, and landing hard on her backside. The Afanc wasn't deterred. It slowly climbed out of the water after Enid, dripping wet and furious.

Enid scrambled to her feet and backed away, holding her hands out in a placating gesture. "I'm sorry. I-I didn't mean to trespass. Please, let me go and I won't come back."

The Afanc continued to advance on Enid. Her knees threatened to wobble at the sight of those needle-like teeth. She thought the situation couldn't become worse until she heard the creature's gravelly voice, "Your death won't be quick this time, human."

When Enid heard it speak, she remembered where she had seen those golden scales, at the lake in the human realm where she almost drowned. *But that was impossible, wasn't it?*

Enid had no choice but to run. She sprinted towards camp, the Afanc hot on her heels. Enid heard its angry breaths and the wet slurping sounds it made as it ran. She wouldn't make it. Just as the Afanc was about to catch her, Enid tripped over a root and went sprawling into the dirt.

The Afanc was upon her in an instant. Its mouth opened. Enid scrabbled frantically away, trying to put as much distance between herself and the creature as possible. She wasn't fast enough. The Afanc caught her by the leg and dragged her kicking and screaming back towards the stream. Enid was going to die.

Suddenly, the Afanc stopped dragging Enid and let out a surprised grunt. Enid looked over her shoulder to see Rhodri standing behind the Afanc, his sword buried deep in the creature's back. Enid had never been so relieved to see anyone in her life.

Rhodri yanked his sword free, and Enid scrambled to her feet. However, the Afanc was not dead yet. It turned on Rhodri with a vengeance, slamming into him and knocking him to the ground. Its strength was petrifying. While the creature was distracted by Rhodri, Enid realized she had to help her friend somehow. She grabbed a nearby baseball-sized stone and ran towards the Afanc, hitting it as hard as possible on the head. The Afanc roared in pain and let go of Rhodri. Enid hit it again with all her might until the creature stilled.

Enid stared down, stunned, and the bile rose in her throat because she had knocked a living thing unconscious. Until that moment, Enid hadn't realized she was capable of such a thing.

She turned away and retched at the sight of the Afanc's chipped tusk, which must have occurred during their struggle. When she finished, she checked on her friend.

Rhodri stood nearby, a little unsteady on his feet. "Enid, are you alright?" He reached out to her and hugged her as if his life depended on it. Then he took a step back, studying her for injuries.

"Y-Yes," was all Enid could stammer.

"You captured an Afanc?"

Enid nodded, with her eyes wide. "I-It was about to kill us."

"Do you remember what Aeddan said they do to people who capture them?"

Enid nodded her head, her stomach somersaulting again. She hadn't thought about the consequences of her actions.

"They grant wishes," Rhodri said in a solemn tone. "Which sounds amazing, except the price is always too high. Someone innocent must always pay. No wish is given for free in Afallon. If you wish for beauty, wealth, or power, it is taken in equal measure from someone unsuspecting. If you try to wish for something good, like bringing Dylan safely back home, another must take his place as Malagant's captive."

Enid swallowed hard. She had to admit it was so tempting. Her friend could be back home with a single wish. But what would happen to the person who took his place? Enid couldn't put another person in jeopardy even to save her friend, nor would Dylan want her to. She hadn't considered a cost to wishing. But for now, she was just glad to be alive.

"Thank you for your help, Rhodri," Enid said. "I don't know what I would have done without you."

Rhodri nodded, his face grave. Enid guessed he was thinking about the Afanc and the price it might extract from them. But they would deal with the creature. Together, they would overcome anything.

Aeddan wouldn't be happy when he found out what Enid had done, but Enid would face it. After all, she and Rhodri were still alive. And that was all that mattered.

They dragged the unconscious Afanc to the far side of the stream. Rhodri set him floating adrift in the swift current, and when the creature disappeared around a bend and vanished, both breathed easier.

When Rhodri finished, they headed back to the campsite, hoping for a small fire.

The Afanc's attack had left Enid shaken, and she wanted nothing more than to curl up in a ball and forget the whole incident. But she knew that wasn't possible. Aeddan would want to know what happened, and she wouldn't lie.

As they approached the campsite, Enid spied Aeddan sitting by the fire, his face grim. He looked up as they approached. She had faced down an Afanc, so surely, she could face Aeddan's anger. But she wasn't looking forward to it.

"What took you so long?" he demanded. "I was about to come looking for you. Human, you look even worse after bathing. What happened?"

"Calm yourself, Coblynau. We ran into some trouble," Rhodri said.

Aeddan's gaze shifted to Enid, and he saw the truth in her eyes.

"You did something, didn't you?" he asked.

Enid nodded, her stomach twisting. "I accidentally captured an Afanc. I didn't intend to, but it was going to kill us," she said, sounding defensive. "What was I supposed to do?"

Rhodri explained they had set the creature free without making a wish after overpowering it. Aeddan was silent for a long moment, and Enid could see the wheels turning in his head.

"You did what you had to do," he said. "I only hope that is the end."

Enid swallowed hard. She knew exactly what he meant.

Chapter II

NIGHT TERRORS

AFTER ENID'S AFANC ENCOUNTER, the trio moved their camp inland and away from the stream. Hopefully, when the creature regained consciousness, he'd be satisfied to leave them in peace.

The shadows lengthened and Enid stumbled more often in the advancing gloom. Rhodri prevailed on Aeddan for the group to rest for a while. They found a break in the woodland that looked ideal for a campsite. Enid could hardly keep her eyes open and thought she might sleep for a week, yet she wanted to reach Dylan as quickly as possible. She protested, but both males insisted. "Human, you will only slow us down with all of that stumbling in the dark. It makes sense to rest a short time in Ellyllon before we reach hostile lands," Aeddan said in a matter-of-fact tone with a smug lift of his chin.

Enid silently objected to his logic but was too tired to argue further. She barely had the energy to sit up and watch as Rhodri rustled around the clearing and gathered some tall grasses into three separate piles. What happened next completely astounded her.

Rhodri placed his hands over each stack of grass. After a brief flash, the piles changed into grass-colored bedrolls. But that was not to be the only impressive feat of magic. Aeddan gathered some wood, and with glowing hands, started a small campfire. He also ringed the fire with rocks glowing from the heat of just his touch.

Enid's tiredness vanished after witnessing these magical yet mundane tasks. Enid gestured to the newly formed bedrolls and the small fire. "Wow. Does everybody here have magic?"

Rhodri nodded. "Yes, most beings on Afallon have some small level of magical skill. It is called alchemy and is about the transformation of matter."

"Are there limits to this skill?" Enid's mouth hung open with wonder.

"It depends more on the skill and energy level of the practitioner and how radical the attempted transformation is. The change from meadow grass to cloth isn't very difficult, but to change grass to metal or stone is almost unheard of," Rhodri said. Enid shook her head in wonder and almost pinched herself again to check if she was dreaming.

The princes roasted the leeks, mushrooms, and berries that Rhodri had gathered. "Would you like some of this, Human?" Aeddan said as he tried some steaming mix.

Typical bully, Enid almost responded. Rhodri growled in reply. "Don't tempt her, Coblynau, or you will have my sword. You know she cannot eat our food. You heard what the wizard said."

"What would happen to me? Mr. Ambrose... Sorry, M-Merlin didn't explain that part," Enid corrected herself.

"It is said that if humans eat our food, they cannot return to their realm. Nothing will ever taste as good or as sweet," Rhodri, flushed with anger, explained while watching Aeddan through narrowed eyes.

"Yes, it's well-known that humans are very weak." Aeddan turned away.

Enid's stomach rumbled. She had a sudden thought and pulled out the horn. She held it for a while, thinking about what she might want to eat. Her father's vegetable broth came to mind. She sensed the horn heating. Enid let the warm cup rest in her hands to chase away the nighttime chill and then took a small sip and smiled. The broth tasted exactly right. She experienced a sudden pang of sadness, picturing her friends frozen in time.

Both princes had finished their meals and looked at Enid with interest. "Enid, do I smell your dad's soup?" Rhodri asked with wonder in his voice.

"Yes. I was thinking of it, and my cup filled with this broth. Oh, it filled again, but I've had enough. Do you want some?" Enid asked.

"I've always wanted to try your dad's soup. It always smelled so good." Rhodri held out his cup and Enid filled it.

She turned to Aeddan. "I don't suppose you'd like to try some as well?"

Rhodri drank his broth with relish. Aeddan held his cup out. Enid filled it to the brim and Aeddan took a small experimental sip and then drained the whole cup.

"That is the best soup I have ever had. Enid, your horn is a wondrous thing. It was fortunate Merlin had it at his disposal," Rhodri said.

Enid was pleased her companions liked the food she conjured and smiled. "I was lucky he had this handy. It would have been difficult to search for Dylan and rescue him from Malagant on an empty stomach."

"Human," Aeddan said, after a lengthy pause, as he stared into the campfire, "why are you doing this? Why are you risking your life to save the dragon prince? He's only one being, and he did not trust you with the truth. He's not even human."

Enid looked at Aeddan, wondering how best to explain it so he would understand. His words stung a little, but she couldn't deny their truth. "Dylan is important to me," she began. "We've been friends since we were very young. We bonded over the loss of our parents. I never had the chance to know my mom, and he was the only one who could relate to what I was going through. He's like family to me, and I love him." Enid's voice caught briefly, and she had to take a deep breath before continuing. "I'm not sure why he didn't trust me with his secrets, but that doesn't matter right now. I'm sure he had his reasons. He is in trouble, and I can't lose anyone else."

Aeddan was silent for a moment, contemplating Enid's words. Then he nodded his understanding. "I see."

Rhodri spoke. "I'm sorry for what you've been through, Enid. I'm glad you had Dylan in your life, and you have my friendship, too. And I'm sorry, but glad you're here with us now."

Enid smiled at her friend, touched by his understanding. She turned her gaze back to the campfire, lost in thought. She was determined to rescue Dylan from Malagant's clutches. Enid would use the items Mr. Ambrose gifted to her to break the curse that had frozen her friends in time and stolen her best friend. She had to believe that there was a way because she couldn't bear the alternative.

Aeddan and Rhodri discussed the trail they would take in the morning. It would pass mostly through the Ellyllon lands. Enid's eyes grew heavy as she listened. After all the hiking and excitement, she was utterly exhausted.

Enid leaned her head back against a tree and closed her eyes, letting the sound of her companions' voices lull her to sleep.

Enid woke with a start. She must have dozed off. It was Rhodri's turn to keep watch. Enid sat up and rubbed her eyes, trying to shake off the drowsiness. She looked over at Aeddan and was glad that he was sleeping soundly. Enid got up quietly so as not to wake him and walked over to where Rhodri stood guard.

"You should get some sleep too," Enid said.

Rhodri turned to look at her. "I will, soon, but I wanted to talk to you first."

Enid nodded and sat down on the ground, facing him. "What is it?"

"I just wanted to tell you I understand why you're doing this," Rhodri said. "And I'm here for you now, like you were for me when I became trapped in your realm. We won't stop until we find and free Dylan. If it is in my power, I will make sure you lose no one else."

Tears welled up in Enid's eyes and she blinked them back. Rhodri's words touched her. "I hope you are right, and I'm so glad you're with me. Thanks for helping me."

Rhodri smiled, and it struck Enid how handsome he looked in the firelight. "It is my pleasure, Enid."

Then Enid yawned, unable to stifle it.

"I think that is my cue to let you get more sleep," Rhodri said with a chuckle. "Goodnight, Enid."

"Goodnight, Rhodri," Enid said as she lay down and closed her eyes. She knew she would dream of Dylan tonight. And she would save him. She had to believe they would succeed. Because the alternative was unthinkable.

Soon Enid floated high above the frozen landscape of her nightmares. As she stared down, she noted the dense blue forests and icy battlements located high on a mountain crag.

It gave her a sense of unease.

She expected no one in the fortification would note her presence except the one she dreaded seeing. As she glided through the battlements, many cadaverous figures could be seen. This time, Enid studied their appearance. With the almost complete absence of color, the figures blended into the mountain terrain. A few had their heads thrown back in agony, and Enid could make out sharpened ears. There was no mistake in that observation. Was this Malagant's castle and their ultimate destination?

Enid's unease turned into fear as she peered closer at the figures and realized their conditions were worse than in previous dreams. Enid swallowed hard against the bile rising in her throat as she continued to search among the countless bodies.

Suddenly, Enid spotted something moving close by. She turned to see a black smoky tentacle slithering towards her. Another followed, and then another, until Enid was surrounded by the writhing mass.

Enid tried to scream, but no sound would come out. The tendrils tightened around her, and Enid got pulled towards the darkness.

She found herself paralyzed with fear. The tentacles tightened their grip as the suckers bit into her flesh. Just before she was engulfed, Enid heard a voice calling her name. The grip of the tentacles loosened, and she floated up out of the darkness and deeper into the fortress.

Enid braced herself for what would come next. The dream never varied. Enid landed on the battlement wall nearest to a widened corridor. The young man looked as he always did in her dreams. He glanced towards her with purpose. An icy fear gripped Enid's heart.

As in her previous travels, he was propped against a wall while any vibrancy he had was being leached away by the dark tendrils which slithered and scraped across his countenance.

Aside from subtle differences, he resembled her Dylan. She could admit that now. This figure appeared taller and more solidly built, like Aeddan or Rhodri. His curly hair was colored a lighter shade of brown. His eyes appeared more prominent and of a bright hue, almost as if he had a fire raging inside against the dull surroundings.

Why hadn't she recognized this earlier?

Enid approached Dylan from the side. Like countless other times, he sensed her presence. His head fell to the side and Enid glimpsed his ear. Like Aeddan and Rhodri, Dylan's ears came to a graceful point in his fae form. His voice rumbled in his chest when he asked, "Enid?"

Enid found her voice and answered him, "Yes, Dylan. I'm here with some friends, and we're coming for you. Don't be afraid. What is this place?"

"It is the end," Dylan said. "The end of everything."

Enid glanced around and witnessed the devastation. The corpses were strewn about. Enid became sickened by the sight. This didn't appear to be any natural disaster. It was something much worse.

"What happened here?" Enid asked, her voice trembling.

"The last battle was fought," Dylan said. "And we lost."

Enid glimpsed the emptiness in Dylan's eyes. He had been through so much.

"How can I help you?" Enid asked.

"You can't help me," Dylan said. "No one can."

Dylan's laugh sounded devoid of humor. Enid experienced a blast of cold air and stepped back. Icy flames licked at her skin, and she cried out in pain. "You always wanted to play the hero." His voice sounded the same, but the tenor sounded almost robotic in its delivery. Dylan looked at her with cold pity, his eyes full of shadows.

"Of course, I'd come for you. We're best friends. I'd do anything to help." Enid tried to sound confident, but her voice wavered.

"And that's your problem, Enid. You're always trying to save people after it's too late." The cold temperature warmed for a moment and Enid could see the real Dylan trapped inside the nightmare surface.

Tears welled in her eyes, and Enid shook her head. "I don't understand what is happening."

"Are we still best friends, now that you know what I am? Would you do anything to help a hideous monster like me? You denied my very existence. If you intended to help, then why didn't you offer any of the other times we met in this horrible place?" Dylan's tone sounded even cooler than the surrounding icy battlements.

"I wanted to help, and I'm sorry I didn't believe you when you showed me who you were." her head bowed as shame bloomed on her cheeks.

"I've seen you cower in fear before. Are you saying you aren't afraid now?" Dylan sneered.

Enid found the lack of warmth in his eyes unsettling. This Dylan appeared to be a darker reflection of her friend. His laugh sounded bitter. Blood stained his lips and teeth.

"I'm trying hard not to be. I wish you had told me all about what was going on sooner. But I'm here now, and I'm listening. What can I do?" Enid said, urgent to get through to her friend.

"You can die," Dylan said, and then opened his mouth. Enid stepped back in horror as a fresh wall of ice spewed forth, straight at her.

Enid recognized what came next. She had witnessed his icy flames in the waking world. If his frozen fire engulfed her, she would burn. Enid tried to appeal to him.

"Dylan, please."

"Dylan is gone, Human. Your human friend never actually existed." The flames grew colder, and Enid's skin blistered.

"Please, stop. I can help you." Enid screamed as the glacial fire spread and realized she wouldn't escape this time. Enid called out to Bendith for help with raw panic in her voice. The flames crept closer. Was this the end? Enid got pulled out of the maelstrom just in time to escape.

Enid awoke with a start. Rhodri was shaking her awake, his face full of worry. "Enid, wake up. You were having a nightmare."

"It was Dylan. But I'm awake now. I'm awake." Enid assured him. She felt like a rag doll after being shaken by Rhodri. His strength was formidable.

"Are you sure?" Rhodri's voice held a note of skepticism. He noted her shivering and offered his cloak.

Enid nodded gratefully. "I'm fine." Enid realized she didn't sound entirely convincing. But she had to find Dylan. And soon. That was a clear warning from her dream self. She had to reach Dylan before it was too late.

Chapter 12

UNEXPECTED VISITORS

"YOU WERE DREAMING AGAIN, and I noticed you emitted a strange light while you slept. This was something I hadn't ever noticed before." Rhodri said with his eyes narrowed in concern.

"What do you mean, a glow? And how could you tell I was dreaming?" Enid asked, shocked.

"Human, with all that dreadful noise you made, it was obvious you were dreaming," Aeddan said snidely. "Although I didn't realize you had some rudimentary magic." He stood nearby with his hand gripping a knife as if preparing for battle.

"I'm sorry. What did you say? I have rudimentary magic. That's not true." Her shock at Aeddan's words shook off the last of her dream. The sharp pain in her chest fueled her fervent denial. Magic had taken Dylan. How could she possess the very thing she was fighting against?

"Our old knowledge claims that dreams are a portal to another realm. A being's basic essence can travel and witness the past, present, or future if they have a touch of magic. Your glimmer while dreaming shows you may have this ability," Rhodri said, while Aeddan nodded.

"I, too, saw the gleam, Human. Do you have wizards in your family? It may explain Merlin's interest in her." Aeddan aimed the last comment at Rhodri and made a show of scrutinizing Enid. Rhodri bristled at the attention.

"Wizards and magic? Me? Since we're in this place, I'm forced to admit that magic is real, but there's absolutely nothing magical about me. Those dreams are just terrifying nonsense, not a glimpse into any future." Enid shook her head vehemently in denial.

Aeddan shrugged, and his mouth pulled down into a frown of impatience. "Have it your way, Human. But your blindness to your power will put us all at risk, even your precious Dylan. From now on, we'll need to be watchful when we sleep. You should be tethered to the present, or you may get lost in time."

What Aeddan and Rhodri said alarmed Enid. She tried to downplay the entire episode, but there was more to it than she was letting on. Enid had always viewed herself as an average person with no skills or talents. But if what they said was true, Enid might have some trace of magic inside her after all. And that could be very dangerous in this strange place.

"What do you see in these dreams? What upsets you so?" Rhodri's brow furrowed in concern for her.

"It's always the same. I'm in a frigid, barren place where some kind of battle raged. There are bodies everywhere, either dead or decaying. I am chased by some type of dark fog or tentacles. I can't let them catch me. As I run, I come upon a figure who looks like Dylan. He recognizes me and asks for my help. When I try to speak, no words come out. My dream ends at that point, but this time, we spoke. Afterward, Dylan tried to burn me with his fire." Enid looked from one prince to the other, wondering what they would think of her nightmare. "It is just a bad dream, right?"

Both princes looked at one another, concern etched across their faces. Even Aeddan's expression lacked his usual contempt. "It is possible to create a talisman for your protection," Rhodri said. "I'm concerned that if you burn in your dream, you might perish here."

"Perish. As in dead? But it's Dylan. He would never hurt me. He wanted my help," Enid protested, though the Dylan in her dreams differed from the boy she knew.

Rhodri reached out for one of Enid's hands and took it into his own. "As long as I've known you, you've suffered these nightmares. If there is danger in them and it is within my power to provide protection, I must." The beautiful green script on his left wrist glinted in the firelight.

Moments later, Rhodri left Aeddan and Enid alone at the site while he searched through the surrounding forest. He came back with his arms overflowing with flowering green and yellow vines. Rhodri set to work, transforming the vines into a beautiful woven belt, buttery yellow and punctuated with star shapes of the darkest green. He held it out to Enid.

"This is a chain of witches' candle and star anise, which should anchor and protect you from your nightmares."

Enid took the belt and scrutinized it. It appeared as supple and strong as the finest leather, velvety soft, and the scent reminded her of licorice. Enid nodded her thanks and threaded the beautiful belt through the loops of her jeans. She was skeptical, but would err on the side of caution. She would let nothing jeopardize Dylan's safety.

Aeddan started to comment, his tongue sharp as a blade, but stopped mid-sentence abruptly. His head snapped to the side like he was startled by something invisible, and he leaped to his feet. He darted towards the edge of camp, squinting into the inky blackness as if searching for something.

"What is wrong?" Rhodri called after him.

"I heard something." Aeddan's voice sounded tense. "A noise... like someone digging."

Despite her jacket, a chill ran down her spine. Aeddan's sense of hearing must be far better than hers. She got to her feet and joined him at the edge of the camp.

"Where is the noise coming from?" she asked.

Aeddan shook his head. "I can't tell... it seems to come from every side all at once."

Rhodri came up behind them, drawn by the sense of unease that filled the air. "What should we do?"

"I'm not sure," Aeddan said. "But we should be ready for anything."

Enid nodded, her hand straying to her bow. Whatever was out there, at least they would face it together.

Aeddan tensed. "There." He pointed over at a clump of bushes.

Enid followed his gaze and could perceive the movement. Something lurked just out of sight.

"Come out." Aeddan called. "If you mean no harm, you have nothing to fear from us."

Enid heard a rustling and then a small, gnarled creature appeared from the shadows. It was the size of a child with white matted hair and dark eyes that seemed to take everything in at once. The creature wore an unusual uniform, which was a mix of dull brown military fatigues and smudged mining garments. In its hand, it grasped a pickax that glinted menacingly in the light.

Rhodri reached for his sword, but Aeddan stopped him with a gesture. "Wait here. Let me speak with him first."

The creature eyed them warily for a moment, then spoke in a strange, guttural language that Enid couldn't understand, but Aeddan comprehended.

Aeddan stepped forward, hands held out in a peaceful gesture. Enid and Rhodri watched as Aeddan nodded in greeting and addressed the visitor in the same language.

The creature saluted to Aeddan and then chattered away in its strange language, and Aeddan listened intently. After a few minutes, Aeddan turned back to them. "His name is Selwyn. He's a member of the Coblynau border guard, instructed to watch for my return since I departed court."

The rustling of leaves signaled the entrance of two more Coblynau into the clearing. They were dressed in similar brown leathers and had weapons glinting on their belts, although not as many as Selwyn. The three Coblynau discussed something fervently with Aeddan, and Selwyn made a wavelike motion with his arm, ordering Aeddan to join him. Aeddan spoke to placate them, and at one point revealed his bargain mark to them. The Coblynau glanced at it with excitement in their eyes, but shook their heads in disagreement.

"What are they saying, do you think?" Enid asked Rhodri.

"I believe they are trying to persuade Aeddan to go back to the Coblynau court, but my language skills are a bit out of practice."

Aeddan turned and beckoned Enid and Rhodri over. "Don't worry," he said. "They were searching for me. Come and meet them."

A little hesitantly, Enid approached the group of Coblynau with Rhodri close behind. Aeddan introduced them and explained that Rhodri and Enid accompanied him to save the dragon prince. He pointed again to his bargain mark and then to Enid. The other Coblynau were named Delwin and Jestin.

The Coblynau stared at Rhodri and Enid for a moment, and then they all started talking at once. Aeddan laughed and tried to keep up with their questions and answers, translating for Rhodri and Enid.

After a bit, Jestin went off into the forest and came back with a small bundle. He handed it to Aeddan, who smiled and thanked him.

"What is it?" Rhodri asked.

"Food," Aeddan said. "For breakfast."

As the princes and Coblynau ate, Enid held the Horn of Bran and tried to picture something filling and warm. She thought back to those chilly mornings when she ran late for school. The warm and chocolaty breakfast drink it conjured was a comforting taste that brought Enid back to her childhood. The drink was sweet and bitter, with a hint of creaminess that made it so satisfying.

As the generous horn warmed in her hands, Enid thought about her father and her friends. What would happen to them if she failed? What would happen to Dylan? Would they ever go back to the way things were?

Her companions interrupted her glum thoughts, asking her what she had for breakfast. She obliged by filling everyone's cups with the chocolate concoction. None of the fae had ever tried chocolate before. Enid filled their cups several times. To her delight, Aeddan grudgingly complimented the humans on their ingenuity.

Jestin enjoyed himself, politely requesting seconds and thirds.

The Coblynau were fascinated by Enid because they had never seen a human, and they wanted to know everything. Enid answered as best she could.

"Tell us about your world," Selwyn said, through Aeddan. "Is it as strange as this one?"

Enid considered for a moment. "It's different, but I wouldn't say my world is stranger. It's just... normal, I guess. Most people go about their lives without ever knowing that magic exists."

The Coblynau looked at each other and shook their heads in disbelief. "How can they not know?" Delwin asked. "Surely everyone must sense the magic in the air."

"Well, some people do," Enid said, thinking of Mr. Ambrose and her mother. "But most people just write it off as coincidence or chance. They believe in a thing called science, not magic, so they don't see it."

"That's sad," Jestin said. "If they can't see the magic, then they can never experience the genuine wonder of existence."

Enid nodded. "I'm still trying to get used to the reality of magic. It's like... opening my eyes for the first time and seeing a vast ocean in all its lethal beauty."

The Coblynau sat silent for a moment, contemplating Enid's words. Then Selwyn spoke up. "If your world is so different, then why are you here? In our world, I mean."

"I'm here to save my friend, Dylan," Enid replied. "He was taken by Malagant, and I'm going to bring him back."

The Coblynau looked at each other again, this time with a touch of apprehension. "Malagant is a formidable enemy," Selwyn said. "You should be careful."

"We will be," Aeddan said. "But the human is right. We must try."

The Coblynau nodded and rose to their feet. "We will show you our path that will help shorten your journey to reach Malagant's castle," Selwyn offered.

"Thank you, my friends," Aeddan replied.

A short trek from their camp, the three Coblynau stopped, and Selwyn showed they should continue along the worn path. The companions bid the Coblynau a fond farewell.

Some distance further, Rhodri called out, "I think I see something up ahead." An edge of caution in his tone put Enid on alert.

Aeddan frowned. "What do you see?"

Rhodri pointed towards some shrubs before them. "I can't be sure, but I think it's their path."

Enid stepped closer to the shrubs and amongst their thick branches was an opening of some sorts. She inspected the area more and realized that what they were looking at wasn't just an ordinary pathway—it was leading down towards something underground.

Chapter 13

THE CRYSTAL CAVE

AEDDAN STUDIED THE OPENING. "It's certainly one of my people's trails. If we take the path, as Selwyn suggested, it will shorten our journey." He motioned for her and Rhodri to follow him as he descended into the entrance of a hidden underground cavern.

Enid and Rhodri exchanged a quick glance before following Aeddan into the cavern. The air was cool and damp, but they could make out some dim light in the distance.

As they descended deeper into the cavern, a sense of unease settled over Enid. She had always been uncomfortable with tight spaces.

"Watch your footing," Rhodri warned as he led them down slippery steps leading to rough-hewn stairs embedded within stone walls.

Enid nodded, clinging to the wall for support as they made their way towards the light. As soon as they emerged into an enormous chamber, Enid gasped in surprise. The cavern was lined with glowing crystals of all shapes and sizes that illuminated the entire room like a thousand stars twinkling within its depths. The surrounding crystalline light emitted a comforting warmth, as if she had finally rediscovered something she had long been missing.

"It's so beautiful down here. I wasn't expecting that," she said.

Aeddan's lips tightened in irritation at her surprise.

What really amazed her was an underground creature unlike anything she had ever witnessed. The creature resembled a tall bat-like figure. Its fur possessed a rich ebony hue, while its enormous eyes shone brightly amidst the darkness. Delicate and thin, its wings emitted a soothing glow ranging from shades of sapphire blue to emerald green.

Enid, speaking in hushed tones, couldn't help but ask Aeddan, "What is that?"

Aeddan responded by saying, "That is a guardian of the crystals. They safeguard these gemstones from those who seek to exploit them for evil purposes."

Enid found herself captivated by the creature's presence as it approached them with gentle movements. Its fluffy fur was so inviting that she felt a desire to touch it. "I've never encountered anything like this before, " Enid remarked.

The creature bowed its head towards Enid and the princes to which they nodded in return as a sign of respect. Enid could sense its presence within her thoughts. Its voice provided solace, akin to a breeze carrying words of encouragement. "Welcome to Afallon," the guardian conveyed through her mind. "We understand what you have lost and why you are searching for the Gwyllion Queen."

It was clear this majestic being held knowledge within.

The guardian continued speaking, revealing the extent of Malagant's plans. Malagant aimed to extend her influence across the land. She had been amassing magic users from various sources, not just limited to Afallon. This strategic move would only amplify her power.

Upon hearing this news, Enid couldn't stop a shudder of unease. A sense of discomfort settled within her as she listened intently to every word spoken by the guardian creature.

Aeddan's expression turned grim, showing that his worst fears were now confirmed.

Taking a breath to steady herself, Enid mustered the courage to ask the lingering question on everyone's mind. "Can you provide any help?"

Regrettably, the guardian shook its head in response. "I cannot intervene in your destined path or alter your fate."

Aeddans' disappointment and frustration were clear as he sought clarification from the guardian. "What does that imply? Will the success of this quest be determined solely by the capabilities of this human?" he inquired with a tinge of urgency.

The creature fell into silence, taking its time before speaking more. There was an ominous quality, to its voice as it said, "You will encounter challenges that will test you, but in the end, your strength of heart and spirit will be your greatest assets."

Enid's heart sank upon hearing the guardian's words. She had hoped for a simple response.

Rhodri broke the silence, his voice echoing through the cavern as he asked, "Is there anything else you can share with us?"

After a moment of contemplation, the guardian replied. Its eyes glowed brightly as it spoke. "There is one thing I can offer you; beware of those who would deceive you. Some may try to manipulate and mislead you for their gain."

Enid furrowed her brow at this warning from the creature, pondering over whom it might refer to.

Aeddan appeared perplexed. "Who would do this?" he questioned.

The guardian shook its head slowly before answering. "That is not something I can reveal. Remember this; trust your instincts and be wary of appearances." As if emphasizing its point further, the guardian gestured towards a stack of crystals. "Coblynau

Prince, you can choose a crystal to take with you. It will be essential to complete your quest."

Enid looked at the pile of stones and asked, "What do these crystals do?"

Aeddan kept his eyes fixed on the glowing stones before carefully selecting one. "These crystals possess a lot of power, which's why they are highly sought after. That's why it's crucial for the guardians to protect them."

A surge of excitement filled Enid's chest. Her father used to tell her tales about crystals. She never imagined encountering them in real life.

Rhodri glanced at the pile thoughtfully and asked, "Should we also take one?"

Aeddan shook his head in response. "No, it would not be wise to take any without permission. While the guardians may seem friendly, they have terrible punishments for those who disobey them."

Rhodri nodded in agreement, not wanting to risk angering the beings.

Enid watched as Aeddan carefully placed his crystal into his pocket. She couldn't help feeling a twinge of envy. However, she understood the importance of respecting the guardian's wishes.

As they turned to leave, the guardian spoke more. "Take care, Enid. Humans have difficulty surviving for long here," it said.

After expressing gratitude to the guardian, they moved away from the depths of the cave. Enid couldn't shake the feeling that the guardian's words held a deeper meaning than what they initially thought. Yet still, she was thankful for the increasing light as they moved further along, until finally they were out and back into the sun.

"That was incredible." Enid said. "I can't believe we got to meet some of your people."

"They're not all as friendly as the ones we just met," Aeddan warned. "But I was surprised they tolerated you, Human."

Enid chuckled nervously. She couldn't tell if that was a good or bad thing. Rhodri smiled at her before turning to Aeddan. "What do you think, Coblynau Prince? Do you believe what the guardian said about Malagant's plans?"

Aeddan scratched his chin. "It's hard to say for sure, but I have heard rumors of Malagant's desire for power. If what the guardian said is true, then we must be careful not to fall into her trap."

Enid nodded in agreement. She couldn't imagine what kind of trap Malagant could set for them, but she trusted the guardian's warning.

As they walked, Enid's mind inevitably returned to her nightmare. Dylan had looked so different in the dream, but she was sure it was him. Why would he want to hurt her? The talisman Rhodri made for her rested reassuringly against her waist. Enid resolved to ask Dylan about her dream when they next saw each other. Maybe he could explain it. Enid quickened her pace to catch up with the princes.

"How far do we have to travel before reaching our destination?" Enid asked her companions. She shaded her eyes and studied the distant mountain. It appeared closer than yesterday, but was still miles distant. The pinnacle appeared impossibly high and shrouded in thick, murky mists.

Her guides conferred. Then Aeddan estimated it would take almost three days to reach the mountain. Malagant's fortress was an additional day's climb from the base. The mountain was called Gorre, which roughly translated to "Land of No Return." *How cheerful,* she thought.

"What is our plan when we get there?" Enid asked.

Aeddan glanced at Rhodri before answering, "Gorre is a cold and forbidding place, heavily fortified at its borders. My people are aware of a secret passage through the dungeons. Since they are far below ground and at the heart of the mountain, it may be less guarded. We will have to fight our way from there."

"Fight our way..." Enid repeated.

"Yes, fight, Human. You did not think we could just sneak your dragon prince away?" Aeddan's voice dripped with sarcasm.

"N-No. No. Of course not." But that was what her plan had been. She and Rhodri exchanged concerned looks as the trio headed toward their uncertain future.

A knot formed in her stomach as they trudged onward, the weight of their mission bearing down on her. Aside from that terrifying encounter with the Afanc, she had never been in a fight before, let alone a battle against a powerful queen and her minions. She had been picked on, but Dylan always stepped in to protect her. But she knew it was her turn to be strong for Dylan and for her friends and family back home.

As they walked, Rhodri took every opportunity to teach Enid some basic self-defense moves. He showed her how to use her bodyweight to throw someone off balance and how to strike vulnerable points on the body. Enid practiced diligently, hoping she would never have to use these moves in a proper fight.

"You're doing well," Rhodri said when finished, patting her shoulder. "But you need to work on your reflexes. If someone comes at you with a sword, you can't just freeze up."

"I know," Enid said, frustrated with herself. "I just... I'm not sure if I can do this."

"You can," Rhodri said. "I will let nothing happen to you, and we will be there to help you save Dylan."

As the sun set, the group made camp for the night. Enid was exhausted from the long day of walking, but her mind was restless. She watched as Aeddan and Rhodri set up the camp, their movements fluid and practiced. Enid had never been camping before, but she had read enough books to know that it was supposed to be fun. This wasn't fun. This was serious. This was dangerous.

Following a rushed meal, Aeddan and Rhodri discussed the trail they would take in the morning. It would pass mostly through the Ellyllon lands. Enid's eyes grew heavy as she listened. After all the hiking and excitement, she was utterly exhausted.

"Rhodri and I will take turns at watch tonight. You'll need all the rest you can get. We need to be up early to make better time tomorrow."

Enid protested when Rhodri spoke. "You haven't been getting enough rest. It's been a long time since you had a good sleep. We will both watch over you tonight. Rest well for tomorrow and the trials to come."

Enid startled a little at Rhodri's observation but remembered he had slept outside her door nightly for months, and occasionally in her room when the dreams were bad. The color of her cheeks deepened. He knew her far better than anyone else.

It wasn't a weakness to need rest, since she was unsure what they would come up against. Whispers in the back of her mind said differently, but Enid refused to give in to their call. "All right. I agree, but after I'm rested, I insist on doing my share," she said. Enid smiled at Rhodri to show she took no offense and snuggled into her bedroll. The princes spoke to one another a while longer as Enid fell asleep to the sound of their voices.

Enid slept soundly that night, lulled by the sound of chirping insects and the crackling of the fire. No haunting dreams disturbed her sleep, thanks to Rhodri's belt of protection.

The princes got little rest, however. They took turns staying awake, watching over Enid, and keeping an eye out for angry Afancs.

Chapter 14

THE MISSING

THE NEXT MORNING, THE trio set off towards the mountain, passing through a nearby fae village. As they walked, the villagers seemed to hide, closing their doors and windows.

The sound of the trio's footsteps filled the air as they made their way through the village. The wind softly rustled the trees, carrying a chill with it. Behind them, they could hear faint voices, as if whispering something.

Aeddan and Rhodri exchanged glances while continuing their walk through the village. They couldn't shake off the feeling that all eyes were on them. Unease emanated from every window, door, and corner. Despite the princes' familiarity with fae lands, they had encountered nothing like this—it was as though everyone here was hiding from a terror lurking just beyond their sight.

Within those walls, nothing seemed to stir except for occasional rustles that ran through thickets of trees surrounding each home's entrance or along rooftops concealed under blankets of mist that sought to hide any wrongdoing.

Enid was less attuned to the undercurrents. Instead, she marveled at all its beauty—houses constructed from flower petals and cobwebs, trees whispering secrets among themselves while swaying in a breeze.

It felt like something out of a dream or an ancient tale.

As they strolled along, Enid's eyes absorbed the breathtaking beauty. She struggled to believe that such a magical place existed. The houses appeared alive, as if each one possessed its unique soul. Unable to resist, Enid extended her hand and brushed a petal on one house, savoring its velvety softness under her fingertips.

A melodious voice called out from behind them. They turned around to find a stunning fae woman standing there. Her wings shimmered in the sunlight with hues of green that contrasted against her skin. Her eyes were filled with a brilliance akin to glistening diamonds. It was difficult to tear from her mesmerizing gaze. "Welcome to our village. I am Aelora, the elder of this village. What brings you and your companions here, Prince Rhodri? We've heard rumors circulating about your disappearance, and now you have reappeared in the company of a human. And just yesterday, some of our own went missing."

Startled by this revelation, Rhodri took a step back.

He had been away, for some time, caught in the human world. Hearing about the missing villagers was shocking to him. "Yes. It's true... I was traveling elsewhere, attending to my affairs." After a pause, he asked, "What has happened to your people?"

Aelora let out a sigh and shared what she knew about the situation. A small group of fae had vanished overnight with no explanation. The remaining members of the community lived in fear, dreading that they might be next.

As Aelora spoke, a sense of unease crept over the trio. Aeddan cast a look at Rhodri and stated, "We should offer our help."

Rhodri nodded with agreement, feeling a sense of responsibility as their prince to assist those who were in need. "We will do everything within our power to locate your missing villagers. Is there anything you can tell us that might aid us in our search?"

Aelora guided them towards a humble cottage on the out-skirts of the village. Inside, she presented them with a map depicting the surrounding area. She pointed out where the fae had last been seen.

Enid studied the map.

The map of the fae village displayed meandering pathways that led into the surrounding countryside, passing by streams, farms and fairy circles.

It showed hills enveloped in mist, towering trees whose roots created a barrier of enigmatic symbols etched onto rocks, ancient ruins emerging from lake beds and glistening creeks winding through fields of wildflowers. Each corner of the map held something waiting to be explored.

As Enid's finger traced along the lines marking locations on the map, a suspicion formed in her mind. "What if they were taken by something... not from this place?" she wondered, hoping not to sound too imaginative.

Aelora's eyes widened in surprise at Enid's theory and re-frained from dismissing it. "It could be a possibility. There have been murmurs of dark magic stirring in these lands. Some believe it may be the actions of the mountain queen who seeks to capture our kind," the elder said.

Rhodri clenched his jaw upon hearing Malagant's name mentioned again. Wherever they turned, Malagant was at the center of all their troubles. "We must uncover what is happening and put an end to it. We cannot allow innocent lives to be taken because of Malagant's thirst for power."

Aeddan nodded in agreement, acknowledging the importance of action. "We must act now. Malagant should not be underestimated."

Enid's heart raced with a mix of excitement and trepidation. This was her first time being part of such a search party. She determined to contribute in any way possible. Turning to the group, she asked, "What should we do first?"

Rhodri shifted his gaze towards Aeddan, his mouth frowning. "Our primary task is to search the surrounding forest for any clues that may shed light on what happened. Finding evidence linking Malagant to these events is crucial. If we're fortunate, we may discover the villagers unharmed. If not, we press on towards her mountain stronghold to confront her and secure everyone's freedom."

Aelora shook her head as her wings fluttered behind her back. "My prince, it's a fool-hardy endeavor. Malagant is an adversary of immense power—none have ever overcome her."

Rhodri's expression hardened as determination filled his face. "We must make an attempt. I refuse to stand by while she inflicts harm upon others."

Stepping forward, Enid raised her chin and voiced agreement.

"We should attempt to rescue those who are missing," Aeddan remarked, nodding in agreement. His eyes glistened with determination as he spoke.

The princes' willingness to assist the villagers surprised the village elder. "Thank you." Aelora acknowledged, bowing her head. She gestured for them to follow her. "Allow me to lead you to the location where they were last seen." With that, she guided the trio through the meandering paths of the village.

After an hour of walking, Aelora halted in front of a glade. "From here on, our friends will guide you. I must return to the village and reinforce our enchantments to prevent any further incidents."

Rhodri expressed his gratitude towards the elder.

Fauns emerged from among the trees, their gazes fixated on the travelers. Enid had come across depictions of fauns in books before. They appeared half-human and half-goat, with small horns crowning their heads. She had always believed them to be mythical creatures, and witnessing their existence firsthand was both astonishing and delightful for her.

The faun's eyes lingered on Enid. She tried her best not to be affected by their scrutiny and instead focused on her surroundings.

Tall trees stood in a ring around the clearing. The ground was carpeted in moss and wildflowers.

One faun took a step forward, addressing Aeddan and Rhodri in a language that Enid couldn't understand. The princes bowed and responded in kind. The faun nodded before turning to Enid with curiosity. "What is that?" he asked, giving her an appraising look from head to toe.

"She's with us. We are her protectors." Rhodri said.

The faun appeared skeptical but stepped back. "Follow me." He gestured for them to follow him.

Enid trailed behind Aeddan and Rhodri, feeling the gaze of the fauns on her back. She pondered why they seemed suspicious of her presence. Was it because she was human? Could there be another reason that made them hesitant to trust her?

As they ventured further into the forest, Enid noticed the trees were growing taller and denser. The sunlight struggled to penetrate through the foliage, casting a glow over everything around them. The air grew colder, causing Enid to shiver despite still wearing Rhodri cloak.

The group came to a stop in front of an imposing tree.

The tree's girth surpassed that of ten men standing side by side and its towering height prevented Enid from glimpsing the top.

To Enid, the tree appeared animated. The leaves moved independently of the breeze. A deep rumble reverberated through the woods. A shiver traveled down her spine as she comprehended that this was no ordinary tree.

Aeddan spoke with reverence, "This is the World Tree. It links all the realms—the nine worlds. We believe it to be the wellspring of all life."

Enid was overwhelmed as her gaze fixated on the colossal tree. She had heard tales about the World Tree from her father, who studied all sorts of mythology. Witnessing it firsthand was an extraordinary experience.

Rhodri approached closer to the tree, his eyes shut tight as he sensed a pulsating energy emanating from it. "It's astonishing. I always intended to visit this place."

Enid agreed—the World Tree was a marvel to behold. Its trunk and roots intertwined like ancient timber while its branches stretched high into the sky, seemingly stretching to every corner of existence. Soft green moss clung to its bark.

The tree's brown hue provided a contrast to the bright green leaves, and as Enid stood before it, she couldn't help but feel a sense of awe and wonder. The faun who had guided them indicated the trunk of the tree and mentioned that it was the last known location of the missing fae.

Rhodri nodded, understanding the gravity of the situation. He asked if there were any added dangers they should know, his gaze scanning their surroundings.

The faun shook his head in response. He admitted that there had been no reports of danger in this area until recently. The faun's tone didn't do much to reassure them.

Acknowledging this information, Rhodri glanced at Enid before gesturing for everyone to approach closer. He began circling around the tree while scrutinizing it. Aeddan followed suit, inspecting each detail. Enid trailed behind them, her eyes absorbing every aspect of this enchanting tree.

However, as they moved away from the trunk, something peculiar caught Enid's attention. A set of tracks resembling those left by a bird led off into the distance. She pointed it out to Rhodri and Aeddan, who both furrowed their brows upon hearing this news.

Aeddan knelt down and examined the tracks closely.

"It's not one bird. There are three birds." Aeddan looked up at Rhodri and Enid, his expression guarded.

Enid's heart raced as Aeddan spoke. Her mind jumped to the worst-case scenario. What if they were being pursued by something?

Rhodri seemed to share her concern. His eyes scanned the surrounding area. "We need to proceed with caution. Keep your weapons at the ready."

Enid nodded, retrieving her bow. She had never used it in a fight before, though her father had trained her well. She was skilled at hitting targets.

As they continued circling the World Tree, Enid couldn't shake off the sense of unease settling in her chest. The peculiar tracks hinted at a danger that she didn't understand. Every rustle of leaves and snap of a twig made her startle.

Just as they rounded the tree, an unexpected gust of wind caught them off guard.

The branches swayed gently, emitting a creaking sound and Enid thought she caught a whisper carried by the wind.

Aeddan grasped her arm, his eyes widening. "Can you hear that?" he asked in hushed tones.

Enid strained to listen. Could only hear the rustling of leaves. "M-Maybe. What did you hear?"

Aeddan's grip on her arm tightened. "Voices." He scanned their surroundings. "Whispers carried by the wind."

Enid strained her ears further. Still couldn't perceive any sound. She looked to Rhodri for guidance. He appeared lost in his thoughts.

"Perhaps we should split up for a bit and search for any clues. Aeddan, stay with Enid while I explore in the other direction." Rhodri said.

Aeddan sighed with irritation and reluctantly nodded in agreement.

Chapter 15

THE BIG BAD WOLF

THE AIR WAS HEAVY as Aeddan and Enid trudged through the damp forest, their breath curling in front of them like tendrils of smoke. The sky had just begun to lighten, giving way to a pale pink and indigo horizon. Just as they were about to give up on their search for clues to the missing fae, Aeddan broke the silence. "Get your bow ready," he said, his voice was a tense whisper.

Enid quickly unslung her bow from its resting place on her shoulder. She could feel Aeddan's eyes boring into her as he handed her an arrow, the fletching brushing against her fingertips. He gave a nod of encouragement and drew his sword.

"Where?" Enid whispered.

Aeddan pointed towards the underbrush at the far end of their path. Aeddan crept forward, with Enid following close behind. They soon entered another part of the gloomy forest. When they drew near enough to their destination, Aeddan motioned again for stillness.

Enid watched in awe as the faint, early morning light revealed a small group of creatures that she had never seen before. Their downy white fur glowed softly, and their eyes shone like two red rubies in the fading darkness. "What...?"

Aeddan cut her off and gave a one-word answer: "Puca."

Enid's father had whispered stories about the creatures before bed, his voice full of mystery. He described them as shape-shifting entities that ranged from playful to deadly but were always unpredictable. The tales had stuck with Enid over the years. "What do we do? Are they responsible for the village's trouble?"

"Nothing. We must be careful not to disturb or anger them. They are cute now but can have a dangerous side. I don't believe they would be involved with the missing fae, but we should be cautious," Aeddan gestured for Enid to backtrack carefully from the way they had come.

"Everything here is dangerous," Enid grumbled when they had moved far enough away to converse.

"You'd do very well to remember that, Human." Aeddan turned and looked at her, his face illuminated by the light of the rising sun. "If you want to stay alive in Afallon, you need to be on constant guard."

Enid kept a few steps behind Aeddan, her feet slipping through the leaf-strewn path that wound its way through the trees. She was constantly glancing over her shoulder, scanning the shadows for signs of the Puca or dreaded Afanc. Luckily, they had escaped silently, and there was no sign anyone had noticed their passing.

Aeddan's feet moved in a rhythmic pattern as they strolled along the path. Now and then, Enid stole a glance at his profile. He seemed content to take in their surroundings without speaking. Even though she wanted to fill the silence with questions, Enid appreciated the peaceful quiet.

Enid craned her neck to view the canopy of trees above her, swaying in the soft breeze. She felt as if she had stepped back in time, surrounded by a mysterious air of enchantment and age-old secrets. Aeddan led them onward with muted steps, careful not to disturb the tranquility of their surroundings.

As they walked, Enid had the distinct sensation that they were being watched, and though she didn't see any malicious eyes following her, it felt like something—or someone—was tracking their every move. Enid shivered as an icy chill ran down her spine.

Lost in thought, Enid didn't notice Aeddan had stopped until she walked into him.

"Ow," she exclaimed, rubbing her nose.

Aeddan glanced about with his weapon ready. After a lengthy pause, he led Enid back towards the World Tree. Enid caught glimpses of something, but Aeddan always steered her clear.

"Are we being followed by something?" she asked.

"I am not sure," Aeddan said. "It's best not to acknowledge them."

Enid nodded, understanding. Even in her world, some creatures should be left alone. She was grateful that Aeddan was present to help her navigate this strange place.

They walked a little further in silence, but Aeddan halted again. He cocked his head to the side as if straining to listen. Enid fought the urge to ask questions.

Enid stopped abruptly and tilted her head, her eyes narrowing as she strained to identify a rustling in the dense undergrowth just off to their right. A soft thud and branches snapping alerted her that something large was moving through the brush.

The sounds grew louder and Aeddan tensed for a split-second. "Run."

Enid spun around and started running in the opposite direction, while Aeddan charged towards the noise, his feet pounding against the soft ground. He soon vanished from sight, swallowed up by the gloom.

Still carrying her bow, Enid found a suitable spot to conceal herself and waited for Aeddan's all-clear signal. She cursed the fact that they got split up. How would she find Aeddan or the camp? Would Aeddan need her help? What about Rhodri, who was searching in the other direction and unaware of the danger?

Her heartbeat sounded in her ears. She was certain whatever was in the woods could hear it pounding.

From her right, movement in the brush was visible. Whatever it was had no fear of her and took little care to hide.

Enid trained her loaded bow in the noise's direction. She started breathing exercises to calm herself, so she could get off an accurate shot.

The bushes parted and Enid got a nasty shock, and then her heart soared. "Dylan. I'm so glad to see you." She exclaimed as she flung herself into her friend's waiting arms.

Enid and Dylan embraced tightly. Tears of relief rolled down her cheeks. She feared she would never find her friend again. But just as she thought she would burst with happiness, doubt crept into her mind, and she pulled away. "Wait, a minute. This is just way too good to be true." She stepped back and poked at Dylan with her index finger. "Is it really you? How did you escape? And how could you keep all of this from me?"

"I'm relieved to see you, too. You can't imagine how much. I don't blame you for doubting. I'm wondering if you're real, myself. I want to get back home, and then I will explain everything. The entire story is so unbelievable, and I didn't think you'd understand. As for my escape, somehow, I overpowered Malagant, and I've been roaming through these woods ever since. It's a scary place. Do you know where we are?" Dylan sounded troubled. "I think something may be following me, and we probably need to go soon."

"What's following you?" Enid tried to read Dylan's expression in the dim light of the forest. She had visions of the Afanc and its terrible teeth.

"No time to explain. Come on. We've got to get going." Enid heard something crashing toward them. Dylan grabbed her hand, and her only choice became to follow him as he ran deeper into the wilderness.

Enid eventually got tired and slowed down, but Dylan dragged her along. "Dylan, wait," she called out. They burst into a small clearing and Enid insisted on stopping to catch her breath.

"Okay, but we must keep moving." Dylan's eyes darted around the clearing. Enid sat down on a log and gasped for air.

"What's going on?" she asked. "Where are we going?"

"I'll explain everything later. I have the location of a portal to get us out of here." Dylan appeared to be about to say something else when the sound of snapping twigs interrupted. Something headed towards them, fast.

Dylan grabbed Enid's hand, and they took off running again. Enid wondered how far to reach the portal, but she trusted Dylan. They ran for a while, but Enid's side ached, and she stopped again.

"Please, Dylan, I'm sorry, but I can't go much further," she begged him between ragged breaths. "Tell me more about what's going on."

Dylan appeared torn, but he relented and sat down next to her. "Okay, but we need to be quiet. I'm not sure if we are safe to talk here."

Enid nodded and waited for him to continue.

"Remember those creatures back in the clearing?"

"You mean the Puca?" Enid's stomach clenched in fear.

"I think they are following me," Dylan said. "I've been hearing noises in the forest, like something stalking us."

Enid's pulse raced as she scanned the darkness, half-expecting something to jump out at them.

"Do you think they know where we are?" Enid glanced nervously in all directions.

"I'm not sure," Dylan said. "But we need to keep moving towards the portal, just in case."

He stood and extended his arm. His hand was warm against her skin, inviting her up from the cold ground. Enid bit her lip and hesitated for a moment before clasping onto him and letting him pull her back to her feet.

Enid was pulled so close to Dylan that she was reminded again of their almost-kiss. She could see his pulse jumping at his throat, and he licked his lips. Was he thinking about their near kiss, too?

A warmth spread through her body, and she smiled, but there was no answering spark of warmth from Dylan. Had she imagined their attraction? Or worse, was it all one-sided?

Enid gazed up at Dylan, squinting in the shadows of the trees. She found it difficult to make out his features in the faint light, and for a moment his face was a blur. Suddenly, his amber eyes seemed to illuminate with a slight crimson hue. *Did the stress of all this madness finally get to him?* Enid wondered.

But then his face snapped back into focus and Enid blamed her imagination.

"Come on," Dylan said, breaking into her thoughts. "We need to keep moving."

Enid nodded, and they set off again, hand in hand. She had never been so grateful for Dylan's presence. She only hoped they would find their way back to safety soon. *Wait. What about Rhodri and Aeddan?* If they kept moving like this, she would lose them altogether, and they'd never know she found her friend. She decided she couldn't let that happen and dug her heels in.

"Dylan, stop," Enid said. "We need to go back to the clearing. I came here with some friends who were going to help me save you, Aeddan and Rhodri. I can't just abandon them. They might be in trouble."

"No, Enid, we can't," Dylan said. "It's much too dangerous."

"I don't care," Enid said. "I'm not leaving them behind."

Dylan argued, but Enid cut him off. "I owe them, and I shouldn't have let us be separated."

Dylan bristled at this statement and asked, "So you value them more than our safety?" Was her imagination playing tricks or did the red color in his eyes deepen?

"No, of course not. But we can't leave them behind. We need to find them, and then we can all decide on how to move forward together." Enid appealed to Dylan's logic.

Dylan stared at her for a moment before sighing in resignation. "Okay, but we need to be careful. Those things could be anywhere."

They started back the way they had come, Enid keeping a tight grip on Dylan's hand. She was terrified of what might lurk in the darkness, but she couldn't give up on her friends. They had to find them, and all leave the forest together.

Glancing at Dylan's profile, something occurred to Enid, and she again stopped. "How did you know Aeddan, and I saw the Puca?"

"You have so many questions. I'm thinking you don't trust me." Dylan's eyes reddened further, and he squeezed Enid's hand in a vice-like grip. She had never seen his expression so cold, even in her worst nightmares.

Enid tried to break his iron-clad hold, but Dylan's strength had increased substantially. Was it because he was a wyvern, or was something else happening?

"Please, Dylan, you're hurting me," Enid said. "Just tell me what's going on."

Dylan glanced at Enid for a moment before his features softened, but he continued the tight grip on her hand. "The witch said for me to fetch you. I wonder if she'd mind if I took a little taste? You smell delicious, just like that other one."

"What?" Enid realized too late that this chance meeting in the woods *was* too good to be true. Dylan's eyes became blood-red, and his teeth elongated into sharp needle-like fangs.

"Dylan?" Enid whispered. Indeed, terror choked the rest of her words because this wasn't her friend.

Enid had been tricked and fooled by a shapeshifter. And now, it was hungry for her. Enid trembled in fear as she stood face-to-face with the monstrous creature. She had no choice but to fight back, or else be devoured alive.

"Don't worry," it said as he moved closer to her. "Just a quick sip, and then all will be over. I am sure I have enough self-control to stop before you die." The impostor pulled Enid closer, and she couldn't break away. Enid's muscles tensed, preparing to fight. The impostor leaned down to breathe in the scent of Enid's neck.

Enid closed her eyes, bracing herself for the pain.

Chapter 16

INTO THE WOODS

JUST BEFORE THE PUCA could do anything further, a bright light flashed all around them, and Enid got pulled away from the impostor. She turned to see a stunning woman dressed all in white with long frosty hair standing between them. The woman had one blue eye and one brown eye, and both were fixed on Enid.

Enid found herself frozen and couldn't move a muscle while being studied by the strange woman. After a moment, Enid was set free. She maintained her distance but realized if the woman wanted to harm her, there was little she could do. Sweat stung her eyes.

"You should never have come to this place, Enid," the woman said. "It's not safe for you here."

"H-How do you know my name? Who are you, and who is that?" Enid motioned towards the still-frozen impostor.

"My name is Viviane, and that is an old friend of mine, whose name is Widdershins. Unfortunately, he has not fed recently, and I forgot how tempting humans are to the Puca." The beautiful woman shook her head in genuine regret. "I did not intend to put you in any further danger."

"What did you intend, then?" Enid challenged, reaching for her bow.

"I needed to pass along a message I was entrusted with a long time ago. Afterward, I will help you find your friends to continue your quest," Viviane said.

Viviane turned to the Dylan impostor and released him from her spell. His movements were jerky as he advanced towards Enid, his voice strident and angry. He spoke in a language she had never heard before, and although she couldn't understand what he was saying, it was clear that he wasn't happy.

The woman in white crossed her arms and scowled at him. Her voice was stern, and her words clipped as she spoke in a language Enid could not understand.

The Puca's reply was a low, guttural sound that rumbled through the air and filled Enid with a sense of dread. The woman's eyes flickered like flames, brightening in intensity until they shone like stars, and she responded in a language that sounded ancient and wicked. As she spoke, her hand twisted into a threatening gesture, nails elongating into claws.

The Puca appeared convinced and nodded his head to Enid in contrition before turning and disappearing into the darkness of the forest, his Dylan form melting back into the white furry creature Enid had spied earlier.

Enid breathed a small sigh of relief when the figure completely vanished. "What are you?" Enid asked.

"I am a witch." Viviane was not what Enid pictured at the word witch. The woman appeared youthful, beautiful, and graceful. The only features that looked otherworldly were her glorious white locks and mismatched eyes. "I've been around for a long time. I originally came from your realm but ended up here." The witch paused for a moment, considering. An azure moth appeared and flitted about, finally landing on the witch's hand. Vivianne lifted the tiny creature to eye level and whispered. After a moment, the moth flew away.

"Come with me." Viviane held out her hand. "We have much to discuss, and only a little time before I take you back to the safety of your friends."

Enid hesitated, and the witch said, "I see you are coming to appreciate the dangers of Afallon. You are wise to be wary, but if you want to save your friend, you need to hear me out."

"How do I know you won't try to kill me like everything else here?" Enid's eyes narrowed with suspicion.

"You don't, it's true. But we do not have the time for me to convince you of my good intentions." The witch replied with an impatient tone.

"So you say, but my friends are probably searching for me right now, and won't be pleased if you harm me," Enid warned.

The witch nodded in understanding and gave Enid a tight smile. "You are correct, one is searching as we speak. You are brave to threaten me, and remind me of your mother."

"My mother? What do you know of my mother?" Despite her fear, Enid stepped towards the witch with her hand outstretched.

"I only met her briefly once, long ago, when she accidentally traveled through. She was about your age and looked very much like you. I was impressed she had the power to make it here through the portal. Is she aware you have traveled here?" the witch asked.

"N-No, she doesn't know. She died when I was three years old," Enid said.

"Oh, I am sorry... such a waste. She was very brave and very determined." The witch observed what sounded like genuine regret.

"Determined? About what?" Enid asked.

"She wouldn't tell me, but I hope she found what she was looking for. Now I'd like to help you if you'd let me." Viviane encouraged.

The witch could just be trying to lull Enid into trusting her, but something told Enid the woman was sincere. Possibly it was the way Viviane looked her in the eyes when she spoke. Enid told herself that it had nothing to do with the claim of knowing her mother.

Enid eventually took Viviane's hand. She needed all the help she could get. They started back towards Enid's friends. Enid hoped this was a good sign.

"How can you help me save my friend?" Enid asked.

Viviane's gaze was intense as she spoke, and Enid's heart fluttered. Viviane's eyes seemed to penetrate Enid's soul. "I know things that can help you on your quest," Viviane said.

Enid weighed her words, not wanting to be taken in by the witch's charms - however sincere they seemed.

"What things?" Enid asked.

Viviane's voice was flat and unimpressed when she uttered the words, "Knowledge that may save your friend's life." A silent moment passed while Enid deliberated. Her face became an unreadable mask as she weighed her options.

"All right," Enid said. "I'm listening."

As Viviane told her story, Enid couldn't help but feel hopeful. Maybe there was a way to save Dylan after all. She just had to trust the witch and follow her instructions. Enid was ready to do whatever it took to save her friend.

"I was given a message centuries ago from a friend to pass on if the dragon prince ever got taken." Viviane smiled fondly at the memory.

"A message? From whom?" Enid's eyes widened in wonder.

"The message is from an infamous wizard. He warned me these events would occur, and I should not have doubted him." Viviane shook her head in regret. "Even as a blight spread over this world, I tried to deny his predictions. I should have known better. He was never wrong." Viviane's eyes crinkled as she smiled, recalling the past.

"You were fond of this wizard," Enid said.

"I was, and for a brief time, he was fond of me, until I betrayed him." Viviane sighed, while Enid almost tripped in her renewed shock and fear. Her head throbbed with panic.

"You b-betrayed him?" Enid squeaked.

"I did, but only because I was tricked by someone I trusted." Viviane's eyes hardened at the memory. "Merlin was his name, and he was a sorcerer. A powerful one."

Enid's heart sank as she realized who Viviane must be. She heard the stories of Merlin, and how he had been betrayed by the woman he loved. Enid always assumed it was a fable, but now she knew it was all true. And the woman who betrayed Merlin—Mr. Ambrose—stood right in front of her.

Enid's voice quavered as she clutched her hands into fists. "What did you do to him?" She whispered, afraid of the answer.

"I offered him as a sacrifice to my goddess, Diana, in exchange for all of his knowledge." Viviane's voice sounded full of sorrow. "It was a mistake which I very much regret."

Enid didn't know what to say. The sincerity shone in Viviane's eyes, and Enid felt the woman's pain.

Enid's eyes widened, and her mind raced. She blinked, unable to form the words she wanted to ask. "A s-sacrifice? Did you... k-kill him?" Her voice quivered.

"No, I didn't kill him, but what happened may have been worse. I took his powers and trapped him in stasis for over a millennium.

The goddess required this of me, and I had no choice but to obey. Merlin knew it would happen, but loved me, anyway. Since you are here, he must be free again. I am glad." Viviane's eyes were full of pain at this admission, but her smile was genuine at the last bit.

"Do you mean Mr. Ambro... Sorry, Merlin? Why couldn't he give me this message himself?" Enid stammered.

"Merlin gave me the message, along with all the knowledge he had and everything else that made him powerful. He may not remember it now. So much was taken from him. The message was *the key lies within the hearts.* I am not sure of the meaning, but he was very insistent." Viviane recited.

"*The key lies within the hearts.*" Enid dutifully repeated. "It sounds like a cheesy greeting card sentiment, not a clue. Do you have anything more concrete to give me?"

Viviane shook her head and said, "I'm sorry the message is not more helpful, but I assure you, it is vital. You have made it this far and have capable companions. Do not doubt that you have what you need to save your friend."

Enid peered around the clearing, her eyes widening as a few clues stood out; a bent sapling here, a familiar rock formation there — she was sure of it. They must be close to the World Tree. The witch followed her gaze and smiled knowingly at the teenage girl. "Remember, Enid, *the key lies within the hearts.* I am afraid our time is up, and I must not be seen by your friends. They might have the power to banish me from this place. I was honored to meet you, and I hope you rescue your friend."

The woman's figure grew increasingly faint as she walked away until her body was but a shimmer. Suddenly, just before fading away altogether, she glowed brilliantly for one moment. "I have one small request. When you make it home again, please tell Merlin that I am glad he is free and that I am truly sorry." With the last word, the witch vanished with a popping sound.

Enid was alone again in the clearing where she started. The sounds of the forest no longer intrigued her, and shivers traveled the length of her spine. She had to find her friends. This wasn't a place for her to wander about on her own.

The witch had met her mother. How had her mother made it here and had she traveled alone? How had she survived? What was she after? Enid swore under her breath, wishing she had taken the time to ask more questions about her mother. Her breath quickened as she heard rustling in the brush nearby. She strung her bow with trembling fingers and held it at the ready, aiming towards the darkness as something large emerged.

A minute later, Aeddan charged into the clearing.

"Human. There you are. Why did you keep running from me? I thought you had been taken by a Puca. I am glad that is not the case, but next time stay with me." He chided. For a moment, Enid was untrusting that this was the real Aeddan. How could she if her senses continuously betrayed her?

But then he said something that only the real Aeddan would say. "Only a human would be so careless."

Enid gave him a wide grin. "I'm glad to see you too, Aeddan."

She almost told Aeddan what happened, but his obvious relief at her well-being made her pause. If they knew she was so vulnerable, would they continue to help her, or would they insist she stay side-lined? After all, she had two deadly attacks in as many days. Aeddan may not care, but she thought Rhodri might insist on her safety. She kept the narrow escape from the Puca to herself.

Aeddan and Enid made it back to the World Tree as Rhodri arrived. Rhodri questioned them about what they had found and acted even less satisfied with the answers.

Enid mentioned the Puca they had seen. Rhodri's mouth tightened in annoyance, so Enid emphasized how cautious they had been. This did little to mollify Rhodri's sudden bad mood.

Rhodri announced he would go for further reconnaissance. Enid offered to come with him, but Rhodri declined, saying that he could scout faster on his own for signs of the missing fae. Aeddan and Enid watched him go, then looked at each other.

"I'm sorry if I am slowing you down," Enid said after a few minutes.

"It's not your fault, Human," Aeddan said. "He's just concerned for the fate of the villagers."

Rhodri soon returned with no further clues to the disappearances.

Enid still couldn't bring herself to tell her friends about the witch, or the knowledge she had gained. They might not understand why it was so important for Enid to know more about her mother. Enid gingerly held on to this newfound information, admitting even to herself that its significance was too hard to quantify.

So Enid silently continued with them on their journey, hoping to one day find out more about her mother's time in Afallon and what brought her there. It was a way for Enid to honor her mother's memory.

Chapter 17

BITTERSWEET SONGS

THE COUNTRYSIDE THE TRIO passed through continued to leave Enid speechless. Flowering trees grew plentiful and taller than three-story buildings. Fields of flowers and tall blue grasses ran as far as the eye could see. Fluffy white clouds dotted the sky against a brilliant bluish-green backdrop. The temperature was as mild as any spring day, and Enid had returned Rhodri's cloak and tied her jacket around her waist. She noted little in the way of animal or bird life, unlike the forest, but gloriously colored bees buzzed and droned about the fragrant blooms.

Enid asked Rhodri questions as they crossed the kingdom of Ellyllon. She remembered Merlin saying the inhabitants focused on natural magic, so she asked Rhodri, "What does that mean?"

Rhodri explained, "Nature's power is defined by spells or potions created using plant lore. Each contains properties that, when combined, make it one of the strongest types that can heal or harm."

Rhodri's explanation reminded Enid of her mother going in search of ingredients in their woods. She fell silent for a moment and then changed the subject to shapeshifting. "How does shifting work?"

"The spark to animate the process comes from magic. The morphing is an actual physical transformation. For most, the first time it happens, the shifter goes through incredible pain. But after a while, it becomes automatic. Some shifters have only limited forms to morph into, while a few can assume limitless shapes," Rhodri said.

"Did your first shift hurt?" Enid couldn't help asking.

Rhodri admitted it had. From an early age, he possessed an uncanny talent for shapeshifting, as well as impressive skills with plant lore. "When the Gwyllion grew bolder with their attacks, I knew I needed to protect my people and my kingdom at any cost."

Enid listened as Rhodri told her about the Gwyllion, that were the sworn enemies of Ellyllon. "They are vicious beings that feed off the emotions of others. They take strength from pain and hatred, or other intense emotions. They love to lure travelers off the path into their dark domain, where they would imprison them or worse."

Rhodri explained the Gwyllion skirmished with the Ellyllon for years, but they grew increasingly bolder. "I needed to put an end to their threat, so I planned to retrieve the dragon prince. I found a portal and traveled through it without my parent's knowledge or approval. I would ask Dylan to return with me, hoping he could fulfill the prophecy and defeat Malagant. But it all went wrong when I passed through and got stuck in my hound form."

"I don't understand. Why try to bring Dylan back to Afallon before he was ready?" Enid asked.

Rhodri shook his head. "It was a plan born out of desperation. I didn't know whether Dylan attained his powers, but the attacks on my kingdom by the Gwyllion happened with increasing frequency."

"What about returning to find someone else to bring Dylan through?" Enid glanced at Rhodri's handsome profile as she asked him.

He shook his head. "Locked in that form and cut off from access to any magic, I wasn't sure which portal would help me return. If I chose the wrong one, I could have been trapped forever somewhere else. In my animal form, I was becoming too attached to you and your family. If I remained much longer, I would have been unable to leave you," Rhodri admitted with his head bowed and face touched with heightened color.

"Please tell me about your family. Do you have any brothers or sisters? Are your parents still living?" Enid couldn't resist asking, suddenly desperate to change topics.

Her friend breathed a sigh, happy to be in safer territory. "My parents were still alive when I left, and I pray that is still true," Rhodri said as he bit his lip. "I have an older brother, Gwynn, and a twin sister, Ceridwen. I think you would like them, especially Ceri. They are headstrong as well, or at least that's how I see them." Rhodri's face lit up with a smile as he thought about his family. His expression turned wistful, considering the months lost with them.

"You have a twin? How cool. Do you two look anything alike or share the same powers?" Enid asked.

"It's funny, Ceri and I are very different on the surface. She is petite, and her talents lie solely with potions. But underneath, I believe our personalities are similar. Ceri was my best friend growing up, and no one can match her intelligence." Rhodri was fond of his twin.

"You were brave to travel to my realm on your own. That must have been terrifying for you, but you're free now with full access to your magic. After we find Dylan, you can return home. You must be so relieved." Enid's eyes ached a little with unshed tears, realizing she'd lost her loyal friend Bendith. Yet she was happy for Rhodri to be free and home.

"Yes, so relieved..." Rhodri rubbed at his left wrist where the mark of his bargain gleamed. "But I didn't endure it alone. You made it bearable, Enid. You helped me."

Enid looked away, her own eyes filling with tears. Rhodri reached out and took her hand in his, giving it a gentle squeeze before releasing it. A sudden warmth flowed through her at his touch, and she hastened her pace, needing to put some distance between them before she did something foolish, like crying in his arms.

After many hours of walking, the trio stopped for a quick rest in a sunny meadow. Enid tried to ask Aeddan similar questions about his family and home, but his replies weren't nearly as pleasant.

"Human do not pretend interest in me, or I'll think you succumbed to my irresistible charms. You're only interested in yourself and Dylan, and how we can assist you. My parents told me much about humans."

"So there are really no humans here?" Enid asked. Rhodri, at least, showed a willingness to answer her inquiries.

Aeddan replied. "Humans only visit this realm. They do not stay. And every time they slink away, they steal objects of power they barely know how to control. I'm surprised your species made it this far."

Enid's face flushed with anger, but she hesitated and mulled over his words. Humans had developed many terrifying things, like atom bombs that proved too dangerous to control. She wanted to defend humankind but only ended up saying, "You have a good point, Aeddan. It's hard to argue with that."

Aeddan's widened eyes and raised eyebrows spoke volumes about his shock at her easy agreement.

Enid experienced a pang of guilt for giving in to Aeddan's words, but she knew it wasn't worth arguing with him. She turned her attention instead to the beautiful meadow they were resting in. The sun was warm on her skin and a light breeze rustled through the tall grass around them.

Rhodri wandered off into the field, inspecting some wildflowers growing along its edges. Enid watched as he plucked one from its stem and brought it back over to where she sat on their makeshift blanket.

"Here," he said before offering her his handiwork - a pale purple flower with dark veins streaking across each petal.

She took it gratefully, marveling at how such beauty could exist even amidst all this darkness surrounding them.

"So tell me about yourself," Rhodri prompted once again. "You've asked us plenty already."

Enid paused before nodding in response. "What can I tell you that you don't already know? You stayed with us for months. Where should I start?"

Rhodri cleared his throat and then asked, "Enid, I'm not sure how to ask you this, or even if I should, but your mother... what do you think happened to her?"

Enid's shoulders slumped as she admitted, "I was only told stories about my parents' fairytale romance until recently. My dad loved her so much and told me about her favorite songs and books, but he never talks about what happened to her. I learned that my mother had traveled to Afallon when she was my age." She paused, biting her lip as conflicting emotions coursed through her.

"Really? How did you find that out? From your dad?" Rhodri asked.

"No," Enid said. "I don't think my dad knows about this place. Someone I encountered mentioned meeting her once."

Rhodri let out a deep sigh and a low whistle as he shook his head in disbelief. He said, "Wow. Enid, that's huge."

"Yes, I guess everyone has secrets. Dylan and now my mother. It's so difficult to decide what I should believe, but I must find the truth about my mom's death no matter how hard it may be. It's the least I can do for her." Enid said.

"I understand the desire to uncover the truth, and if there is anything I can do to help you, just name it," he replied, his voice echoing with determination.

"Rhodri, you've been so kind to me already, but..." Enid began her response.

Rhodri interrupted her, "There are no 'buts'. I'm here for you, Enid."

Enid looked at Rhodri with gratitude, and tears welled up in her eyes as she said, "Thank you. You don't know what that means to me."

Rhodri reached out and took her hand gently in his own. He gave it a reassuring squeeze before he spoke again. "Enid, there is no need to hesitate. I'll always be here for you." There was a pause as he looked at her with intensity in his eyes. "And not just because of a sense of duty or obligation, but because I...."

Enid's heart skipped a beat as Rhodri trailed off, the intensity in his eyes making her breath catch. For a moment, she thought he was going to confess something personal, but just as quickly as the expression had appeared, it disappeared as he cleared his throat awkwardly.

"I mean, we're friends, right?" he said, his voice slightly hoarse.

A mix of disappointment and relief washed over her. She had been so caught up in the moment that she had forgotten the reality of their situation - they were on a mission to find Dylan and save both their worlds.

"Of course," she replied with a small smile, giving his hand a reassuring squeeze. "You're one of my closest friends."

Rhodri nodded slowly before letting go of her hand. They sat in silence for a moment before Aeddan's voice broke the peacefulness of the meadow.

"Come on, lovebirds," he sneered. "We have to keep moving if we want to find Dylan."

Enid's cheeks heated in embarrassment at Aeddan's taunting tone, but she brushed it off and stood up, brushing grass off her clothes.

"Yes, let's keep moving," she said, determined to push aside any distracting thoughts or feelings.

Rhodri nodded in agreement, and the trio set off once again, their focus on the task at hand. But Enid couldn't help but steal glances at Rhodri, wondering what he had been about to say before he stopped himself.

Enid couldn't shake off her thoughts about Rhodri. Despite her best efforts not to be preoccupied, she studied him as they walked. Why was she drawn to him when she liked someone else?

Rhodri had always been there for her, no matter whether he was Bendith or a prince, and had saved her life. Even now, he kept watch on their surroundings, missing no detail. But she had saved him too. No, it was something more.

As they walked across a meadow, a beautiful bird song began. Enid thought it was lovely. The song came from a trio of stunning birds not too far away. They resembled large sparrows and had wonderfully colored plumage. Spots covered the wings, and their tails fanned out with colorful stripes. The birds sported lilac and snowy white plumage with a dark-purple speckled crest in the center of their heads.

Enid turned back to ask Rhodri about the birds. He had stopped, sat down, and his eyes were closed. Aeddan also appeared to be napping. Enid considered waking them, but both had been up most of the night. Instead, she settled in for a private concert by the beautiful bird trio.

The birds never stopped singing. It was uncanny. They hopped around in the meadow, but never ceased their ditty. As Enid focused on the melody, it morphed from a pleasant tune to a sinister one. One minute Enid enjoyed their harmony, and the next moment a faint dissidence gave her the shivers. The ring on her hand pulsed in time with the bittersweet melody.

Enid tried to awaken Aeddan and Rhodri, but both continued to slumber. Spasmodic movements revealed both experienced some discomfort. Enid tried unsuccessfully to shake them awake. She was panicking. Enid hadn't forgotten her previous experiences with the deadly Afallon residents.

Mumbling the refrain, *please wake up,* didn't seem to help, either. Tears of frustration were very close. No matter what she did, neither prince woke, though both moaned in pain as if from the surrounding cacophony.

Was it Enid's imagination or had the bird song gotten louder? So focused on trying to wake her companions, she temporarily lost sight of the birds. When she glanced around for them, she jumped, startled at their size and proximity. Their plumage was still breathtaking, but close-up, their faces were fearsome. They each had a dagger-like beak full of razor-sharp teeth and their talons appeared to be metal-tipped. They were no longer just pleasant songbirds.

Their eyes disturbed her the most. There was no life in them. They had the dull eyes of a carrion eater. Enid was reminded of a vulture's eyes. She inched toward her bow. She didn't know what to do but thought keeping her weapon on hand was a good idea.

One bird raised its beak and focused on Enid. It cocked its head to one side and stared at her through cold, black eyes. It bobbed its head forward in an eerie, jerky motion. For a moment, Enid froze in fear.

The song grew louder as the birds neared. A sharp pain stabbed behind her eyes, and blood trickled from her nose. Aeddan's warnings from earlier about the dangerous wildlife were now clanging in her ears. She pulled the bow into a ready position and retrieved an arrow from her quiver. After taking a calming breath, Enid silently aimed at a bird, drew back the bowstring, and let her arrow fly.

Within seconds, the arrow hit its mark. The hawthorn arrow struck through the closest bird's eye, and it fell to the ground, dead. The other two birds stopped their song and squawked at Enid, baring their teeth. After poking at their fallen comrade, both birds hissed in Enid's direction. Forked tongues slithered from their sharp beaks.

There was no time to waste as Enid shook a confused Rhodri and Aeddan and pleaded with them to wake. The princes appeared disoriented, but both quickly recovered and drew their swords. The two remaining birds flew as one at the princes, who stood back-to-back with their swords drawn. Enid was nearby at the ready with her bow and arrows.

The birds were almost the same height as the princes and used their talons as daggers. The four figures thrust and parried across the fields, making it difficult for Enid to get a clear shot. As she watched, helpless, her arms shook with frustration, tired from holding the bow taut.

Aeddan and Rhodri made a formidable team, but so were the deadly raptors. The fight might have been a choreographed ballet, considering all the precisely executed movements. But it was a vicious battle, with blood and feathers flying everywhere.

Rhodri scored a glancing blow on the wing of one bird. The other raptor turned and rushed at Enid before she could fire another shot. The bird impaled her shoulder with its beak, and Enid cried in pain. The carrion bird withdrew and licked the blood staining its beak, and lunged again, biting down on Enid's wrist. She screamed in pain. Suddenly, Rhodri reappeared stabbing with his sword. The bird turned and flew off, leaving its wounded companion behind.

Rhodri gently lowered Enid to the ground, laying her on her back. The wound on her shoulder caused a burning sensation like molten fire, and the numbness spread from the bite on her wrist. The sensation spread throughout her body. *The bird must secrete poison.*

Rhodri's face paled at the sight of blood on Enid's face and shoulder, and asked, "Where else are you hurt? Did they bite you?" She tried to answer but couldn't move her lips. The numbness had spread rapidly. Rhodri surveyed her wounds and called to Aeddan, his voice cracking with desperation. Rhodri's body shifted slightly, and Enid witnessed Aeddan and the remaining bird squaring off.

She wasn't sure if what happened next was reality or merely the effect of the poison, but before the remaining bird resumed the offensive, a red-hot, molten stream of fire erupted from Aeddan. The vicious bird curled up in the inferno and moved no more. The flame kept pouring out of Aeddan until the bird was nothing but a blackened husk.

Rhodri called again to Aeddan, who rushed to Enid's side. "A raptor attacked Enid and I think she's been bitten," Rhodri told Aeddan, who hurried to Enid's side. "I know these things secrete poison. Please, can you watch over her in case it returns? I don't want to leave her unguarded, but I must get something to counteract the poison."

Rhodri ran off to search, and Enid was left to study Aeddan's face. His gaze fixed on her, and his lips tightened at her injuries. Enid saw Aeddan gripping her hand, but she couldn't feel it.

"Human, that was a brave thing you did. You could have easily left us to our fate. Instead, you stayed true and slew one of Rhiannon's fierce raptors. I'm not sure we'd have survived without you. Those beasts are deadly. Please do not die before I can thank you properly." Aeddan frowned. His molten eyes, however, lit from within. Enid hadn't imagined those flames. She tried to speak but couldn't move.

Soon, Rhodri returned with some herbs, which he set about preparing into a soothing mixture. Both princes leaned over Enid. "This poultice will slow the poison in your system, and I made another one to slow the bleeding. You've lost a lot of blood, but I know a place we can take you. Please hold on, Enid. Please don't leave me," Rhodri implored, his voice strained with emotion.

Enid closed her eyes. Because of the numbness, she didn't experience any pain. Her companions lifted her from the ground, and she had the impression of great wings.

Then Enid knew no more.

Chapter 18

REUNIONS

ENID AWAKENED IN A bed whose posts resembled living trees. *Were those actual leaves?* The bedding had the softness of cashmere in shades of green. This didn't look like Enid's bedroom at all. Everywhere were green, purple, and wood tones. Her gaze returned to the ceiling, and she noticed more leaves and branches interwoven in a beautiful pattern. Where was she?

Enid bolted upright but instantly regretted moving so fast. Her shoulder ached.

Shoulder ache...

She remembered those terrifying birds. She looked down at the delicate green nightgown she wore and pulled at the neck to view her shoulder. The skin was flawlessly smooth.

"They healed the worst of your wounds, Human," Aeddan drawled from a nearby chair.

Enid jumped at the sound of his voice. "Where are we? Where is Rhodri? The last thing I remember was that run-in with those awful birds." Enid fired questions at Aeddan, unable to control a shudder.

"Those awful birds were Queen Rhiannon's minions. Rhiannon was Malagant's mother. The raptors were her pets. Some say they were also Rhiannon's assassins. They must belong to Malagant now and are helping her gather captives," Aeddan said, his mouth turned down in disapproval.

"So friendliness runs in that family? Wonderful. Where are we now? Is Rhodri okay?" Enid asked, her brow wrinkled with concern.

"After you got wounded, we took a detour to the Ellyllon capital. Rhodri's mother has a gift for healing, and you certainly needed that," Aeddan said. He got up and crossed over to the door. He opened it and spoke briefly with someone unseen waiting outside. When he finished, Aeddan resumed his seat.

"So Malagant's mom kept those awful things as pets? Their birdsong had a terrible effect on you two," Enid said.

"Yes, their song is famous for bewitching and lulling their prey right before their fatal strike. We got lucky you remained unaffected by it and didn't run away," Aeddan said.

"I wanted to run, believe me," she confessed. "I've never been so scared, but I also didn't want either of you hurt. I wasn't sure if my arrows would be effective, but I couldn't think of any other way to shut them up," Enid finished, biting her lip.

"As I said before, Human, you did well," Aeddan said.

"You mean I did well for a *human*?" One eyebrow lifted in challenge.

"No, I mean you did well for anyone in such a circumstance. I was shocked you had some skill with a bow." Aeddan rolled his eyes but kept his tone patient.

She smiled. "You can thank my dad for that one. He insisted that being good at archery would honor generations of our Welsh ancestors. It's quite different, though, shooting a living thing versus a target." Enid's mouth tightened in distaste.

"I agree with your father. It is good to honor those who came before. He is wise. Unfortunately, sometimes taking life is necessary," Aeddan said.

Was it Enid's imagination, or did his eyes just blaze with flames? She almost asked about Aeddan's fire when he resumed speaking.

"Human, you asked me some questions about my family, and at the time I refused to answer because I doubted your motives. Now I'm forced to admit I may have misjudged you."

"Aeddan, it's okay. You don't have to apologize." Enid's face scrunched as if biting a lemon, expecting an awkward scene.

"I'm not apologizing. My caution was warranted. However, you have proven yourself trustworthy, so I will answer you now," Aeddan said in a matter-of-fact tone.

"Oh, okay." Enid leaned forward in anticipation.

"My parents are still living. They sent me to your realm to persuade Dylan to return to Afallon. I also have an older sister. Her name is Anna. We're close, though she is nothing like me." Aeddan's face lit with a brief smile, which gradually faded. "I mentioned I was unconcerned with the dragon prince's fate until it affected my family."

Enid guessed what was coming next.

"Two weeks ago, Malagant's forces took my sister hostage and imprisoned her in her fortress, just like Dylan. My parents sent me to your realm to ask Dylan to return in the hopes he would fulfill the prophecy and save her. It was easy to convince Dylan to help. He seemed human to me, but Dylan has courage. His only request was that he wanted to attend your party before leaving. I admit I thought it was frivolous, but now I think Dylan may have suspected he would never see you again." Aeddan's frown deepened.

"Oh," was all Enid said for a moment. How amazing that Dylan would worry about her while shouldering such a terrible responsibility. How horrible for Aeddan's family to have a daughter in captivity. It would be agony if she never saw Dylan again. Her eyes filled with useless tears. "Our goal is obvious, then. We must save both Dylan and your sister and stop Malagant." Enid's quiet voice never wavered.

Aeddan's eyes widened in surprise. "You will help me then? Even though you don't know Anna and can barely tolerate me?"

"I promise to do all I can to help, which may not amount too much. But I want to help. I have never met your sister, that's true. But everyone deserves to be free," Enid said. A glowing green script appeared on her left wrist. She should be concerned about making bargains, but she meant every word.

A light tapping at the door interrupted the intense scene. Aeddan straightened and went to admit the visitors. Enid was relieved to see Rhodri and intrigued by the unfamiliar but stunning woman as they entered the room. A beautiful, dark-haired girl trailed both.

The woman appeared to be in her mid-thirties and dressed in a sumptuous gown of dark green with gold thread embroidered in leaf patterns. Unlike Rhodri, her hair was in golden ringlets that cascaded down her back. In her hair, she wore a gold circlet in the pattern of vines with leaves. The dark-haired fae girl wore a simple frock of the palest pink. Both women had Rhodri's friendly brown eyes.

When Rhodri saw Enid, he came over and perched on the bed. "I'm glad you're awake. How are you doing?" His smile was like a comforting ray of sunshine. His gaze studied her, looking for any signs of discomfort. When Rhodri spotted the glimmering green script on Enid's wrist, the smile faded, and his warm brown eyes narrowed.

"I'm much better now," she said, "but I never want to see another songbird for as long as I live." She said, then attempted to cover her wrist. Rhodri and the girl laughed. Aeddan and the older woman exchanged glances.

Rhodri stood and escorted the stunning lady forward. "Enid, I would like to present my mother, Queen Dona of the Ellyllon. This is my lively and lovable twin, Princess Ceridwen." He turned to his family to introduce Enid. "This is Lady Enid from Wales. She is a close friend of the magician Merlin and my constant benefactor and companion while I was cursed and trapped in her realm."

"Oh, Your Majesty, it's an honor to meet both you and the Princess," Enid stammered. She was mortified that she was still in bed—in a nightdress, no less. *What's the protocol? Should I kneel?*

"I am honored to meet the lady who saved my son and took care of him when we could not." Queen Dona's angelic voice quavered as she spoke. Ceridwen gave a perfect curtsy.

"Your son made it very easy to be kind, Your Majesty. I'm honored to have him as a friend," Enid assured Rhodri's mother.

The princess spoke, "Is this Rhodri's human? I don't think she's *that* pretty." Her friendly tone resonated with faint disappointment.

Rhodri laughed in response. "Yes, Ceridwen, this is my human, and I think she's lovely."

Enid blushed furiously as they discussed her appearance. His human, she fumed. But then, hadn't he been her dog for months? *I guess that's fair*, she concluded.

"Well, Lady Enid, you have done the impossible by restoring my son to me." Queen Dona's voice choked with tears. Rhodri gently took his mother's hand and squeezed it reassuringly.

Enid became emotional at the sight of Rhodri surrounded by his family. How terrible to not know the fate of a loved one. Her thoughts flew to her family and friends back home. Her dad had known so much loss. How would he feel if she never returned?

What about Dylan's parents? Dylan was their only son, and he was the center of their world. It would devastate them to lose him. What if Enid never saw Dylan again? What if she didn't find him? Or save him? Could she live with the failure? *Stop this,* she told herself. These thoughts weren't helpful. Enid forced her thoughts back to the present.

"We came to check if you were any better, my dear. When Rhodri and Prince Aeddan brought you to me, there was not much hope. But you have a powerful spirit, and we are all relieved that you responded to treatment," Queen Dona said. Ceridwen wandered through the room and stood, admiring Enid's horn and bow.

"Prince Aeddan mentioned you were a skilled healer. I appreciate your act of kindness. I'm doing much better," Enid said.

"Oh, I am gratified to hear it. Prince Aeddan and you must join us tomorrow night to celebrate Prince Rhodri's return. You will be the guests of honor at our revelry, of course." By the time Queen Dona finished speaking, Ceridwen had finished her perusal of the room and returned to Rhodri's side to take his hand.

Enid's thoughts raced as she considered how to answer. Dozens of voices in her mind were shouting very unhelpful advice. She wanted to decline the invitation because she was in a desperate hurry to find Dylan and save him, but she was unfamiliar with the customs of Afallon. She remembered Merlin cautioning her to be polite. *Do we have time for a party? Haven't we lost too much time already?*

She looked from mother to son and observed how tightly Ceridwen held Rhodri's hand. They all smiled so much and laughed frequently. Tears stung at the back of her eyes as she considered how Rhodri had spent months separated from his family. Enid took a calming breath and tried to picture what she would want if she got parted from her friends and family for as long.

"Your Majesty, you honor me. I would be happy to attend," Enid accepted graciously.

Rhodri's eyebrows lifted in surprise and Aeddan's mouth hung slack, but Enid recognized it was the right thing to do. She closed her eyes and sent an earnest plea for Dylan's and Anna's continued safety in the interim. Enid and the two princes would continue their quest immediately following the celebration.

"Good, then it is settled. Enid, it was a delight to meet you. Now we should leave you to get some rest. Rhodri, when you finish here, I would like to speak some more. Come, Ceridwen." Queen Dona took a polite leave with the princess in tow. Ceridwen kept glancing back at Enid until the door closed softly between them.

As soon as the door shut, Rhodri grabbed Aeddan, pinned him to a wall, and placed a knife at his throat. The expression on Rhodri's face reminded Enid of that deadly hound she met their very first day. "What did you make her promise? Tell me, Coblynau."

"Unhand me, Rhodri. This was not my doing." Aeddan snapped. Aeddan's eyes caught fire again. This situation could grow out of hand quickly.

"Rhodri, calm down. Aeddan didn't make me promise anything. He told me about his sister, who is also Malagant's captive. I agreed to help him save her. I-I don't understand how these bargains work, but that doesn't matter. I meant what I said," Enid lifted her chin defiantly.

"Your sister? Do you mean Anna is also Malagant's captive?" Rhodri loosened his grip on Aeddan and reluctantly put the knife away.

"Yes, Anna was taken just before I traveled to the human realm. I was as surprised as you that this human offered to help. I did not expect such a response. She is a strange creature," Aeddan said, glancing at Enid. Oddly, the fire had not left his eyes.

"Why is Malagant taking these hostages? What does she want?" Enid's gaze darted between the two princes.

"We believe she's after additional power to fuel her spells," Aeddan said. "The Gwyllion can use other beings' powers to heighten their own. Anna is an exceptionally powerful mage in her own right and is first in line to inherit the Coblynau throne. Malagant may use Anna to fuel the spells she's been casting." His fists opened and closed in frustration.

Enid shook her head, discouraged. "This just keeps getting worse."

Chapter 19

A GRAND TOUR

ENID AWOKE THE NEXT morning refreshed. The stiffness and pain from yesterday were a distant memory. Enid supposed it was a small price to pay, considering that she'd narrowly escaped a deadly attack.

Rhodri was currently meeting with his mother and father over breakfast, and food for Aeddan had been sent to Enid's room. Enid contented herself with the horn's version of Scottish pudding. They had just finished when there was a soft tap at Enid's door. Aeddan answered and Princess Ceridwen entered, looking stunning in a pale lilac dress. Enid was delighted to have someone else to talk with. This time Enid was out of bed, dressed in borrowed clothes, and able to perform a serviceable curtsy to greet the princess. "I am glad to meet you again, Your Highness."

"You are looking much better today, Lady Enid," Ceridwen said.

"Yes, Princess. I feel much better. I appreciate your visit."

"My family is busy with meetings, which are all so boring. I wanted to ask some questions about you and your human realm," Ceridwen said with wide eyes.

"Of course. I'd love to answer questions," Enid responded. This began an animated discussion about Enid's friends, home, and the nearby village. Ceridwen asked Enid to share some of her favorite memories, and Enid's stories involved Dylan, Zoe, and

Rhodri. This topic involved a lot of laughter from the girls while Aeddan listened attentively.

"You must have been extremely close," Ceridwen said.

"Dylan and Rhodri are my best friends, but I also have another friend, Zoe, from school," Enid confirmed with a smile. Ceridwen's eyes lit at the mention of school and asked about the classes Enid studied.

"We study topics like science, math, and human history," Enid said.

"Do the humans in your world learn about Afallon?" Ceridwen asked with a narrowed gaze.

"To us, Afallon is just a legend. I didn't know about this place until right before I traveled here," Enid said.

After Ceridwen asked about magic in the human realm, Enid explained that humans mostly relied on science and technology. They discussed the mechanical marvels of the human world, like phones, television, airplanes, and space travel. "You make it all sound so marvelous, Lady Enid," Ceridwen concluded, her eyes shining in wonder.

"Well, humans have a lot of issues, too, like poverty, disease, and war. There are as many wonders as there are terrible injustices," Enid said with the corners of her mouth turning downward.

"You mentioned the cities in your realm. What about nature? Are there many animals?" Ceridwen asked, leaning forward in interest.

This question involved lively back-and-forth comparisons of all the animals that Enid could recall. Many animals appeared similar across realms, but some, like elephants, whales, and kangaroos, sounded as fantastic to Ceridwen as wyverns were to Enid. The morning flew by with much laughter as the two girls became more comfortable with each other.

Before breakfast, Rhodri mentioned his father had wanted to meet Enid, and so Ceridwen offered a guided tour of the palace on the way to the throne room. Enid stared at the variety of Ellyllon folk who lived in the castle. There were many birds and mammal species, as well as reptile and insect inhabitants. They all moved with purpose. The most surprising was the walking plants, moving easily amongst the other residents. Enid had to reconsider her understanding of plant life.

Enid commented to Ceridwen about the many guards she noted at almost every doorway. They wore forest green uniforms and most carried an array of deadly weapons. "We've had to triple our Royal Guard due to increased attacks by the Gwyllion," Ceridwen said.

"Have there been any attacks on the palace?" Enid asked.

"Not yet, but Father wants us to be ready, just in case," Ceridwen said, a frown tugging at the corners of her mouth.

Too soon, they ended the tour outside a throne room guarded by a half dozen soldiers. "This is where I must leave you. A dancing rehearsal is scheduled before the party this evening. Maybe we could get together again before you leave?" Ceridwen asked in a hopeful tone.

"I would love that, Princess. We appreciate the tour, and I hope to see you again soon." Enid grinned from ear to ear.

After Princess Ceridwen left her and Aeddan, there was nothing to do but wait for their audience with Rhodri's father. Enid recalled what Rhodri had told her the previous evening. His father's name was King Urien, who oversaw the military and had always been a strict disciplinarian.

The guards soon summoned Enid and Aeddan into the throne room. The vaulted ceilings were so high above her. Looking up at them made Enid dizzy. Every surface was drenched in sumptuous forest green, gold, and purple. The room was very long and narrow, and the only furniture was two green and gold thrones at the far end, placed on a raised dais.

An imposing male with brown hair and bright amber eyes that reminded her of a wolf occupied one throne. Enid didn't see Rhodri's mother, but stationed one step down from the throne platform was another individual who strongly resembled Rhodri, only with light blond hair and tawny eyes.

That must be his brother, Prince Gwynn, she thought.

Aeddan performed a flawless courtly bow and nodded to both males. "Greetings, Your Majesty, and to you Prince Gwynn."

Enid performed another curtsy and echoed Prince Aeddan's words, silently thanking her teachers' instructions on how to curtsy. Who knew it would come in so handy?

"Greetings, Prince Aeddan. We thank you for escorting Lady Enid to our presence, but you are now dismissed," King Urien said with a gracious nod of his head.

"I find, Your Majesty, that I cannot leave the lady's side, but do not let that delay the proceedings. Please continue." Aeddan delivered this statement in a mild tone. However, his hand moved to his sword and his eyes lit with twin flames.

Prince Gwynn noted Aeddan's movement and mirrored a move for his weapon. Enid recognized she needed to say something to break the tension. "Your Majesties, it's a pleasure and an honor to meet you both. I appreciate your help in my recovery and your hospitality until we continue our travels."

King Urien's eyes narrowed. "Do you intend to travel to the Gwyllion realm and stir up further hostilities?"

"Were you sent by Malagant to cause unrest in our realm? Does the wizard Merlin have anything to do with this?" Prince Gwynn followed his father's questions as his hands clenched his sword pommel.

"Your Majesties, I don't understand. I was just traveling through your kingdom to help a friend who got kidnapped by Malagant. I wasn't aware of Afallon and its struggles until Malagant came into my realm and took my friend. Now, I plan to save him and stop her." Enid's chin was raised as she finished her statement.

"How can I be sure that you and that scurrilous wizard Merlin didn't cause this? Did that wizard hold my son captive in your foul realm?" King Urien gripped the throne's armrests as he awaited Enid's response.

She hadn't expected these questions and was momentarily left speechless with anger.

A sharp voice spoke from somewhere behind Enid and Aeddan. "Because I told you so, Father. I can't believe you are addressing Lady Enid in this manner. Maybe we should be more focused on our missing fae." To Enid's relief, Rhodri stalked up and stood on her other side.

"Rhodri, these humans are well versed in the art of deception, and you mentioned the wizard Merlin's involvement. That magician has tricked this family enough. How do we know he is not the mastermind?" King Urien slammed a fist down on an armrest.

"That was Merlin, Father, not Enid. She didn't know about any of this, me, Merlin, or the dragon prince. Enid discovered it all just before we traveled through the portal. I can't believe you're making me repeat this all again and being unforgivably rude to the girl I... to the girl who saved me." Rhodri protested with a tone that sounded more like a growl.

"Father, I think maybe we should..." Prince Gwynn began with eyes darting between his brother and Enid.

"Quiet, both of you. I heard what you have to say and now would like to hear from the young lady," Urien's insistent gaze locked with his youngest son's.

"Your Majesty, I understand your suspicions. Your missing son returns with a strange human in tow, which is enough to cause anyone alarm," Enid said. She looked into King Urien's eyes. "You just got him back, yet he is already pledged to travel to Gwyllion to free captives. I assure you I hold your son's and Prince Aeddan's safety above my own."

"Do you swear it, human?" King Urien pressed, leaning forward.

"Enid, no." Both princes on either side of her spoke at the same time.

But Enid didn't listen. "Yes, Your Majesty, I promise." Enid sensed when the second line of shimmering green script appeared on her wrist. It was like a gentle brush of feathers against her skin.

When the King viewed the proof of Enid's bargain, he sat back in his chair as if relieved of a heavy burden. "I appreciate your candor, Lady Enid. I sincerely hope for all to return safely from this adventure."

Prince Gwynn had witnessed the vow. He gave Enid and her princes a tight smile and suggested they all adjourn to get ready for the evening's festivities.

All the way back to Enid's room, both princes didn't utter a single word. When they were ensconced in her room with the door closed, Aeddan said, "Human, I don't want or need you to make a foolish sacrifice for my sake. You don't even like me. Why would you make such a bargain?"

Rhodri chimed in, "Enid, I don't want you to risk yourself for me, and neither would Dylan."

Enid placed her hands on her hips and gave each prince a warning look. "Both of you listen closely. It's my life and my decision what to risk. You're jeopardizing everything to help me. Can I do less? Now, I don't want any more lectures. I have a party to get ready for. Aeddan, quit fishing for compliments. Even though you can be a real jerk, we are friends. Now go somewhere and bother somebody else," Enid declared. Both princes looked at each other, speechless, and took their leave. Enid collapsed on the edge of her bed with her head in her hands, overwhelmed by the daunting task before her.

Another gentle knock sounded on her door. It had to be a prince ready to talk her out of the promise she made. She flung the door wide open and was shocked that Queen Dona was at the threshold.

"Oh, Your Majesty, forgive me. I was expecting someone else."

"A certain prince, perhaps?" Queen Dona quirked a knowing eyebrow.

"S-Something like that…" Enid stated, recovering from a deep curtsy.

"The King mentioned what occurred when you met with him, and I am here to offer my apologies. Losing Rhodri for so long almost destroyed our family, but he should not have forced you to make such a promise. You are too young to make such a commitment." Queen Dona reached out and took one of Enid's hands.

"I don't mind the promise, Your Majesty. I meant what I said. Your son has been a good friend of mine for months. I would hate to see him or Aeddan come to any harm. They promised to help me save Dylan. The least I can do is guarantee to help them stay safe in return," Enid reasoned.

"You are quite courageous," Queen Dona remarked, her brow furrowing as she recalled a distant memory. "It is almost uncanny how you remind me of a human girl I met so many years ago."

"Do you remember anything else about her? What was her name? What was she looking for?" Enid's mind raced when the queen mentioned another human.

"I clearly remember her bravery. She was on some sort of quest, but I never discovered what she was searching for. She had a name... Liesel, Lottie, or maybe Lilli. I am not sure."

Lilli, but Enid forced herself to stay calm. "Do you recall who she was with? Or when she was here in Afallon?"

The queen shook her head sadly. "She was alone the last time I saw her, and if I had to guess, she might even have been your age."

Enid's mind raced with possibilities. Was it possible that this girl was Enid's mother? Enid knew she needed to find out more.

"Thank you, Your Majesty, for sharing that with me. Is there anything else you can tell me about this girl? Any other details or stories?" Enid asked, hoping for any clues that could help her unravel the mystery.

Queen Dona paused for a moment, lost in thought. "I'm afraid that's all I can remember, my dear. But I hope your journey is successful, and that you all return safely. I will do all in my power to assist you. In the meantime, my attendants have brought your clothes back mended, and my seamstresses fashioned something for you to wear to the revelry. I hope you don't mind."

The Queen summoned her attendants from the hallway, and they brought a stunning creation in dove gray into the room. Enid was relieved that it wasn't a floor-length ballgown. She had enough of uncomfortable clothes.

The outfit consisted of a smocked blouse, a long-sleeved hooded jacket, and breeches made of a fabric like velvet. The jacket had a lace-up bodice, bell-shaped sleeves and was decorated with swirls that resembled growing vines. In addition, lace-up dove gray boots were also provided. Delicate azure moth appliques were so skillfully applied to the sleeve and hood trim, they appeared to be paused in flight. A huge grin spread across Enid's face.

Enid thanked the queen and watched as she left her room. As soon as the door closed, Enid collapsed onto her bed, deep in thought. The mention of another human girl on a quest had stirred such curiosity within her. She couldn't shake the thought that her mother's death was related to Enid's current quest.

It made her feel connected to her mother, knowing she was retracing her steps through Afallon, no matter how fantastical that seemed. Enid needed to find out more.

With a start, Enid realized the time had flown by. She had to get ready for the revelry.

First, she laid out everything she would need for travel afterward. She studied her clothing from home and found no trace of any holes or bloodstains from the dreadful incident with Malagant's raptors. She liked to think the seamstresses were talented, rather than her clothes being mended by magic. Would the magic wear off and the holes reappear?

Enid continued to the adjoining bath and marveled at the unique yet functional facilities. The bathtub appeared to be a natural pool set into the floor, with warm water constantly being replenished. The shower resembled an actual waterfall. Enid shook her head again in amazement. Would anyone ever believe her back home if she tried to describe this place?

Enid focused on a dressing table topped with a giant silvered mirror. She grabbed a wooden brush and tried to tame her unruly mop of black hair, deciding to let her hair hang loose in gentle waves.

When she got her hair looking tamed, she studied the various cosmetics scattered on the table. After some hilarious experimentation, she discovered the cosmetics contained magical, face-altering powders that made her appear like a goldfish or a tabby cat. Enid sighed. She rewashed her face and settled on a light application of non-magical lip rouge.

Before she tackled getting into the outfit, Enid had a snack from her horn. It became harder and harder to resist the mouth-watering solid food that was everywhere. She experienced a sudden pang of homesickness, and her thoughts strayed to her dad. Would she be brave and clever enough to see this adventure through? She fervently hoped so.

After downing two cups of her father's favorite potato and leek soup, she just decided a cup of tea would settle her nerves when she heard a gentle tap on her door.

She answered the door and discovered Princess Ceridwen, checking to see if Enid needed any help. Both girls sat down to share cups of Enid's tea and giggled over magical cosmetic mishaps. It was good to have the company. Too soon, the princess politely excused herself to get ready.

Finally, Enid was dressed and ready for the celebration. When she looked in the silvered mirror, Enid almost didn't recognize herself. The dove-gray outfit reminded her a bit of Robin Hood, and she looked ready for anything. She didn't know where the party was being held, but trusted one or both princes would be along to escort her. She was glad the dove gray boots that the Queen had provided were so comfortable.

What was a fairy revelry like? Would there be dancing?

Another knock sounded at her door. This time when she answered, the two princes were standing outside, ready to escort her. Enid had to acknowledge that both princes were ridiculously attractive.

Rhodri wore a forest green uniform with gold buttons which appeared tailor-made to fit his imposing form. His dark brown hair was tamed and combed back from his handsome face. Aeddan, too, had elected to dress in a uniform of the darkest khaki trimmed in crimson. As if Aeddan had hurried to be ready, his hair was still damp and unkempt. Aeddan had his sword strapped to his side and wore gloves.

Both princes appeared to Enid to have stepped out of the pages of her favorite fairy tale until Aeddan started speaking. "Human, you are running late as usual. It is rude to be tardy to a revelry held partly in your honor." Aeddan said with an eyebrow raised in challenge.

"Oh." Enid's face turned rosy in frustration.

Chapter 20

EVERYONE LOVES A PARTY

WHEN THEY ARRIVED AT the revelry, the scene was unlike anything Enid had ever seen. The enormous Great Hall was entirely ringed with giant conifer trees, and its ceiling was left open to the night sky overhead. The heavens had never looked so clear and full of stars. Enid imagined reaching up to touch the moon. Translucent floating lanterns added to the whimsical atmosphere. Four ponds were spaced throughout the hall, and an ornate, scrolling, and sculpted flower hedge outlined the spacious dance floor.

Enormous tables were placed around the edge, loaded with a mountain of delectable foods and desserts. Giant sugar cakes decorated with frosted flowers made Enid's mouth water. *Oh, if only I could eat.* Elaborate drinking fountains located strategically at the four corners of the hall proved popular. There appeared to be enough food and drink to feed her entire town for a month.

The throng of beings who attended the bash was overwhelming. It was a crush of all unique life forms. Many beasts, fowl, reptiles, trees, and flowers turned out to welcome their missing prince home and greet his human companion. The upbeat atmosphere reminded Enid of a carnival.

Enid and the princes wove their way through the crowd to the far side of the hall, where the rest of the royal family stood. In their wake, Enid heard lots of murmuring and saw pointing and gesturing in her direction from the fae. She had to remind herself that humans were rare on Afallon and tried not to be too self-conscious.

When the trio arrived, King Urien and Queen Dona stepped up onto a dais to address the crowd and took turns reminding them of their lost prince's bravery and good deeds. Rhodri was called to step forward, but before doing so, Rhodri squeezed Enid's hand and then moved into the spotlight. The crowd went wild with cheers, whistles, and clapping. It sounded like a roar of approval.

Rhodri's voice carried over the throng. "Greetings to Ellyllon. I have missed you." Another roar of approval sounded from the crowd. "It was very hard to be away from all of you, but fortunately I found the best of companions to aid me while I was away. I would like to thank my good friends for bringing me home."

The crowd's roar of approval was deafening.

Enid overheard her name and Prince Aeddan called next to come forward. Surely, they wouldn't be called forth. Yet both were summoned, and Aeddan kept his hand on the small of Enid's back as he guided her into the spotlight. Again, a roar of approval came from the crowd. In her wildest dreams, Enid never thought that a crowd would be wildly applauding her. Thankfully, Enid and Aeddan didn't have to speak.

After the introductions, the band struck up a song that sounded like something Enid would hear on the radio. She had expected an orchestra that played waltzes, yet the band was more in line with a rock group, which surprised her. The musicians had string instruments, keyboards, pipes, and drums. The music they played had a strong base rhythm, which set Enid's pulse thumping in time to the music. Singers weaved beautifully strange harmonies, and Enid was moved by their voices though she couldn't understand their words. It all blended into a hypnotic and exhilarating experience.

To Enid's horror, the dancing began. Rhodri appeared before her with his hand held out. She gave him a panicked look, and Rhodri said, "I think we're supposed to join the dancing. Aeddan will be paired with Ceridwen. Is something wrong?"

"I've never been to a school dance, and I don't really know how. I'm pretty clumsy. Why didn't you warn me?" Enid hissed in his ear.

"Don't worry, Enid. I won't let you fall." Rhodri's joy and confidence were contagious.

"I'll hold you to that, but I'm not apologizing if I step on your toes." Enid's laugh bubbled up from somewhere inside.

"We'll figure it out together." Rhodri beamed at her. He took Enid's hand and led her out to the dance floor, where the King and Queen were already sailing around the floor on feather-light steps in unison. Aeddan and Ceridwen glided gracefully out there as well, moving effortlessly to the beat. Enid trusted Rhodri's lead because she wasn't sure what else to do. *What was the worst that could happen?*

They joined the other couples, and Rhodri held her close, swaying in time to the rhythm, as opposed to trying the complicated steps of the others. Enid relaxed a little, and let the melody take over. They were dancing. At that moment, Enid believed she could do anything. Her steps and Rhodri's fit perfectly in sync. *Dancing must not be that hard,* Enid decided.

The dance floor soon swelled with fae doing many dance styles. As they bumped into another couple, Rhodri held Enid even closer and whispered in her ear, "You look so lovely tonight. You took my breath away when I first saw you."

Enid blushed at his compliment and stammered a little. "Y-You look nice too."

Rhodri's smile lit his face, and then he tilted his head. "We are in a hurry to reach Dylan and get him to safety. Why did you agree to come to this?"

Enid sought the right words. "Rhodri, everything you went through was so unfair. You were separated from everything you loved, and it must have been awful. I thought about what I wouldn't give to spend a single moment with my mother. I'd give almost anything. After witnessing your reunion with your family, how could I take you away from them so soon? I would understand if you wanted to remain behind. No one would blame you. I would gladly release you from your promise. Everyone should have a choice."

After a moment, he said, "You were wrong the other day."

Enid's footing got a little tangled. "Sorry." She refocused on her dancing partner. "How was I wrong?"

"You're magic, Enid Davies, and much rarer than you realize. I started this quest for my people, but I find I want to help you more." They were so close that she could feel Rhodri's heart pound as he confessed this in her ear.

"Wow. That's the nicest thing anyone has ever said to me." Enid blushed again. Shivers ran down her spine at the words being whispered in her ear. This had never happened to her before.

"Hasn't Dylan ever given you a compliment?" Rhodri's tone sounded unbelieving.

Enid laughed self-consciously. "I'm not saying he never gave me a compliment, just not one as nice as that." By the end, she was blushing again.

"My confinement in your realm was bearable because you treated me like a member of your family. I'm not sure you realize how unusual that generosity is." His low tones caused more shivers. It was like there were only the two of them on that dance floor.

"I'm sure anyone would have done the same, Rhodri." She laughed again. *What is wrong with me? Is he flirting? Am I?*

"I know how you feel about Dylan, but I wish you would see yourself the way others do—the way I do. I choose to accompany you on this quest for my people and our friend, but mostly for you." Rhodri's eyes never left Enid's as he made his declaration.

The song ended, and Rhodri was whisked off to dance with another partner before Enid gave him a reply. What could she possibly say?

An unsmiling Prince Gwynn wanted to take a turn with Enid around the dance floor. She welcomed the change in partners. Her reactions to Rhodri were confusing. She liked Dylan but had to admit Rhodri was very handsome, and for all she knew, she and Dylan were just friends. *You did nothing wrong,* she reminded herself, but a sense of guilt chased her jumbled thoughts.

As the evening wore on, Enid danced far more than she expected. Most partners were curious because she was human. Her most exciting pairing was with an actual tree, who proved an excellent dancer. She was amazed at how the tree roots twisted into lower limbs, like legs, which enabled the tree to move about. Thankfully, her dance partner was a smaller tree and light on its roots.

The party wound down, and the attendees started trickling home. Aeddan appeared before Enid and held out his hand. "Enid, would you do me the honor of dancing with me?"

Enid's mouth hung open in shock from his politeness, but she shrugged and took his hand in hers, which seemed sweaty to the touch. She had danced with practically everyone else. Why not dance with Aeddan? The floating lamps had been snuffed out one by one, and Enid wondered if it was some signal or countdown to the end of the celebration. The gathering gloom made it difficult to see across the floor, and Enid stumbled more frequently while dancing with Aeddan. Was it because of the dimming lights, or was it because he made her uncomfortable?

They completed their first dance in almost total silence. As another tune began, Enid thought they would part. However, Aeddan held on to her hand and continued into their second dance without asking permission. Enid decided this would be her last dance of the night. She felt a little weird. The music became too loud and the dim lighting too bright.

"Enid, I must confess something to you," Aeddan said into the shell of Enid's ear, making her shiver.

"What is it?" She backed away. Was that a trick of the light, or did his face blur for a second? Enid shook her head slightly to clear her vision.

"I'm uncertain about continuing our mission into the mountains. I've reconsidered things and concluded that we have no chance to succeed against the Gwyllion. Unfortunately, Malagant has been one step ahead of us the entire time." Aeddan frowned as he made this statement.

Was it her imagination that they twirled faster than before? Enid sensed her stomach churn and acid rise in her throat. Enid opened her mouth to speak, but Aeddan interrupted her again.

"I'm also anxious for you. I think about you all the time and I can't risk your safety. You've become too important to me."

Aeddan danced Enid into a darkened corner of the Great Hall, a spot that appeared to be secluded from onlookers. They had the alcove all to themselves. Her dizziness persisted.

She tried to speak, her words faltering. *What is going on tonight?* "Aeddan, I-I'm flattered. I am, but now isn't the time for this discussion. We can't start doubting what we have to do. What about your sister, Anna? What about our promises to free them?"

"It is because of Anna's safety and yours that I think we should let Malagant keep the Dragon prince. Don't you see? It's the only way everyone I care about will remain safe." Aeddan's lips tightened, and his eyes bored into Enid's.

"What? I'm not going to let that to happen. I've come too far to turn back now." Enid stopped dancing and swayed a little as the room spun.

Aeddan grabbed Enid to steady her and gently lowered her to the ground. "That is precisely why you need to be eliminated, Enid." His lips curled in contempt, but his eyes held no trace of a flame.

Maybe those flames had been a product of her imagination all along?

"What are you saying?" Her brain didn't seem to work. *Wait.* Was that a second Aeddan with eyes blazing like an unholy fire?

"You there. Get away from the human. Why are you wearing my likeness? Who sent you? Malagant?"

Enid must be seeing things. The next second, the real Aeddan stormed toward them, his throat glowing as if containing an inferno. Her head spun faster, and she experienced indescribable pain.

Through her agony, Enid heard another voice. It was Rhodri.

"Aeddan? What's going on? What is wrong with Enid?" Just a moment later, "Ceridwen?"

"Ceridwen?" Rhodri repeated.

The false Aeddan stepped away from Enid and faced Rhodri with a lifted chin. "You can recognize my energy then? Interesting."

"But I don't understand. You've never possessed the power to shapeshift." Rhodri's eyebrows furrowed, trying to fit the puzzle pieces together in a shape that made sense.

"Correction. I didn't have the power to shift before, but I do now. Isn't Malagant generous to her friends?" The false Aeddan bared his teeth, then he melted a bit like wax left too long in the sun. After a bright flash, Ceridwen stood in her celebration finery with a sneer twisting her beautiful face.

"Never mind all that now. What have you done to this human?" Aeddan's throat glowed with liquid fire barely contained.

"All of this concern over a useless human. It's such a waste. She won't be with us much longer. It's a pity." Ceridwen pouted her lips in mock sympathy.

"Ceridwen, please don't do this. What hold does Malagant have over you? You are better than this." Rhodri took a half step forward with his hand reaching out for his twin, his loyal sidekick he'd taken on so many childhood adventures.

"No, brother, I'm not. I used to be the powerless one. The one who always got overlooked. Poor Ceridwen. Nothing magical about her. She will never rule Ellyllon. But now I have all the power I need, thanks to Malagant, and can strike you where you are most vulnerable. And I've developed a solid talent for curses, don't you think?" Ceridwen winked, nodded at Enid, and turned before Rhodri caught hold of her arm. In the next moment, she shifted to a small bird, a swift, and darted away into the night.

Rhodri turned back to Enid and Aeddan, his eyes wide with shock. Aeddan held one of Enid's hands. Still conscious, Enid's eyes widened with fear. "Rhodri…" Enid tried to say more. The words caught in her throat and her stare became fixed.

After assessing her for physical injuries, the princes found no apparent wounds. Then Aeddan noticed Enid's hands, which peeked out from her cuffs and called Rhodri's attention to them. Her hands became an unnatural pale shade and cold to the touch.

"Enid has had frozen moments before, but never like this." Rhodri's voice cracked with tension, and he ran his hands through his hair.

"You have no ideas? Come on. Is it poison or a spell?" Aeddan urged. As they watched, the paleness progressed further.

Enid could only listen helplessly as her friends discussed her fate. She experienced a searing pain and then mercifully nothing. It was crawling up from her feet, and if it got to her heart, she was dead. Was this how her rescue mission was going to end? Her father and Dylan's parent would be devastated if they never returned, or would they remain frozen in time for all eternity? The weight of her failure was crushing her every bit as much as Ceridwen's deadly spell.

"I don't know. This could be anything. If I guess wrong, Enid could die." Rhodri confessed.

"We must try something. She looks like she's turning to stone." Aeddan said. The paleness had progressed further as they debated and was at the base of Enid's neck.

"Stone... It might be a petrifying curse." Rhodri breathed out. "That might be what Ceri chose because there is no known treatment for it." Rhodri bowed his head mournfully. He gripped one of Enid's unresponsive hands in his own. Her temperature was frigid to his touch. Rhodri's heart would become stone if his sister's curse succeeded.

Aeddan let out an expletive, grabbed his knife from its sheath, and slit his index finger. He gave a squeeze until a tiny, gleaming crimson droplet the size of a single tear formed. It hung suspended from his finger for an endless second, then the scarlet drop crystallized and fell. Aeddan caught it in his other hand. "Place this under her tongue. Hurry, before this thing goes further," he ordered Rhodri.

Rhodri took the shimmering drop and did as Aeddan instructed. Nothing happened. Did Rhodri guess wrong? Or was Aeddan's cure ineffective? Both princes just knelt beside their friend, just as frozen as she was, but for very different reasons.

"The human was too trusting..." Aeddan murmured and lowered his head in sorrow.

Rhodri opened his mouth to reply, either to shout a denial or agree, but never got to finish. At that moment, a tiny red sparkle shone at the tips of Enid's fingers. A heat so intense followed, which forced Rhodri to drop the hand he'd been holding.

The red sparkle expanded until it enveloped Enid's body. The air around Enid shimmered with the waves of heat coming from her. Moments later, she convulsed. Her back arched and lifted her off the floor. Enid's lips parted in a silent scream.

The red glow faded, and she collapsed again. Her color slowly changed from red back to normal. Enid groaned and rolled to her side. Thousands of needles stabbed her arms and legs as her circulation painfully resumed.

The princes helped Enid to a seated position. She spat a tiny white pebble from her mouth. She sat staring in shock at what she held in her palm. The drop of Aeddan's blood must have changed color after adsorbing the petrifying curse from her body. Rhodri gave Enid a bone-crushing hug. "Oh, Enid..." After a long moment, he eased his hold a bit. "I can't believe this. I'm so sorry. Are you okay?"

"I'm fine," Enid assured him. "It's not your fault. How could you have known?"

Rhodri shook his head. "I should have paid more attention instead of always trying to be a hero. Ceri always appeared so sure of everything. I didn't realize that's not how she saw herself."

"Those closest to us are sometimes the hardest to see clearly. We don't blame you." Aeddan placed a comforting hand on Rhodri's shoulder.

Both Rhodri and Aeddan helped Enid to stand as she shook out the last of the stiffness. "Aeddan, you saved me. I don't understand how, but I appreciate it."

The fire in Aeddan's throat disappeared, but his eyes still burned. "Human, I don't wish to see you die. Against my better judgment, I've grown accustomed to you."

At Aeddan's statement, Enid pointed toward him. "I should have suspected something when I danced with your clone. You never call me by name, and you appeared... blurry. And the things you said..." Enid broke off and shook her head.

Rhodri looked at Aeddan and said with a voice cracking with emotion, "I owe you a debt, my friend. I didn't know dragon's blood cured such a foul thing."

Dragon. Of course, that explains the smoldering fire in Aeddan's eyes I've witnessed. It was real. Enid looked to Aeddan. "Wait, a minute. Are you a dragon-like Dylan? I thought dragons were rare."

"We are rare. My people have kept my secret for many years to protect us from the Gwyllion. I am unaware of any others, though Dylan and I are different dragons. I am an earth-firedrake with fire from the earth's core, while Dylan is a sea wyvern with water magic that burns with a glacial fire. We are both deadly creatures, but a dragon's blood can also cure many ailments. I wasn't sure it would work, but I'm glad it did." Aeddan's molten gaze locked on Enid.

Chapter 21

MAKE A WISH

THE TRIO LEFT ELLYLLON in secret and as quickly as possible. The friends couldn't be sure if anyone else at the castle was in league with Malagant. Ceridwen would have been the person Rhodri trusted the most, and she had betrayed them all. How far did Malagant's reach go?

Ceridwen had an enormous head start on them and would reach Malagant's fortress first. They had lost some element of surprise. Malagant would expect them.

Back in her room, Enid gathered her belongings and changed. She left the horn behind. Ceridwen probably cursed it when they shared tea. Enid mentioned her suspicions to the princes, and they agreed. Deadly potions, like curses, needed to be administered directly to the victim. "I thought we became friends. I liked Ceridwen."

"Malagant's followers will do anything for her. She must be stopped," Aeddan vowed.

The trio made their way to the palace stables, where the royal menagerie was kept. Enid's mouth hung open when they entered at the sheer variety of creatures, both familiar and unfamiliar.

The spacious stalls were full of shire horses, unicorns with silver manes and horns, blue kelpie with spiked green manes and sharp teeth, a dark Pegasus with iridescent wings, and other creatures she couldn't even name. All were comfortably housed, with plenty of room to roam.

"Wow," Enid had never seen such a variety of exotic creatures in one place before. The horses seemed happy and well cared for. She made her way over to them, wanting to get a closer look, wishing she had slices of apple or mints to give.

Rhodri paused in front of some gryphons housed in large stalls. Enid glanced over at him for further details, but he was busy gathering saddles and tack. Aeddan, who followed behind Enid as she tried to make friends with the unicorn, explained, "These fierce beasts are known as Gryphons. They are powerfully loyal and are the Ellyllon royal family's preferred mode of transport."

The creatures had the snowy-feathered head, giant wings, and front talons of a fierce eagle, with a dark-red body, hind legs, and tail that resembled a mighty lion. The beak looked as if it could tear a man in half, and the sharp talons and claws on the massive hind paws resembled deadly scimitars made of brass. The gryphon's eyes shone, alert with intelligence. For the moment, the gryphons seemed calm around Enid but acted skittish around Aeddan.

"They must sense your hidden firedrake," Rhodri concluded.

Rhodri almost finished saddling the three gryphons when a commotion occurred at the entrance of the stables. Prince Gwynn and a small detachment from the Royal Guard arrived. Not sure what to expect, Aeddan and Rhodri drew their swords and Enid had her bow out and ready to fire. Prince Gwynn stepped forward, weaponless with hands out, and spoke first.

"Rhodri, are you really leaving without saying goodbye to us?"

Rhodri stepped forward. "We find we must resume our travels earlier than expected." He and Aeddan still held their weapons at the ready. "What brings you to the stables at this hour, brother?" he asked.

"We are searching for Ceridwen," Prince Gwynn explained. "She disappeared at the celebration and has not been spotted since, nor is she in her rooms. Have you seen her?"

Rhodri's mouth tightened and pulled down. "We have seen her." He paused, not sure where to begin. "I'm unsure how much you know, Gwynn, but Ceridwen has been working with Malagant all this time and has left Ellyllon to join her. We are following Ceri to Malagant's fortress and must hurry if we are to catch her. If there is any way to bring Ceridwen safely home, I shall try," he said.

Prince Gwynn's eyes widened, but he didn't appear as shocked by his brother's pronouncement. "I realized something was going on but did not suspect that. Tragically, over the months you remained missing, Ceridwen changed from the sweet girl we knew. Be careful, brother. I sense much rage in her, and powers that should not be. Our parents are in denial and do not suspect any of this. I must confess I'd hoped I was mistaken."

Rhodri nodded. "I, too, wish it was a mistake. What will you do now?"

"After I break this news to mother and father, I can follow you with a detachment of the Royal Guard and do whatever I can to assist you in ending this travesty and bringing our sister home." The brothers embraced, and then Prince Gwynn left the stables, calling out orders.

After his brother left, Rhodri turned back to face Enid and Aeddan. "Riding a gryphon is much like riding a horse, only these are much more intelligent. I have communicated what we need from them, and these three will join us on our quest. Don't be afraid of Bellerophon, Enid. He is the gentlest of companions." Rhodri stroked one of the gryphon's feathers as he spoke.

Enid approached her mount from the left side and grasped the reins. She stroked the feathers and enjoyed their downy softness. She murmured a greeting to her gryphon and introduced herself. After Enid's gentle pats, the gryphon gave a throaty purr, like a giant house cat. Heartened by this, Enid put a foot into the stirrup and pulled herself up into the saddle. It was remarkably like being on horseback.

She took time to fasten her bulky coat and slick her hair back into a ponytail with the holder around her wrist. She secured her hood in place as the princes mounted their steeds. They set off at a canter, which morphed into a full gallop. Enid was in her two-point stance with her hands on the reins up to the snowy feathers of the gryphon's neck. She clucked to Bellerophon, who picked up speed to keep up with their companions. With little warning, the three gryphons rose from the ground and climbed skyward.

It was awe-inspiring and terrifying all at once. The gryphons made a steep climb, but Enid never considered that Bellerophon would let her fall. They leveled out well above the tree line, and Enid got used to the rhythm of the beating wings.

She was flying. It was such an incredible experience. The wind blew past her as they soared over the moonlit landscape. The valleys they glided over appeared like intricate patchwork quilts of forests and fields, painted with a twilight haze. A warm light occasionally shone from the dwellings and appeared as bright as the moon and stars overhead. She heard all the sounds of life at night. Birds, animals, and insects all sang the same poignant, haunting tune, which rang out over the sound of the wind whistling past.

It would take them several hours to reach the mountain and see what awaited them there. *Would Dylan and Aeddan's sister, Anna, still be alive?* Enid shivered, and the gryphon emitted a toasty amount of body heat. She snuggled closer to Bellerophon to take full advantage of his warmth. Bellerophon didn't seem to mind and would emit a purr that signaled his contentment. Enid took comfort from the sound.

As the trio flew, however, a gradual tension grew in Bellerophon's neck and shoulders. He sensed something that Enid could not. The closer they got to the mountain, the more nervous he became. He began to fly erratically, swerving back and forth as if trying to avoid something.

It scared Enid. "Something's wrong." she called out. She heard an answering shout from Rhodri, but the wind carried away his words.

Bellerophon focused on whatever he was sensing. Enid clung to him tightly, not knowing what else to do.

Bellerophon let out a roar and dived toward the ground. Enid screamed as they plummeted toward the trees below. But at the last second, Bellerophon pulled up and flew into a clearing. He landed roughly, throwing Enid from his back.

"What were you doing?" she asked, getting to her feet. "We could have been killed."

But Bellerophon didn't listen to her. He stood in the middle of the clearing, sniffing the air.

Enid sensed something too, a dark presence, like a storm brewing on the horizon. She sensed they weren't alone. She searched the night sky in vain for any sign that the princes had seen where they landed and followed.

At her side, Bellerophon tensed and turned towards the trees. Enid followed his gaze and saw nothing. Was something lurking in the fading darkness?

Bellerophon let out a challenging roar and stepped forward, but Enid grabbed the reins to stop him. She almost didn't have the strength but held on anyway and kept the gryphon firmly by her side. She glanced upwards again, but no princes were speeding to their location. This forest wasn't somewhere she wanted to wander on her own.

Enid mounted her gryphon again and held Bellerophon's reins, ready for anything that lurked in the darkness. No matter how scared she became, Enid was determined to face whatever danger awaited them head-on. The princes were almost there. She just had to hold her ground until then.

Enid prepared her bow for a fight. The wind whistled through the trees, carrying with it an eerie warning. Their fate was uncertain… but Enid knew it was time to test her courage. Enid tightened her grip and stared into the darkness, knowing that no matter what happened, it was time to take control of her destiny.

Something was coming. The ground shook as if something was rushing closer and closer. And then she spied it—an Afanc emerging from the shadows of the trees, its snarling face a mask of rage. Enid gasped in horror. When she spied the chipped tusk, she knew that this was not just any monster they were facing. This was her nemesis—the beast must have been hunting them since they escaped its grasp days ago.

Enid remembered with fresh horror that it now owed her a wish, whether or not she wanted to make one. But she also knew that if she didn't, it would take her life instead. She glanced up, hoping to see Aeddan and Rhodri. They had been right behind her. Where had they gone?

"Your friends cannot assist you, human," the Afanc said. "They have interfered too much already. I have confused their mounts and sent them in another direction. It is time for us to talk."

Enid swallowed hard and nodded, though blood was pounding in her ears. She had no choice but to face this creature on her own with just Bellerophon at her side. As if sensing her thoughts, the gryphon nodded its head, making her feel less lonely. "What do you want? I have released you without obligation. I don't want your wish." Enid's voice echoed in the clearing.

"A human who does not want a wish—I find that very hard to believe. There must be something you desperately desire?" The Afanc studied Enid for a reaction.

Enid thought about Dylan but didn't speak his name out loud. Could the Afanc read her mind? She was unprepared for this moment.

"Hmmmm... I sense an unspoken wish. Are you sure you do not want to give voice to it?" The Afanc smiled and its razor-sharp tusks and teeth were on full display.

Enid took a deep breath and looked the Afanc directly in the eyes. "I have nothing to wish for," she said. "I don't need your wishes to accomplish what I want in life."

The Afanc seemed to consider her words for a moment before letting out a low, throaty laugh. "You are a brave one, human. But do not underestimate the power of magic. It is what separates us from the mortal world."

Enid's hands were slick with sweat. She knew the Afanc was right - magic was powerful, but she refused to rely on it solely to achieve her goals. She had come too far and fought too hard to let a wish dictate her future.

"How did you find me?" Enid changed tactics. "It has been days since our run-in. Aren't you relieved to be set free without granting a wish?"

"That is no fun for me, human. I must eat, and it has been so long since I feasted on one of your kind." Again, it gave her a blood-chilling smile.

The Afanc moved closer, its eyes narrowing. It had grown twice as tall since she had last seen him. The ground shook beneath her feet as it shifted its weight. Bellerophon snorted in fear and Enid tightened her grip on the reins and gave her mount reassuring pats. She had to stay strong no matter what happened.

"I'm not intimidated by you," Enid said, meeting the Afanc's gaze without flinching. "Your power has no hold over me."

The Afanc roared, but Enid refused to break eye contact. Its eyes gleamed with malice. "Your mother," it intoned. "You have questions about her. I met her once long ago."

A shiver ran down her spine as the creature continued its tale. "She came seeking something."

Enid's pulse skipped a beat. "What did she seek?" she asked, her voice barely above a whisper.

The Afanc grinned wickedly. "Ah, that is something I cannot reveal to you so easily. But I can tell you this - your mother knew what she wanted. And she gladly paid the price to get it."

Enid's mind raced. She had always wondered about her mother's murder. Could this creature really know something that could help her? Or was it just trying to lure her into a trap?

"Why are you telling me this?" Enid asked, eyeing the Afanc warily. "What do you want?"

The Afanc's eyes glittered with amusement. "Oh, nothing much. Just a small wish from you in return for information."

Enid's heart sank.

Suddenly, a familiar presence was behind her—Aeddan and Rhodri had arrived. Enid glanced back at them with relief and realized that they were ready to fight if necessary.

The relieved smiles on the princes' faces quickly morphed to gaping mouths as they beheld what she faced. Both rushed forward but were stopped some distance away. Rhodri pounded ineffectively on something invisible in frustration.

Enid's relief at their arrival was short-lived because there was a barrier between her and her friends. The Afanc had created an invisible wall separating Enid and Bellerophon from Aeddan and Rhodri.

"Now," the Afanc said, "are you sure you do not want to make that wish? One tiny little insignificant wish? I have power over life and death, and reality itself, after all. Nothing is beyond my reach. Nothing," It smiled menacingly as if daring Enid to challenge its might.

Enid stared at the beast with determination in her eyes before finally speaking up. "No. You won't get my wish today. I am stronger than everyone gives me credit for—you can't tempt me. Now leave me alone." Enid shouted.

The Afanc stomped in anger, making the ground tremble and Bellerophon tensed beneath her.

With a deep breath, Enid dug her heels into Bellerophon's sides and charged toward their enemy. The fight had begun. Enid raised her bow and released an arrow straight toward the Afanc's eye.

The arrow veered harmlessly away at the last second. "Are you sure, human, that there is nothing you want to ask for? The path of your arrow does not lie. There are desires written upon your heart. I can sense them."

Is that what Merlin meant by aiming with a pure heart? There were so many wishes on Enid's mind. She wanted her friend back. She wanted to see her loved ones unfrozen. She wanted to know her mother. But the cost of all those things was far too high. Someone else would lose a friend or family member if she spoke the words, yet she couldn't defeat this creature with force.

Enid had to use cunning. She had to think fast.

Enid took a deep breath and steeled her gaze on the Afanc and spoke with conviction. "My dearest wish at this moment is to not have to wish for anything from you." Enid raised her useless bow again, ready for battle if needed. But instead of attacking Enid, the Afanc cackled in dark delight.

"Very well, Human of the Woods. I am furious that I have lost a tasty meal this day, but you have amused me. I must grant your wish and allow you to live without consequence, but we may yet see each other again." The Afanc waved its golden foot and the invisible wall evaporated. A wave of relief washed over her as Aeddan and Rhodri galloped toward them.

The battle was over. Enid may not have won by force, but she had outsmarted the Afanc instead. The creature melted away into the night, leaving Enid with a sense of satisfaction and accomplishment. She had stayed alive, despite all odds—and that was victory enough for now. Enid shared a smile and hugs with her relieved friends before once more taking to the air and flying onwards towards Malagant's fortress.

Chapter 22

NO RETURN

DAWN BROKE AS ENID and her companions arrived at their destination. The gryphons huddled together and still acted uneasy. After a brief discussion, the trio sent them back to the Ellyllon border to wait. Enid's lower lip trembled as she said goodbye to Bellerophon. She hugged him and whispered her appreciation for an incredible experience, even with the heart-stopping conclusion. Bellerophon responded by giving a throaty purr. Soon the gryphons became airborne and disappeared into the clouds.

They landed partway up the slope of Malagant's mountain. A dense forest surrounded them. Snow lay on the ground in patches where the sparse gaps in the trees allowed it to fall. The frigid air stung Enid's cheeks, and her breath became visible. She was aware trees grew tall, but the surrounding silvery conifers appeared as if they brushed the sky. She felt lost in a primeval nightmare.

Enid's companions, Rhodri and Aeddan, unstrapped their weapons, preparing to enter the trees. Enid gathered her wits about her, determined not to cause any delay.

As they began their trek, Enid's uneasiness increased with every step. It seemed as if countless eyes watched her from the shadows between the tree trunks. More than once she saw movement out of the corner of her eye, but when she turned to look, there was nothing. The forest appeared lifeless except for them. She tried to take comfort in Rhodri and Aeddan's presence, but their grim expressions did little to reassure her. They acted as if they expected an attack at any moment.

Enid also noted the odd quality of the light, obscured by a thick layer of mist floating overhead. She was reminded of going on a school trip to the aquarium as a young girl and passing through one of those aquarium tunnels. Dylan had been with her that day, and even held her hand when she became frightened by an octopus.

Enid glanced around, almost expecting to see tropical fish and sharks looming above. The colors became deprived of all vibrancy, and everything got shrouded in tones of blue, including her red concert tee.

Aeddan, always impatient, scouted up ahead, looking for any signs of trouble.

"How far ahead of us do you suppose Ceridwen is?" Enid gave a side glance to Rhodri, who kept pace beside her.

He considered a moment before answering. "Swifts are one of the fastest birds. In that form and with her head start, she'll have reached the fortress several hours ago. But Ceridwen and Malagant won't expect us so soon. They believe you're dead, and we are in disarray."

Enid studied Rhodri as he finished speaking. He avoided eye contact with her. The set of his shoulders slumped, sick over the betrayal of his sister. "You couldn't have known that Ceridwen teamed up with Malagant. I'm so sorry it turned out like this. The whole situation is horrible."

Her friend's head nodded in agreement. "I keep thinking that I should have known. She is my twin, after all. We were once very close and told each other everything. We had no secrets. Why would she do all those terrible things?"

"Aeddan had a point about not seeing the people closest to us," Enid offered. "As much time as Dylan and I spent together, I had no clue he was going through any of this. Maybe your sister had problems she thought no one would understand, so she sought help elsewhere," she said as the corners of her mouth turned down.

Is that what happened to Dylan? Did he assume I wouldn't accept him? How lonely he must have been. How did I miss something this big?

"She should have realized her family would be there for her, no matter what," Rhodri insisted, his head bowed in disappointment.

"Sadly, there is often a big gap between what people should know and what they actually know." Enid shook her head and considered all the important people in her life still frozen in time. Would she ever see them again? Would she get the chance to express how much she loved each one? *Did they know?* Enid hoped so but made a promise to herself to tell them if she ever made it back home.

The friends grew quiet for a moment, each lost in their thoughts as they walked. She changed topics, "Your mother told me she met a human once, who called herself Lilli. I think she must have met my mother."

Rhodri's eyes widened. "Your mother? But that means..." His voice trailed off as he looked up at Enid, realizing the significance of what she had just said.

Enid nodded, her thoughts racing. Could it be possible that she had found a connection to her mother's past?

Rhodri took a step closer to Enid, gazing deeply into her eyes. "Did she tell my mother anything about her quest?"

Enid experienced a jolt of awareness as Rhodri stepped near. She'd experienced nothing like this before, not even with Dylan. Was she having the same feelings for both of them? *How was that possible?*

"I-I'm not sure," she replied, stepping hastily back.

Aeddan called out interrupting them from up ahead. "I've found something."

Both Enid and Rhodri hurried to catch up with Aeddan. He stood in front of a large tree, his hand running over the rough bark.

"What is it?" Enid asked.

Aeddan pointed to a symbol carved into the tree. "This is a mark of warning."

Rhodri's eyes widened in surprise. "A warning about what?"

Aeddan shook his head. "I'm not sure, but I think it says 'Beware.' We have entered the Gwyllion's lands and need to be careful." After that ominous remark, Aeddan continued to scout ahead.

As they moved further into the forest, Enid's unease increased. Her eyes darted all around, trying in vain to pierce the murk, but visibility remained difficult because of the all-encompassing mist, like being submerged in the ocean. What did it conceal?

To distract herself and Rhodri from gloomy thoughts, Enid asked him a question that still troubled her. "Rhodri, when I met your father, he mentioned something odd about Merlin and how he tricked your family. He seemed pretty mad about it. Do you know what he meant?"

Rhodri smiled a little at the change in topics. "Merlin knew my grandparents. He was given the power to shapeshift by my grandmother."

Enid encouraged Rhodri to continue. "Merlin was a prophet, a wizard, and an advisor renowned in all the realms. My grandmother was a young queen with many suitors vying for her hand in marriage. Merlin came to our court, and he was young and handsome. According to her, they fell in love. Merlin taught my grandmother some enchantments, and she gifted him with some abilities, like the power to shapeshift, and old heirlooms, like our family's sword. Because Merlin had a wandering eye, my grandmother broke off their relationship. He kept his abilities and gifts. Though it ended badly, my grandmother still remembered Merlin fondly, because he was her first love. But our family, especially my grandfather, who loved my grandmother fiercely, remained outraged on her behalf."

Enid had sympathy. "Wow. I can understand why your father was so upset. What was your grandmother's name?" Enid asked.

Rhodri gave a genuine grin as he remembered that powerful lady. "Her name was Queen Nimue. My grandfather was jealous of Merlin, and my father grew up listening to endless stories. I did as well."

Enid stumbled in her surprise. "So, are you telling me that your grandmother was the Lady of the Lake? And your family blade... Was it called Excalibur?" Her eyebrows rose in amazement.

"Well, our family always referred to it as Caliburn." Rhodri tugged at his ear. "Wait, have you already heard this story?"

Enid nodded. "I have, but I never guessed that your family was so connected to our King Arthur legend. It's an incredible story."

Rhodri agreed. "Yes, it is. And one that my father still holds onto anger about. He's never forgiven Merlin for what he did."

Enid understood King Urien's hostility. After all, his mother had been wronged.

Enid shook her head, and the friends continued for some time in silence. She struggled mightily to reconcile the fashion-challenged, kindly old wizard as a ladies' man.

The trio took a quick break just after midday, partway up the slope. The weather was frigid, and the mist overhead was a looming presence. They had seen no sign of any creature, human or otherwise, since leaving the castle. Even the birds deserted the place.

After a few quiet minutes, Enid said, "Are there any other tales of Merlin that I should know?" Enid asked and waited for Rhodri to respond.

To her surprise, Aeddan spoke. "I grew up on stories of his exploits. We know him as the dragon tamer," Aeddan smiled as if he were recalling cherished childhood tales, and Enid had an errant thought. Aeddan should smile more often. It was surprising to her how changed her outlook had become. She had started out fearing Aeddan to now being friends with him.

Rhodri picked up the story. "My favorite tale is that dragon story. He faced off against two angry dragons and by the end had put them both to sleep."

"Yes, humans know that story as well. Are you saying it is true?" Enid's eyes opened wide with wonder.

"Yes, that tale is true. It started with a disagreement between a mighty earth-dragon and a sea dragon over some land. Merlin arrived and spoke at length to both dragons. He said some words that put both creatures to sleep. When they awoke, their disagreement had been forgotten, and the dragons parted as friends." Aeddan shook his head and grinned in admiration.

Rhodri laughed in delight, and all three companions chuckled at the tale. "In our version, Merlin would have been sacrificed if he hadn't calmed the dragons." Enid bit her lip, wondering if that detail was also a fact.

"Hmmm... It might explain the creativity of his solution. I've found survival instinct to be a great motivator," Rhodri said, his brow creased in thought.

Aeddan then asked about the white pebble that Enid saved from her brush with death. She was unsure why she had kept it, but she fished it out of her pocket and handed it to the brooding prince.

He studied it briefly and then requested three of her hawthorn arrows. Aeddan's hand glowed, and the pebble turned to liquid. He dipped and coated each arrow tip into the potion. He then scorched the opposite ends of the projectiles to mark them and gingerly handed them back to Enid. "Careful, Human. Do not cut yourself on these. Use them only in the gravest emergencies."

Enid nodded and slipped the arrows into her quiver, fervently hoping she wouldn't need them. "Wasn't that dangerous for you? To hold that awful potion in your hand in liquid form?"

Aeddan gave Enid a cocky grin and a quick wink. "Are you worried about me, Human? Never fear. I had no cuts on my hands, so the risk was minimal. But if it turned me to stone, don't you think I'd make a beautiful statue?"

Enid shivered and shook her head. "I would not wish that fate on anyone." She had to admit, though, that her confidence increased with the additional potency of her weapons. "Have either of you ever been to Malagant's fortress? What should we expect when we get there?"

Rhodri shrugged his shoulders, but Aeddan spoke. "I went there once, long ago, as a child. As I mentioned before, it is a frozen, lonely place. I remember guards stationed all around, but we should be able to find a hidden underground entrance. Tunnels are everywhere in Afallon, thanks to my people. But that's not the most dangerous part of the journey, Human."

"It isn't?" Enid dreaded Aeddan's next words.

"Well, the mountain's name Gorre roughly translates to 'Land of No Return.' This strange mist completely shrouds these peaks, and they say the forests surrounding the fortress are haunted," Aeddan noted.

"Do you mean haunted, as in ghosts?" Enid's eyes widened.

"Human, there are much more dangerous creatures than ghosts in these forests, namely the Dienw or the unnamed ones. They are deadly and very real, but no one knows what they look like. Few live to tell the tale after an attack, and they always claim to have seen nothing. We've only been told the stories and seen the horrible scars left on the pitiful few survivors," Aeddan said.

Enid glanced around once more. They had held their conversation and now were encircled by the mist. The light grew even dimmer, if possible. Traveling in the fog was akin to heading into a fun house at a summer fair. Outside, the sky looked bright and clear, but inside it was murky, and many deadly monsters could easily be concealed.

Enid glanced at her companions and noticed that their eyes lit with a golden glow, much like a cat's eyes in the headlights of oncoming traffic. She hoped that meant they saw better than she could through the dense, unremitting vapor.

The farther up the slope, the trio traveled, the more their conversation lagged. It wouldn't do to alert whatever beings guarded the place to their presence. Enid had little breath to talk, and she found it difficult to keep up with her companions' stealthy movements during the climb. What she wouldn't give for some cool water. Enid desperately missed Bran's horn.

As they continued their ascent, Enid could feel her muscles burning and her chest heaving with each breath. The harsh terrain was unforgiving, and the mist only made it more challenging.

She was glad for the company of her two companions, who were moving silently and confidently through the terrain.

Enid had been traveling with Rhodri and Aeddan for several days now, and she was feeling a sense of camaraderie with them. They had been through many perilous situations, and each time, they had emerged victorious. She relied on their knowledge and knew that without them, she would have long since perished.

Enid was deep in thought when Rhodri's whisper broke through the silence. "Do you see that?" he asked, pointing to a boggy area on the mountain slope that reminded Enid of the chilling moors of Scotland.

Her body tensed as a chill ran through her veins. Something was watching her, and she could feel it as keenly as someone whispering in her ear. Her gaze darted between her friends, who had all taken on stiff postures, and Rhodri's hand slowly slipped towards his sword's hilt. She felt like prey being stalked by an unseen predator, yet there was nothing to be seen around them. Everywhere she looked, the darkness seemed to linger like an omen of evil.

Aeddan sniffed the air. Then his eyes flared with molten heat. "Human, can you climb a tree?"

Without waiting for her to answer, he grabbed her and lifted her to a lower branch of a nearby tree. Rhodri drew his long sword and covered Aeddan's back as he helped Enid onto her perch. The princes then stood back-to-back with weapons drawn. She climbed a level higher and unslung her bow.

For a moment, the woods stood still, as if time itself had stopped ticking. No birds sang, and no wind rustled through the trees. Only their labored breathing cut through the air like a hammer against an anvil.

"No matter what happens, Human, you must stay in that tree." Aeddan's voice sounded gruff. His eyes appeared as twin flash points of flame, and his throat appeared to be full of molten lava. "Rhodri and I can't afford a distraction."

Enid slowly nodded, her eyes wide and uncertain as she studied the forest floor. Aeddan was right of course. Perched amongst the tree's branches, she became a harder target for whatever lurked beyond their line of sight. Her bow and arrows were better used from an elevation. But what would she shoot at? All she could see in the clearing below them was the three friends.

"Aeddan, do you sense anything?" Rhodri asked just before the screaming began.

Chapter 23

THE UNSEEN

THE SOUNDS OF SCREAMING almost undid Enid's courage. Who was screaming? Where did the sound originate? Aeddan and Rhodri remained ready, standing back-to-back, with weapons drawn, so neither of them made that awful sound. Yet no other creatures were visible.

The sky darkened further, as if in response to the chilling cries. The princes stood nearby, yet she could hardly see them through the cloying mist. Her last clear view was of Rhodri, nodding encouragement to her. Then total darkness descended.

She steeled herself, knowing calling out would gain nothing. Enid fought to keep her breathing steady as she groped around in the darkness, listening for some sign of the others. Something snaked around her leg, almost pulling her from her perch. Enid yelped and put a hand out to the tree trunk to steady herself. *That was too close,* she thought.

Enid shuddered, imagining many monsters lurking in the darkness, just waiting to snatch her up. Enid tried to silence her mind, but the dreadful screaming had resumed, now coming from all around her. It came from the very trees themselves. Would the sound drive her mad?

A shout of surprise came from what seemed like a great distance. Was that Rhodri? *What happened?* The sudden clang of weapons clashing rang through the clearing. Enid dared not call her friends. The slightest distraction might prove too costly, as the princes fought for their lives.

Stuck in a tree and unable to see, Enid experienced alternating bouts of frustration and indecision. If she shot an arrow, she might hit her friends. Her bow was called Fail-Naught, but Enid didn't assume that meant shooting blindly into the fray. She might hit her companions.

Something brushed against her hand. The sensation reminded her of walking through cobwebs. She shook her hand in disgust and focused on the sounds all around her.

She heard Aeddan cry out in pain and Enid froze. *No, please don't let them be hurt.* Enid wrapped her arms around herself, trying to quell the rising panic. Something touched her hair and Enid yelped in disgust.

From below the tree, screams, grunts, and occasional shouts of surprise increased in frequency. How did the princes fight something invisible? *Was that another cry of pain? Who was it?* Her eyes strained, trying to pierce the veil of darkness, but Enid couldn't see a thing. Something tapped on the nape of Enid's neck. She rubbed her neck a moment later and felt nothing.

Although her attention focused on the clearing, Enid sensed scrutiny directed at her. The creeping sensation intensified. Was it her imagination, or did something snag her hair again and pull? She ran a hand carefully over her head. Her hair strands pulled tight and then loosened. *Was something in the tree with her?* She stared into the darkness behind her but witnessed nothing out of the ordinary. Enid swallowed hard, past her dry throat.

She picked up the sounds of battle from below and another grunt of pain. Enid wanted to help. What did she have that would work in such a situation? Her bow was useful only if the creatures revealed their position. She needed to help Rhodri and Aeddan now.

Jabs at her ankles caused Enid to reach down to brush at her feet. *What caused that?* To her shock, something with a squishy consistency pushed back. Hard. Enid cried out in disgust and swatted at it, only to be rewarded with a sharp, stabbing pain in her hand.

She snatched her hand back and scooted farther out along the stout limb. She put a hand out to steady herself and encountered still more slimy consistency. *Ugh.* For a moment, she lost her balance and almost fell, but regained her equilibrium at the last second.

Enid inched along the branch until she was as far away from the trunk of the tree as possible. Something oozed over her shoe, and Enid shuddered in revulsion. *What was happening?* She had to climb up from this branch before whatever it had reached her. Enid hoisted herself onto the neighboring branch.

Unnamed... Darkness... What did Merlin say about the dark? The pain in her hand affected Enid's ability to concentrate. Merlin mentioned something about lighting the way. Enid held on to the idea like a life preserver, noting her surroundings were still bathed in an inky blackness.

She used her throbbing hand to sling her bow back onto her shoulder. With difficulty, she brought out the chrome-plated torch Merlin provided. Was there something magical about this flashlight? If so, would the magic backfire and cause more harm? Her hands shook so much she almost dropped it.

Is this a mistake? She wondered. The light might attract more monsters like moths to a flame. Or worse yet, give away their position. With so many negatives to consider, Enid hesitated to flick the switch. The seconds ticked by in total darkness until she heard another shout of pain from Aeddan. The cry tore from his throat, and Enid's hesitation evaporated. She had to know if her friends were seriously hurt.

The moment she switched on the torch, the strong beam cut through the mist and darkness like a lighthouse beacon. Her eyes had grown accustomed to the dark, so the light proved blinding, but slowly, her eyes acclimated. At first, she couldn't comprehend what she saw. Then she recoiled in revulsion.

Monstrous crawling forms clung all over her tree, surrounding Enid and the clearing. One of those things hung down from the tree limb just above her head, ready to pounce. She moved away from it. As Enid watched, tentacles shot out, stretching, grabbing, and trying to pull the thing toward her face. With a yell, Enid swung the torch and knocked it out of the tree. She refocused the light toward the clearing.

What Enid saw next caused her to cry out in terror.

Below her, Rhodri and Aeddan fought against an onslaught of monsters. The creatures looked unlike anything Enid had ever seen before. They had bulbous bodies with many legs, and their tentacles writhed and snapped at the men. Enid's friends did their best to fight back, but they were outnumbered, and Enid could tell they were tiring.

The creatures' sizes varied. Some appeared the size of a large dog, while others looked only inches long. But there were so many of them everywhere. They appeared translucent in the torchlight. With no light, they perfectly blended into the background as if camouflaged. The torchlight revealed the creatures' hideous forms, much like an octopus. The multitude of limbs resembled tentacles with sharp claws at the end.

The monsters had bulging eyes which appeared empty and life-less. The horrible screeching noise came from them. Of that, Enid was sure.

Is it a language? A battle cry?

Enid wondered where the mouths might be located. She witnessed one screech, realizing its mouth was at the bottom of its gelatinous head, full of milky, razor-sharp fangs. Each tentacle had barbs at the tip, and those hideous claws and teeth were aimed directly at her friends. In the light from the torch, Enid noticed a smear of dark blood on Aeddan's face. Her heart raced.

Rhodri and Aeddan were moving so fast that their actions appeared to blur. The princes cut an effective swath through the invisible horde, yet the monsters didn't stop when the princes cut them down. They simply multiplied as smaller but still deadly versions, and they kept coming.

It only took seconds for her friends to realize they could see what they fought. Rhodri's efforts redoubled, but Aeddan paused. To Enid's amazement, Aeddan changed forms to become a fire-drake. She knew he was a dragon, but his morphing was still a shock. His body elongated and then grew to the size of a small elephant.

Shiny red scales covered his new form, but his molten eyes remained the same, only larger. He had four legs tipped with lethal claws and a spiked tail. Aeddan's wings resembled a bat, but his deadly mouth contained a double row of long, sharp incisors.

Aeddan's eyes and neck blazed before he let his fire loose in the clearing. Every monster touched by his flames was fried, including the ones climbing Enid's tree. His flames just missed Rhodri, who crushed the few remaining smaller creatures underfoot.

Enid nearly fell out of the smoldering tree, stunned by what happened. The obscuring mist cleared a bit, and it became obvious there was little time left before the sunset. Aeddan's fire and a flashlight saved Rhodri and Enid, who gave each other grim smiles of relief. They had faced challenges together on this journey, but this was by far the strangest.

"Well, that was way too close," Enid said.

"Yes, indeed. Are you alright?" Rhodri asked as she landed next to him, clicking off the torch.

"Yes, I think so." Her hand throbbed in pain despite the numbing coldness of the surrounding air. "You?"

Rhodri nodded and moved toward her, reaching for her hand. At that moment, the firedrake roared his disapproval. Aeddan's eyes appeared as twin flames zeroed in on Rhodri and the hulking firedrake took several menacing steps toward him.

Rhodri didn't back down, though the firedrake was intimidating. His glowing eyes narrowed, and Rhodri stepped toward the firedrake with a sword in hand, ready to defend them both. Enid noted this and placed herself between them. She was unsure what kindled Aeddan's wrath, but she was done with fighting.

When she approached the firedrake, she noted blood oozing from a massive cut on his face. "Aeddan, are you okay?" The firedrake's attention shifted reluctantly from Rhodri back to Enid, and the glow of his irises intensified. The firedrake lowered his face to a level where Enid studied the wound. "Oh, you're hurt."

Enid ripped a long strip of cloth from her T-shirt and pressed it to Aeddan's cut, which appeared to run deep. She spoke soothingly to him and brushed at his scales. They seemed hard and smooth simultaneously, like the texture of polished gems. If the gash had been any deeper, he might have lost his sight in that eye.

When Rhodri moved closer to Enid, the firedrake again roared his disapproval. "Now, why are you doing that? Aeddan. You're going to alert the entire mountain to our presence. It's just Rhodri. You remember him, right?"

Rhodri deliberately moved to Enid's side. The firedrake huffed his disapproval, but this time didn't roar. Rhodri took Enid's injured hand in his and looked at her seeping wound. He took his flask and washed her puncture as gently as he could and then ripped a strip of cloth from his shirt to bind Enid's cut.

After he finished, Enid took the flask from Rhodri, whetted her fabric, and cleaned as much of Aeddan's gash as she could. "Why is he yelling at you? You didn't cut him," Enid asked Rhodri.

"I think he and I are both feeling overprotective of you right now. His native form heightens his instincts even further." Rhodri's hand absently rubbed at the back of his neck, his cheeks turning red with embarrassment.

Oh... Oh. Her cheeks turned rosy as well. "We're all on the same team. Correct? No need to be cranky. We don't have time for that," Enid said while still tending Aeddan's cut. Aeddan huffed in annoyance again, at Enid this time, who shrugged her shoulders in response.

"Firedrakes are notoriously temperamental." Rhodri had still not sheathed his weapon.

She guessed shapeshifters were temperamental, too. "Aeddan mentioned his people kept his a secret, so how did you know he was a firedrake?" Enid's forehead wrinkled in puzzlement.

"I got the surprise of a lifetime when you were injured by the raptors. We needed fast transport for you to Ellyllon. When you passed out from the blood loss, he changed forms almost immediately." Rhodri kept his attention on Aeddan as he talked. "Firedrakes are unpredictable, but extremely loyal."

Aeddan took that risk for her. He could have kept his secret safe, but he helped her, a human he barely knew.

Enid realized then it would be a mistake to think of these princes as only human boys. The reality was so much more complicated than that. These beings weren't human. They might not react as expected.

Enid wondered why she wasn't terrified by her warrior-like, inhuman companions. No matter what the princes were, they were loyal, brave, and kind, just as any girl would want in her friends—as Enid wanted in her friends.

"Why do you think he hasn't changed back?"

Rhodri shrugged his shoulders. "He may heal faster in this form or can fight more effectively. Who knows? We probably should get moving, though. There's no doubt this fire won't go unnoticed. We need to be a long way from here when they come to investigate."

Enid wholeheartedly agreed with this plan. As she glanced around the smoking clearing, she shuddered.

The three friends quickly left the bog behind. A firedrake led a fae prince and a human girl on a dangerous quest to save their friends, families, and both realms.

Had Merlin foreseen this unlikely chain of events? Is that why he equipped Enid with the torch? She was grateful, yet more disturbed than ever. Was there a predestined outcome? Could she save Dylan and Aeddan's sister, and both realms, from Malagant? The time fast approached when she would get her answers.

Chapter 24

THE DUNGEON

THE TRIO MADE THEIR way from the site of the confrontation with the Dienw. Enid understood why those creatures had gotten the name. She shivered, remembering how they'd remained invisible until lit by Merlin's torch. Without that light, would her friends have prevailed? Would those things have kept coming until she and the princes were overrun? She trembled again, though not with the cold.

Enid couldn't shake the sense of unease. She wondered if their luck would continue to hold. Even with the princes' magical abilities, they were still facing a powerful adversary.

The worry etched into Enid's features must have been obvious, for Rhodri reached out and took her hand. His touch was gentle, and she drew comfort from it. "We'll make it through this," he said, his reassuring.

Enid bit her lower lip and nodded, silently acknowledging the truth of their situation. Despite being surrounded by newfound friends who were just as determined to save Dylan, she couldn't deny the overwhelming dread at the thought of what lay ahead. She only hoped that their combined abilities would be enough to allow for success.

Up ahead, Aeddan moved with a snake-like gait. His scales caught the moonlight and sent it scattering into a thousand pieces. They were deep red with brown spots like a speckled eggshell. A silver fringe ran along his flanks and tail, that shone like dappled sunlight on water. His eyes gleamed like embers in their sockets. Enid admired the way the firedrake moved with such effortless grace and power.

Rhodri noted her fascination with Aeddan, and he smiled knowingly. "He's quite something, isn't he?" he said.

Enid blushed, embarrassed by her obvious admiration. "I suppose he is."

Rhodri squeezed her hand gently, his touch sending a jolt of electricity through her body. "Just don't forget we're all in this together. We must work as a team if we're going to succeed."

Enid's chin jutted out as she nodded. The cold air chilled her to the bone, but it sharpened her focus. They were walking into unknown danger, and she feared to disappoint the friends who helped her get this far, so she steeled herself to move forward.

Enid trudged along the winding path, her mind swirling with both wonder and dread. She had stumbled into this strange new world full of enchanted creatures and mysterious beings—so different from the mundane life she left behind.

Enid couldn't ignore the drumming that had taken root in her anxious heart. Despite the princes' bravado, they were taking a monumental risk. She wanted to believe they would prevail, but a part of her was afraid of what would happen to both realms if they failed.

A thought suddenly occurred to Enid. "Do you think I'll ever be able to return home?" she asked, her voice just above a whisper.

Rhodri glanced at her with concern etched into his features. "What makes you ask *that*?" he said.

Enid shrugged. "I guess I'm just wondering if I'll ever be able to go back to my old life. To the way things were before all of this. Will any of us?"

Rhodri placed a comforting arm around her shoulders. "I wish there was a simple answer, Enid. But the truth is, I don't know what the future holds. All I know is that we must focus on the task at hand and do everything in our power to save our friend and both realms."

Rhodri was right. They couldn't afford to think about the past or the future. They had to concentrate on their current mission and the here and now.

Enid wondered what other obstacles they would face. As she observed her companions, each one so different from the other, a sense of gratitude and admiration washed over her.

They were a firedrake, a fae prince, and a human girl. Three beings from different worlds and different backgrounds, brought together by fate and a common goal. It was an unlikely alliance, but it was one that had the potential to change both realms for the better.

Enid took a deep breath and focused on the present. They still had a long way to go. But she also knew that she had the support of these princes, her friends, and that was finally enough to give her some hope.

They walked through the night. Each step bringing them closer to Malagant's fortress. They were on a quest and would stop at nothing to succeed.

Aeddan eventually changed from his firedrake form back to his fae persona. The cut over his eye looked much improved and had ceased oozing blood. Enid was thankful for Aeddan's quick healing powers.

After he changed back, Aeddan seized Enid's hand and removed Rhodri's bandage. He sniffed at her wound, wrinkled his nose with distaste, and then redressed Enid's hand with a torn strip of fabric from his shirt. Enid's eyebrows raised at how gently Aeddan handled her injured hand. She hadn't expected gentleness from him. The fae were very odd territorial creatures.

They headed up a steep incline where plentiful trees masked their progress. The night was drawing in, and an icy wind blew. Enid was grateful for her jacket and pulled her hood over her head.

They trekked now far beyond the bog and were closer to the fortress than Enid realized. Conversation ceased altogether. Aeddan walked out in front, with Enid in the middle and Rhodri covering their flank. Aeddan held up a hand to stop, and the group halted in front of a boulder that blocked the path.

In the distance, Enid spotted the fortress. Her heart skipped a beat as she looked at the imposing structure she'd seen only through dreams. It was the home of their greatest adversary, and they would have to enter it if they wanted to save Dylan.

Rhodri turned to the companions, and his expression serious. "We've arrived," he whispered. "Are you ready?"

Enid took a deep breath and nodded. They were facing incredible danger, but they had come too far to turn back now.

Aeddan had a fierce glint in his eye. "Let's do this," he said, his voice filled with determination. "For Dylan and my sister."

Wordlessly, Aeddan motioned to Rhodri that they needed to move the boulder. Both princes strained, displacing the giant boulder just enough to reveal a cave opening in the rock face. After the three squeezed through the tight gap, they entered a series of tunnels that led into the dark heart of the mountain.

In hushed tones, Aeddan explained how his people had tunnel systems all over Afallon, which elicited a raised eyebrow from Rhodri, though he made no comment.

Deep within the mountain were ancient caves, carved in long ago by flooding waters that had run for thousands of years. The stone passage twisted and turned through the maze of tunnels. Stalactites hung from above like giant fangs, dripping water into pools below. Glowing lichen speckled the uneven floor and helped to light their way.

"We are traveling outside the fortress tunnel system," Aeddan said in hushed tones, "but we'll intersect and enter the fortress at the dungeon level."

In some places, the dank air chilled Enid's face. There was barely room for the three of them to squeeze single file through narrow gaps in the rock walls. In other parts, huge boulder fields littered their path. This made Enid nervous. She watched the tunnel roof for any signs of falling rocks. Hopefully, there would be no cave-ins.

After an eternity, Aeddan slowed and informed them they were nearing the intersection with the fortress. The tunnel got narrower and shorter, and the trio ended up crawling the last bit of distance to an unexpected rocky dead end. Enid was confused. *Were we at the correct spot?*

Aeddan put his hands on the wall and gave the block three sharp taps. The next instant, the block crumbled to dust, even as the wall above it still held. Aeddan motioned for the other prince to follow him. He slid through the opening, followed by Rhodri.

Enid heard scuffling and then a sharp tug on her arm and the warmth of a hand on hers as it pulled her through the gap. As her feet touched the ground, she noted a dimly lit corridor with Rhodri standing beside her, illuminated by a single ray of light.

Two slain guards lay in a heap at one end of the hallway, their dead eyes looking back at Enid like accusing phantoms. A chill ran down her spine as she realized what had happened here, and what they must now do.

Up ahead, Aeddan flew down the hallway, searching each cell for his sister.

Enid and Rhodri crept cautiously along the desolate corridor, their footsteps echoing off the walls. Searching each cell, they found prisoners, wasting away in a living nightmare. Gaunt faces stared back at them in abject terror, their hollow eyes pleading for help. Like something out of a horror movie, Enid had seen this before - in her nightmares. The same twisted scenes were now playing out before her very eyes. All around them lay only suffering, fear, and despair.

"What is Malagant doing to these poor people?" Enid asked Rhodri, trying not to avert her gaze from the suffering. These poor souls deserved a witness.

"The powers of others fuel Malagant's magic. She can absorb their power to use as her own. If done too often, it also drains a being's vitality. These must be the missing fae. She must have used their prisoners as fuel for her foul magic." Rhodri's lip curled in distaste.

Few prisoners had the strength to leave their cells after the doors opened. Enid was terrified she would find Dylan in the same condition as these prisoners.

"I don't understand. Is she like a vampire? Is that a real thing, too?" Enid stared at Rhodri with eyes full of concern.

"As long as the Gwyllion have existed, they have needed a being's life force or lifeblood to fuel their magic. I know this sounds terrible to you, but it's not always an evil thing. Certain fae are burdened with too much power, which can cause them to burn out and die young or go mad. So, some viewed Gwyllion's talents as a healing force. Any powers wielded with pure intent can be used for a society's benefit or its destruction. But this isn't healing. These people have been drained against their will almost to the point of death. This is unbridled evil." Rhodri's fists clenched.

Enid glanced down the endless hallway of despair and shook her head. "There can't be any sane justification for this."

Aeddan entered a cell. She reached for Rhodri's hand and squeezed. "I think Aeddan may have found his sister."

When Enid and Rhodri entered the room, they found Aeddan on his knees beside a cot. On it lay a gaunt figure wrapped in soiled linens. Enid could see the striking resemblance between Aeddan and the girl. Anna's eyes were closed, but Enid knew that if they opened, she would be greeted by the same startling blue of Aeddan's. The girl appeared starved. Her face was ghostly pale, and her features hollowed as if carved from marble. Despite appearances, Enid prayed she was still alive.

"She won't wake up," Aeddan said, sounding a little lost as he patted Anna's hand. "I've tried to wake her, but she won't stir. I'm afraid she's too near death."

"Can't we do something? A potion or magic spell? We must help her." Enid glanced between the two princes, looking for a solution. Enid surprised herself by suggesting a magical cure. Maybe she wasn't that different from her mom, after all.

"I can try a spell, but it would take time we don't have." Aeddan jerked a hand through his hair, his eyes welling with emotion, as he brought out the Guardian's emerald crystal from the cave.

"It's all right, Aeddan. Rhodri and I can continue looking for Dylan. Stay here and help Anna. I would do the same. We both understand." Enid patted Aeddan's shoulder to reassure him. His quest culminated at this moment. Enid recognized he had to do all he could to revive his sister. She would feel the same about Dylan.

Aeddan closed his eyes for a moment and when they reopened, they shone like twin suns. "Human—no… Enid, I owe you a debt I can never repay. You once claimed me as your friend, and I can think of no higher honor, except one. Remember that you will always have a tiny drop of firedrake's blood, so I can claim you as part of my family." He held her gaze for a moment before those brilliant eyes turned to focus on Rhodri. "I trust you to keep my family safe, Prince of Ellyllon. I know how precious she is to you." Aeddan then took a knife strapped to his back and handed it to her. "This is my blade, which has never failed me. Use it to keep yourself safe until I can rejoin the quest."

Enid's jaw dropped at Aeddan's use of her name. She hastily accepted the knife, and the weight of responsibility to not let Aeddan down. Carefully, she fastened the knife to her belt and experienced a sliver of comfort that something of his was with her.

Rhodri placed a hand on the prince's shoulder. "I wish you luck with Anna, my friend. Don't doubt that I will guard Enid with my life until we see each other again." Rhodri handed a small pouch to Aeddan. "This potion should also help with Anna's recovery when she awakens."

"Thank you, my friends, and stay safe." Aeddan's gaze lingered for a moment on his companions before focusing on his sister.

Chapter 25

A STOLEN KISS

ENID AND RHODRI RUSHED down the long hallway, as quietly as possible. As they neared the locked gate at the end, a guard appeared. Without hesitation, Enid unleashed her arrow with fierce precision. The guard had to be silenced before he could raise an alarm. The arrow hit its mark with a sickening thud and sprayed blood like a macabre paint splatter. Despite being an inherently peaceful person, the cruel despair in this place called for nothing less.

Rhodri snapped the lock that held the gate in place. He motioned for Enid to be silent, and they began their ascent up the circular steps, a stairwell that seemed to stretch on forever.

As they reached the tower, another guard barred their way. Rhodri moved with chilling speed, dispatching the guard with a single blow, and sending him tumbling down the stairs in an avalanche of deathly silence. Enid reeled from what she had witnessed, her hands still shaking from firing her bow just moments before. Her stomach twisted in knots and bile rose in her throat.

She forced herself to look away from the corpse lying at the base of the steps and embraced a new determination. She must keep herself from thinking about what she had just done to keep her sanity. This was no time for hesitation. As long as she could keep moving, she wouldn't have time to think.

"Where would Malagant keep a kidnapped prince?" Enid asked.

Rhodri pointed to a door at the top of the tower. "There."

The tower door was made of dark wood, studded with large iron nails. A thick metal lock was embedded in its center. Its sturdiness suggested that it could withstand any attempt to break it down.

He reached inside his leathers and pulled out a small tool set, as Enid watched with mouth hanging open. He used them to pick the lock with precision until finally there was a click as the mechanism released. He opened the door, and they stepped into an empty bedchamber. Fortunately, there were no more guards.

Enid and Rhodri surveyed the room. The huge four-poster bed was topped with sumptuous silk sheets, a brocade counterpane, and an antique comforter. Opposite the bed was another stout door, firmly locked, and the window looking out upon the misty landscape was barred. Stone walls were softened by elaborately detailed tapestries depicting ancient fae battle scenes, and two plush velvet chairs rested near a crackling fireplace.

Draped across one chair was Dylan's blue suit jacket. Enid gasped and motioned for Rhodri to join her. Her thoughts raced because Dylan had recently been in this room.

Before either could discuss this discovery further, the threatening sound of voices and clattering keys echoed from the direction of the other locked door.

Rhodri grabbed Enid's hand and tugged her behind the closest tapestry, pressing his body against hers so tightly she could barely breathe. The heavy hangings pooled around their feet, masking them in a shroud of darkness to hide them from detection.

It sounded like two people were shoved into the room. From their voices, it was a man and a woman. The sound of the door slamming and locking echoed through the room. When the couple spoke, Rhodri had to restrain Enid and place a hand over her mouth, so they wouldn't betray themselves. The man's voice was Dylan's. The female's voice sounded familiar as well.

"Enid, I can't believe you're alive. I thought Malagant had killed you that night. When she brought me to the throne room, I thought it was to kill me. I can't believe you're here." Dylan said, his voice filled with relief. It sounded like the couple was fiercely embracing.

"Of course I would come here to save you, Dylan. Nothing could keep me from my best friend. When Merlin offered to send me here, I jumped at the chance to be where you are. I would gladly cross worlds to find you," the female replied.

That voice. That was Enid's voice, but Enid was behind the tapestry with Rhodri. *Who was impersonating me? Ceridwen?* Enid's heart dropped. Ceridwen had been lying to her all along. Every seemingly harmless question about the human realm suddenly seemed too probing, almost like she was taking notes on Enid's life to take her place.

Enid's stomach churned, and she imagined a litany of dangerous possibilities. She bit her lip so hard that the tang of blood filled her mouth. As she tensed against the wall, Rhodri's hand slipped over her lips, reminding her to keep quiet. His grip tightened as he shook his head with urgency, their eyes meeting in a silent agreement of danger ahead. They had to tread carefully around Ceridwen. Exposing her would mean putting their lives on the line. More information was needed before they could act.

Rhodri's proximity was enough to make Enid's skin tingle with anticipation. Wherever their bodies touched, sparks ignited. Enid's pulse pounded as if trying to beat its way out of her chest, and Rhodri's eyes burned with fire as they locked gazes behind the veil of fabric. *Too much, too soon*—Enid had to escape from the suffocating enclosed space.

"We must get you out of here. You shouldn't have come, though it means so much to me you did. I thought once you knew what I was that our friendship would be over. You wouldn't want a friend who was a freak." Dylan's voice turned husky with his admission.

"Being a wyvern complicates things. I'd be lying if I said it didn't," the faux Enid agreed. "Do you think Malagant meant it when she said she could turn you fully human? Oh, if that were the case, then we might be together forever back home, where we both belong," the false Enid confessed in a breathy tone.

The real Enid went ice cold at the thought of what Ceridwen suggested.

Enid stood motionless, hidden by the thick and ornate tapestry, her ears straining to make out the conversation. The sound of Ceridwen's voice filled the silence, laced with an eerie familiarity, as if it were Enid herself speaking the words. She silently listened for Dylan's reaction, her heart hammering against her chest, horrified and mesmerized all at once.

"Merlin didn't tell me much, only that you were a Dragon Prince and Malagant kidnapped you to this awful place. Why didn't you say anything to me about what happened to you?"

"I'm not sure. When I first arrived in the human realm, I remember being so scared. My parents had just died, and I didn't understand why. I'd been taken from everything familiar that I loved. But the Roberts family had been so kind to me. They made me feel wanted. I had no powers then, so I told myself a fairytale."

Dylan paused for so long, Enid almost jumped out from behind the covering. Rhodri, reading her body language and expression, again shook his head and squeezed her hand, and continued holding it as Dylan continued.

"I know this is going to sound bad, but I pretended to myself that I was human. Like you. I told myself I had no powers and didn't belong in Afallon. Everything from this place seemed like a hazy dream anyway, so I almost convinced myself that none of it was real and that my birth parents' murder hadn't happened."

"That's understandable, Dylan," the false Enid said. "You were very young and what happened had to be traumatic. I can understand the desire to forget it all and try to fit in."

It was strange for Enid to hear her voice from Ceridwen's lips. With great effort, she tried to control her racing pulse.

"You can? That surprises me, Enid. From the day we met, you were always so unique and brave. I wished to be more like you so many times." Dylan's voice rose and faded, almost as if he were pacing the room.

"Well, sometimes, no matter how well we think we know people, they can always surprise us. How did you discover your powers?" Ceridwen asked.

Dylan sighed. "Do you remember when I left for school? My powers started manifesting during that first week. Until then, I'd convinced myself I was human, and then some weird stuff occurred. My senses kicked into overdrive, and I started getting migraines. The colors appeared too bright, and the smallest sounds hurt my ears. During those months, I also started losing time. Thankfully, my parents had paid for a private dorm room, or else I would've been caught many times."

He described how one night he lost time. He came to the school's basement, still in his wyvern form. He'd been nesting near the boiler room.

He panicked because he didn't know how to change back to his human form. To calm himself, he closed his eyes and pictured what Enid would do. It came so clearly to Dylan then that if she got stuck as a wyvern, she would try to be the fiercest one possible. Just picturing it made him laugh and relax. He changed back into his human form. From then on, he practiced changing forms and exploring his powers, but only in isolated spots where no one would see.

"And you didn't consider sharing any of this with me?" For a split-second, Ceridwen sounded hurt and so much like the real Enid that even Enid was almost convinced.

"I thought about telling you so many times, Enid. I tried writing, but only wasted a lot of paper trying to find the right words. How could I explain any of this? Could I have come to you and told you all of it? Would you have believed me? Would you have decided I was evil or been disgusted by my reptilian appearance? I still remember how you looked at me the night of the party. I-I didn't want to lose you."

Enid's heart broke over Dylan's fears. She didn't want Dylan to think it mattered to her he wasn't human. She would never want him to change, in any shape or form. Enid loved Dylan no matter what. They had been friends since she was six years old and had always had each other's backs. Nothing would ever change that, or so she hoped.

Becoming human isn't even possible, is it? Isn't Malagant planning to kill him? Why does she need his cooperation?

Dylan continued his tale with Aeddan, his cousin, who appeared before Enid's birthday. "He came asking for my help to rescue his sister. When I thought about you and what you'd do, I agreed to help him. But when I saw you at that party, I got angry."

"With me?" Ceridwen asked.

Enid held her breath and inched closer, desperate to catch every word that fell from Dylan's lips. Steeling herself, she brushed against Rhodri - a solid wall of muscle. Rhodri's body tensed at her touch, and the sensation sent shivers through her veins. Time seemed to freeze as his warmth wrapped around her. Rhodri shifted, and the moment shattered. Focusing back on the conversation, Enid shoved down the feelings bubbling up within her.

"No, I wasn't mad at you. I was disgusted with myself. I'd kept all of this from you and was leaving for Afallon, possibly never to return or see you again. I lost any chance to explain. I'm afraid that when I saw you that night, all my noble intentions flew out the window and I wanted to stay so badly. Enid, to me you have become home." Dylan paced back and forth while talking, but now he halted.

"W-What are you saying, Dylan?" Ceridwen's voice sounded breathless and uncertain.

Yes, what is Dylan saying? Can't he tell that's not the real me standing in front of him? Shouldn't he know somehow? Can't he sense it with his inner wyvern or something?

The atmosphere on the other side of the tapestry felt charged. When a muffled exclamation of surprise came from Dylan's side, Enid could wait no longer. *What was happening?*

Enid stepped back and, in a single motion, shifted around to face the opposite direction. She darted out from behind their hiding spot, feet barely touching the ground. Rhodri followed closely on her trail, but when they both peered beyond the partition, they were met with a scene far too surreal to comprehend. They were rooted to the spot, gazes fixed forward with stunned expressions.

Ceridwen, wearing Enid's face and clothing, fiercely embraced Dylan. Their lips met in a searing kiss as they seemed to meld together. Dylan's hands dug into her hips as if his life depended on it. Ceridwen's eyes were laid shut in blissful oblivion. At the same time, Dylan's were open wide with shock at the intensity of their kiss - unaware of anything around them save each other.

A sharp pain stabbed her chest as Enid gazed at the scene. Words failed to form within her mind, yet she couldn't look away.

The two lovers looked like a perfect fit in each other's arms, but she knew it was wrong. All she wanted to do was run away from the sight, and yet her feet were glued to the ground.

Rhodri pulled out his swords and Enid aimed her bow at the couple, but Ceridwen was too wrapped around Dylan to get a clear shot. Enid was concerned her arrow would pierce Dylan instead. After a brief hesitation, Rhodri cleared his throat, and the two young lovers sprang apart.

Dylan's eyes flashed an icy flame at the interruption, but his murderous expression softened to one of astonished confusion. "Enid? What is this? Who are they? Who is *she*? "

Enid had to hand it to her doppelgänger. At first, Ceridwen seemed flustered, then looked afraid. "Dylan, stay away from them. They are dangerous. Before I made it here, I traveled through a land of shapeshifters. They tried to k-kill me. These two must have followed me here. They're working with Malagant."

Enid rolled her eyes, irritated by Ceridwen's damsel in distress routine. "Dylan, it's me, the real Enid. That impostor is a shapeshifter who tried to kill me. Her name is Ceridwen, and she's working with Malagant. We've come all this way to rescue you." Enid lowered her bow as she tried to convince her friend of her identity.

Dylan, shaking his head, backed away from everyone in the room. When Rhodri saw Dylan's confused expression, he made a desperate suggestion. "Dylan, use your fae senses. You have known Enid most of your life. Your wyvern should recognize the real thing."

Dylan's eyes flashed with a charged neon intensity that could outshine the sun. His throat took on an icy blue glow, as if he were about to unleash a power from some ancient world.

The flickering gaze of his eyes, like bolts of lightning, focused with laser precision on Rhodri. Enid, who had spent time with Aeddan, recognized the telltale signs of an oncoming tantrum - one that could bring down everything in its path and be lethal for Rhodri and anyone standing in the way.

She stepped between the two princes. "Dylan, this really is me, Enid, your friend. I'm here to save you. Rhodri is Bendith. It's complicated, but please don't hurt him. You'd never forgive yourself."

"Enid?" The light in Dylan's eyes sputtered out, and he shook his head in confusion. This loss in concentration proved costly, because Ceridwen, looking much like a wicked reflection of Enid, came up behind Dylan and struck him hard in the side of the head. Dylan crumpled to the floor.

Enid cried out in surprise, "Dylan."

Chapter 26

FROZEN

RHODRI REACHED FOR ENID and placed her behind him. As he faced his twin, he shook his head in disappointment. His eyes lit with an unnatural gleam. "Ceridwen, there's still time. You don't have to do this. Nothing has been done to anyone that can't be forgiven."

Unmoved by his plea, his sister cackled. "Brother, you've been away too long. You don't know the full extent of what I have done to gain my powers. Is your offer of forgiveness only because I failed to kill your beloved Enid? Would you still forgive me if I had succeeded?" Ceridwen, wearing Enid's face, lifted her chin and gave her brother a vicious sneer.

"But you didn't succeed, Ceridwen. I'm still here," Enid retorted. "You won't win in the end. Please listen to your brother before it's too late."

"I'm afraid it's already too late. My bargain was made years ago, and I can't give up all this magic I've gained. Don't ask me to go back to being that powerless girl. I can't do it again. I had only one regret in getting to this point, but I'm glad for the chance to see you again, brother. You see. I knew you would try to go after the dragon prince, and I was the one who cursed you all those months ago. I'm the reason you were stuck in the human realm."

Ceridwen's eyes sparkled with an odd gleam and a bright flash. When Enid's eyes adjusted, Rhodri's sister had transformed into a large, menacing bear.

"Enid, whatever happens, please stay behind me. And if I fail, you need to run," Rhodri warned as Ceridwen charged at him.

The bear was giant on all fours, coming up to Rhodri's shoulders. When she got close to him, the bear stood on its hind legs and towered over the prince. Ceridwen swiped her deadly claws at Rhodri, who deflected the attack using two swords. He pulled his punches against his sister, not wanting to cause her significant harm. Enid wanted to help, but the two were locked together. They moved so fast. It was difficult to keep focus. Enid feared shooting Rhodri by mistake.

As the two siblings were focused on each other, Enid took a risk to check on Dylan. He was breathing, but unconscious, with a lump forming where he'd been struck.

Rhodri's voice pulled Enid's attention back to the unfolding sibling drama. He tried again to reason with his sister. "Ceri, I don't want to hurt you. Please give this up. We can help you. I'm sorry we didn't realize how powerless you felt."

The bear paused for so long that Enid was filled with a wild, desperate hope this mess would somehow not end in tragedy. "Don't feel too bad, brother. No one noticed me until you left. I'll admit you were always the best of them, but I have gone too far to turn back now."

It was unnerving to hear the high-pitched, sweet voice of Ceridwen come out of the fearsome bear. Enid left Dylan's side and readied her bow, arrow nocked. She needed to be ready.

"You can't imagine what it's like with all this power finally coursing through my body," Ceridwen crowed. "It was like I was sleeping before, but now with all this power I'm finally awake. I've made too many promises, and I owe Malagant too much. So, I intend to see this through to the end. From the start, Malagant was the only one who listened and understood me. She helped me when no one else would. I can't abandon her now, even for you." The bear paused, sniffed the air, and tilted its head in consideration. "I just realized something, Rho. I haven't seen you morph a single time since you've been back. Isn't that funny? You used to change forms just to show us you could. My cuddly bear should be no match for the invincible Prince Rhodri, champion of all Ellyllon."

Ceridwen swiped at Rhodri, but he still did his utmost to deflect her attack. Enid hesitated to shoot. After all, Ceridwen was Rhodri's twin, and he didn't want to harm her. The bear seemed to taunt Rhodri, who refused to launch any blows that would seriously hurt his sister. Ceridwen took a swipe at Rhodri's face and made contact. His cheek was laid open with four deep, bloody gouges.

"I'm afraid to shift now, Ceri. It's true." Rhodri's confession was ripped out by his pain. "It terrifies me to think I won't change back to this form and lose my voice again, which I just regained. You trapped me in the human realm for months as a canine. I couldn't express myself, and no one even tried to understand me except for Enid. So, I may understand what you went through a little better now than I did before," Rhodri admitted to his sister.

Ceridwen paused and bowed her head, looking away from Rhodri. "For that, I feel some regret, but not enough to stop me from trying to win, Brother." Ceridwen redoubled her attack. She found an opening and bit down on Rhodri's neck and shoulder. She lifted and shook him mercilessly. Rhodri could only mount a token resistance. Enid found a clear shot and fired an unmarked arrow at Ceridwen. It sank deep into the bear's collarbone.

Ceridwen roared in pain and dropped Rhodri to come for Enid. "Worthless human." she seethed, her eyes glowing a sickly shade of amber. "Why couldn't you have died at the revelry? You had to come here and mess up our plans and force me to kill my brother. I will enjoy ripping you apart. You will beg for the petrifying curse before I'm done with you."

Suddenly, Dylan appeared behind the menacing bear. His eyes and throat burned with a fierce, glacial fire. Like in Enid's nightmares, the blue flames erupted around Enid and engulfed both her and Ceridwen in their paralyzing grasp.

Enid squeezed her eyes closed against the bright flames and braced herself to endure the icy cold bite through her skin into her bones. Was this how she would die? Would she experience pain when she became frozen? Would it be as awful as Ceridwen's curse? Enid waited, but nothing happened. She took a chance and opened one eye. She wasn't frozen, but Ceridwen was.

What was left of Ceridwen resembled an ice sculpture of a ferocious-looking bear captured in mid-attack. The bear's jaws were gaping with its deadly fangs visible, and the enormous paws with their dagger-like claws poised to take a killing swipe at Enid. However, the beastly princess was frozen solid. No hint of natural color remained. The bear was a pale, permafrost shade of ice blue.

Dylan stood beyond Ceridwen, his mouth gaping open in horror. "Oh, no. I-I didn't mean to... She was going to..." His eyes closed for a minute, but when reopened, his neon gaze focused on Enid, waiting to see how she would react. Waiting for her judgement.

Enid didn't hesitate. She lunged forward and grabbed him, hugging him with all her might. Unchecked tears fell. She held on to him for dear life and kept muttering, "I was so worried. I'm relieved you're alive and still in one piece. You're still you, right? Did we find you before Malagant could do something terrible? It's not too late, is it?"

Dylan grabbed Enid and held on to her just as tightly. "Enid, I'm so afraid that being here with you is just another rotten trick. But when I'm this close, all I sense is you. I know it's weird, but I finally feel safe. My wyvern senses are telling me I'm home. I still can't believe you came for me."

They released each other, and Enid took a couple of steps back. She had to clear the air before they went any further on this quest. "Of course, I'd come for you. I don't care what you are. It doesn't matter to me if you're human or not. It never has and it never will. I only care about what's in your heart. That's all that should ever matter to anyone, and you have the truest heart I know."

"How can you say that Enid, when proof that I'm a dangerous monster is staring you in the face?" Dylan bowed his head, unable to meet Enid's gaze.

"It's true that I wouldn't wish this on anybody, but she was going to *kill* me and Rhodri and trick you into a bargain with Malagant. Ceridwen made her choice, and you made yours by protecting me. How can you think I would call you a monster for protecting your friends? If so, then I'm a monster too for what I did to get here. Don't you know me better than that?" Enid grabbed hold of Dylan again for another hug, still shaking from the close call.

A soft moan filtered through the air.

"Rhodri…" Enid let go of Dylan and raced to Rhodri, kneeling over his unconscious form to check his wounds. They looked serious. If she hadn't distracted Ceridwen, Rhodri might be dead now.

Four ragged gouges marred the right side of Rhodri's face, and blood was everywhere. Thankfully, Ceridwen had missed his eye. Rhodri had other scratches and cuts, but the wounds that concerned Enid the most were the punctures in his neck. Ceridwen had missed his jugular vein, but blood flowed freely from the injury. One of his arms twisted at an odd angle from being flung, appearing broken.

"We need to stem the blood," said Enid urgently, looking up at Dylan. "I need something to use as a bandage."

Dylan didn't hesitate. He immediately ripped the sleeve off his shirt and handed it to Enid. Using it, Enid applied firm pressure to Rhodri's puncture wounds to slow the bleeding.

"Can you get me some water?" Enid asked Dylan while maintaining the pressure. "And I'll need more bandage strips. Take the knife from my belt and cut up the sheet."

By the time Dylan was back at her side, the blood flow from Rhodri's neck had slowed. Using the strips of material from Dylan, Enid cleaned and bound his neck. Then she wiped his face clean.

"I wish there was something more I could do," she said, looking at Dylan with tears in her eyes.

"Let's make him more comfortable," suggested Dylan. "Should we move him to the bed?"

Enid shook her head. "No, we might reopen his wounds if we move him. Let's bring bedding to him."

Working together, they made Rhodri as comfortable as possible, with pillows and soft blankets from the bed. Although she wished there was something more she could do, she knew this would have to do until they could find a healer.

Enid's gaze traced Rhodri's profile, and she gave his hand a gentle squeeze. "I know it hurts, but please keep fighting. Don't leave me."

Enid left Rhodri's side and crept over and slowly opened the door leading down to the dungeon. There was no sign of angry guards charging up the steps. After closing her door, she motioned for Dylan to listen at the other locked entrance. After a few minutes, he indicated he heard nothing unusual. Reassured the fight hadn't been heard, Enid sat on the bed holding her head in her hands.

"Who is this, Enid? You said he was Bendith, but how is that possible? You have known Bendith for months." Dylan's brow knit with concern.

"It's a long story. The short version is that he came to our realm looking for you and got trapped as a dog, and his shifting magic was stripped away, courtesy of Ceridwen's curse. When Merlin sent us through a portal to save you, Rhodri regained his fae form. Everyone back home is fine but frozen in time by Malagant's spell." Enid gave Dylan the short version. There would be time to fill in the more colorful details later.

"Well, it explains why I sensed Bendith's presence."

Enid looked across at Dylan. "I can't lie. My instincts are screaming at me to get you and Rhodri out of here and far away from Malagant as soon as possible."

"Is that an option?" Dylan sounded less than convinced.

"Unfortunately, no. Merlin mentioned the portal to take us home would open when I set everything right. Since we're still here, I think time must still be frozen back home and there is more to do here, besides Malagant won't stop coming for you." Enid ran a trembling hand through her hair.

"Are you about to suggest we take on the queen? I don't like our odds on that one." Dylan shook his head a little.

"I agree, yet Merlin foretold you would stop her. He even sent me a clue. *The key lies within the hearts.* Does that mean anything to you? Did anyone ever explain how you win?" Enid went across to Rhodri and checked his bandages for signs of fresh bleeding. There was none. She watched him for any sign of consciousness with chin in hand.

"I don't remember much from being in Afallon before, but I recall that stupid prophecy. I don't remember any details about how the dragon prince was supposed to succeed. I think it's what ultimately got my parents killed."

"I'm so sorry." Enid's heart hurt remembering those precious few times that she and Dylan pretended his birth parents, and her mother were international spies or banished royalty who would return to them someday.

Dylan nodded. Enid blinked the moisture away and changed topics. "Something has been bothering me. Why didn't Malagant drain your magic? Why does she need your permission? Can't she take what she wants?"

"She claims she can transform me into a human, but only if I agree to give her all my powers. There must be a limit to a Gwyllion's ability to drain power from an unwilling victim. She could become a full-fledged wyvern if I gave her all my power."

"Is that something you would want to do? Be human?" Enid asked.

"I'm sure you heard what I told the other... you. When I was younger, I'll admit I would have wanted to be human, but now I just want to be the best me possible. Whatever that is." Dylan rubbed the back of his neck and gave a nervous laugh.

"Do you know if she can do what she claims? Is becoming a wyvern her endgame?" Enid frowned.

"That's my best guess, but I'm not sure she'll stop there. She also asked questions about the human realm. I didn't cooperate. Not because I wasn't tempted to become human, but because I know she has to be stopped." Dylan shrugged and shook his head.

"So, she brought Ceridwen here to persuade you to take her deal?" Enid's frown deepened as her gaze was drawn to Ceridwen's frozen form.

"Yes," Dylan admitted. When he realized who Enid was looking at, his gaze fell to the floor.

Enid turned back to Dylan. "Could *she* have talked you into changing who you are?" They both knew who Enid meant.

"N-No. She... You couldn't have persuaded me to become human. I had a long time to consider things as I went through those changes at school. It was fun to pretend for a while that I was human, but I could never forget my birth parents and my people, no matter how tempting the offer." Dylan blushed as he looked at Enid's lips.

"Couldn't you tell that wasn't me?" She had promised herself she wouldn't ask, shouldn't ask, but she had to know.

"I don't know what to say. I thought Malagant had killed you the night of your party, but then you showed up here. I was so relieved you were still alive that I didn't stop to consider if it was real. She knew things, little details... but when she kissed me, it was different. My senses told me I was kissing the wrong girl, though I couldn't figure out how that was possible." Dylan met Enid with an unflinching glance.

"From where I stood, it looked as if you didn't mind kissing the wrong girl." She felt bad, but it had to be said, at least once.

"I've never kissed anyone like that before, Enid. You... She surprised me." Dylan's neck turned crimson with this admission.

Hadn't she been fooled in the same manner by the Puca? What about her confusing reactions to Rhodri? "Oh. I-I see." Enid's cheeks turned pink, considering all the times she'd been tricked or tempted.

She decided to get back to important topics. "What powers do you have besides that icy fire? Do you think it could be a specific talent that Malagant wants?"

He ticked his powers off on his fingers. "I have control over all forms of water and ice, and I can use them in very creative ways as weapons. My wyvern can fly, which is great, though I need more practice. As you saw, I can use my icy fire as a weapon. I can cast spells and curses and influence weaker individuals. My armor is virtually impenetrable." Dylan deliberately glanced away from Enid's lips and toward the ceiling as he detailed his list of abilities.

"Yep, I'd trade all that for bad breath and mortality." Enid's eyes bulged at his list of talents. "What type of spells are we talking about? Can you cast a cloaking spell on me to make me seem less human and more like Ceridwen? After all, she pretended to be me, so Malagant shouldn't be alarmed if I accompany you in her presence." Enid cocked an eyebrow.

All the color drained from Dylan's face. "Why would you want to be in Malagant's presence?"

"I may have the plan to defeat Malagant. I can't believe I'm saying this, but it relies on magic spells, some play-acting, and a bunch of luck." Enid had come a long way from the girl who scoffed at such things.

A heated debate erupted after Enid's statement, with Dylan trying unsuccessfully to plead with his friend to run. She adamantly refused to leave him and continued explaining her plan. Enid would pose as Ceridwen, who had been posing as Enid. Malagant had no reason to suspect since she thought the real Enid was dead. They would demand an audience with Malagant, pretending Dylan was considering her offer. Once there, they would attack.

It was almost midnight before they agreed on all the details. It was time to confront Malagant.

Chapter 27

THE BIG BLUFF

DYLAN MUTTERED SOME WORDS over Rhodri and Ceridwen in a language that Enid didn't understand. He waved his arms with a certain flourish, and a flash of light occurred. He turned to Enid. "Well, what do you think?"

Enid saw Rhodri lying on the floor and a frozen Ceridwen in her bear form. "A flash of light appeared, but I can still see them. I'm wearing this ring as protection against enchantments, though, and that could be the reason."

"Can you take off the ring to check?" Dylan suggested.

Enid went to do as Dylan suggested, and then hesitated. "Dylan, Mr. Ambrose mentioned to me to never remove this ring, even for a second. I'm so sorry, but I think I'd better listen. There is no telling why he said that."

"If he instructed you to keep the ring on, then you should listen. I've been away from Afallon for so long that I'm not sure what the fae are capable of." Dylan's words reassured her.

Soon he said some words over Enid, with another flourish and flash. Enid said, "I don't feel any different. Are you sure you did the spell correctly?"

Dylan leaned closer to Enid and inhaled her scent and wrinkled his nose. "You still look like you, don't worry. But you're different.

I've known you almost my entire life, and I made the spell, but my sense of smell tells me you're Ceridwen right now."

"Do I smell that different?" Enid tried and failed to sniff herself.

"I usually sense a combination of sweat with a dash of mint, but now all I sense is blood and clove, like her." Dylan wrinkled his nose.

After Dylan finished, they both pounded on the door and bellowed for the guards to demand to take them to Malagant, as Dylan had some questions about the Queen's proposed deal.

The concealment spell that Dylan had cast on Rhodri and Ceridwen must have been effective because the guards who answered their shouts didn't so much as a glance in the siblings' direction. Enid breathed a relieved sigh.

Enid hoped Dylan's healing spell on Rhodri would work just as well.

A half-dozen guards dressed in white livery escorted them through the palace. As they trudged through the dark and forbidding corridors surrounded, Enid tried to steel herself for the coming conflict. Both she and Dylan realized they had only a slim chance of success. Malagant's magic was far too potent, but they knew they had to try.

Enid was nauseous again. Was this what it was like to be in constant fear for your life? What if she failed her father? Dylan? She glanced over at him, and the slumped shoulders told her everything. He thought they were going to their doom. Her stomach flipped over at that thought. She grabbed his hand and gave it a gentle squeeze. Dylan's shoulder straightened a little, and they both managed weak smiles.

Too soon, they were ushered before an enormous, domed double door made of solid brass. Both sides were carved with elaborate runes that reminded Enid of a medieval cathedral entrance.

Each door was fitted with a large knocker that the guards used to request admittance. When the door swung inward, the guards shoved Enid and Dylan through. As they entered the throne room, Enid's mouth went dry, and her pulse was off the charts. She tried instilling calmness by counting to herself while she breathed. It didn't help.

The throne room defined opulence in the extreme, which was meant to intimidate. The floors were white marble with veins of gold. At regular intervals, the thick, carved white marble columns had gilded sconces in the shape of small cephalopod-like creatures with their tentacles opened to emit firelight to brighten the room. The ceiling was domed, reached incredible heights, and was painted with golden scenes of battling fae creatures. A blood-red carpet runner ran from the carved brass doors to the steps of a dais where Malagant's throne sat.

It was an imposing chair made of solid, dark wood. Carved onto the throne's surface, seat, arms, and legs were exquisite renderings of the same exotic fae beasts that battled across the ceiling. The seat and chair back were padded with blood-red velvet that further enhanced the moody, Gothic vibe. The top back of the throne came to a ninety-degree point. Carved into the apex was a medallion with a minutely detailed cephalopod, appearing much like the Dienw.

Dylan and Enid weren't fooled by the empty throne room, knowing Malagant lurked nearby. Enid kept up her act of trying to persuade Dylan to become human. "I hope Malagant can deliver on her promise to make you human. Then we can go back home, where we belong, and forget all of this."

"I'm still not sure it's even possible. And why would she want to help us? Her people killed my parents, and she tried to murder you at your party," Dylan said.

Enid, looking like herself but acting like Ceridwen, said, "Still, if there is even a slight chance she can help, I think we should hear her out. Don't you?" She laid a hand on Dylan's arm and batted her eyes flirtatiously at her friend. Inside, she experienced queasiness at how conniving she sounded.

Dylan's eyebrows shot up in surprise, and he almost forgot what to say next. "I want to ask some questions and get some assurances from her about our parents and you. I don't want her to turn around and murder us all after she gets what she wants."

"Oh, I'm sure she will keep her word. Isn't that what a fae promise is supposed to do?" Enid patted Dylan's arm as she spoke.

As they stood discussing Malagant's proposition, a whirlwind of mist formed on the throne dais. It grew larger and larger until, from the center, a cloaked figure emerged, reminding Enid of that cursed night of her party. She almost expected to turn around and see the other guests still frozen in time.

This time, the petite figure wore a forest green cloak. As she pulled her hood down, Malagant's otherworldly beauty again struck Enid. Her silver snake tresses were threaded through a beautiful silver crown studded with green gems. Malagant's eyes lit with a vibrant light reflected in the ethereal green gown she wore.

"Have you decided yet?" Her laser-green eyes bored into Dylan.

In response, his eyes lit with an intense blue flame. "No, I haven't decided, but I do have questions that need answering before I make any further promises to you."

"I see some progress has been made. At least you aren't telling me no. I guess it was good that your human survived me, after all." Malagant's bright gaze drifted to Enid and lingered for a moment before moving back to Dylan.

Dylan's throat took on that eerie shade of ice blue. "If anything happens to Enid, I will slay you without hesitation."

Malagant's eyes narrowed to slits. "I believe you would *try* to kill me, but I doubt you would succeed. If I decide your human should die, she will."

"Come on, Enid. Our host isn't in the mood to answer questions." Dylan made a move for the brass doors and gestured for Enid to precede him.

"Maybe your human should stay behind and entertain me while you return to your cell. I'm suddenly bored with you and curious about how well humans can defend themselves." Malignant waved a dismissive hand and bared her serrated teeth at Dylan.

In response to Malagant's challenge, Dylan morphed into his wyvern form. The flash and change were almost too quick for Enid to process. Dylan now towered over the petite Malagant, but she didn't appear helpless. Dark tendrils oozed from the Queen and flowed down from the dais. Enid stepped back, not wanting to be anywhere near that magic.

"Interesting. I see you're not as mindless as I thought." Malagant eyed Dylan up and down, her tongue flicking out to taste the air.

"If Enid needs to defend herself, I will stay by her side, and you'll get nothing from me except my fire." Enid knew that was Dylan talking, but the words chilled her, coming from a mouth full of razor-sharp fangs.

As both fae beings faced off against each other without a trace of fear, Enid couldn't help but study the paintings and carvings of previous battles that echoed this scene. The only thing missing was spilled blood.

She realized the creatures bristling in front of her might erupt into a killing frenzy with the slightest provocation and dug deep down inside herself to remain calm. She recognized on some level that it was supposed to be Ceridwen in her place and the shapeshifter wouldn't be anxious, as she was a secret ally of the mountain Queen.

"C'mon Dylan, we requested this meeting, and we should get all our questions answered before leaving." Enid made a show of studying Dylan's wyvern form. "Malagant is just kidding about my safety. After all, she's the one who brought me here, and we need her help."

Dylan allowed himself to break the staring contest between himself and Malagant and glanced at Enid with wide-eyed disbelief. "Enid, I'm not sure you appreciate the danger you're in, but you have a point. We did request this meeting. I can continue if Malagant does not threaten you further." Dylan sounded reasonable, but he remained in his wyvern form with his tail thrashing back and forth animatedly. When his gaze swept back to Malagant, his upper lip curled back to reveal fearsome teeth.

Malagant watched this byplay with narrowed eyes. "Your time in the human realm has robbed you of any sense of humor, I think. For the time being, your human is in no danger from me as I await your final decision."

Enid understood the thrumming undercurrent of the Queen's words—if Dylan's decision didn't go in Malagant's favor, Enid's life would be forfeited, and doubly so if Malagant realized she wasn't Ceridwen. Dylan sensed this as well and pressed their host further. "I'd be more inclined to decide if you guaranteed Enid's safety *now*."

Malagant stared so long at Dylan that Enid shifted a little in discomfort. Did they push too far? Would Malagant lash out and kill them both? After a long pause, the Queen nodded. "Very well, Dylan, if it means so much to you, I promise your human will come to no harm from me." The mysterious green script appeared on Malagant's left wrist. "Ask your questions."

"You have drained countless others of their powers but are asking for mine by consent. I would like to understand why." Dylan's tail paused mid-motion as the wyvern's gaze locked onto the Queen.

Malagant's lips tightened in displeasure. This was the question she wanted most to avoid. "I'd rather not go into all the details. Let's just say giving consent to yield your powers will correct imbalances in mine. Can we leave it at that?"

Enid nodded her agreement, as she thought Ceridwen might, but Dylan shook his head and glanced toward Enid. "You're aware of why I want to be human and remain in that realm. It's only fitting I should understand what you want with my powers. Are you planning to ravage this realm and, later, the human one? Don't you already have access to more power than any single individual would ever need?"

Malagant's hands tightened into fists, and she exploded, "What do you know of my powers? Do you have any idea how it works? How it *feels*? I must constantly supply my power with other sources, or it feeds on my life essence. I have experienced paralyzing pain for years trying to resist. My only respite comes from draining the life forces of others. But I don't want to be this monster anymore." The Queen's entire body trembled with the effort to keep her emotions in check.

Enid forced herself to look away from Dylan and instead focus on Malagant. The truth of the Queen's words were clear in her wild eyes and Enid understood what it would be like to be on the edge of an abyss. Whatever Enid expected, it wasn't this raw admission. Judging from Dylan's raised brows, Malagant's words caught him by surprise, too. "I didn't realize your power caused you such turmoil."

"No one was to know. We eliminated anyone who discovered this information, first by my mother, and then, after she died, by me. I will need you to keep my secret, or it will force me to silence you and your human in other ways." Malagant ran her blood-red nails through her snake-like tresses.

Enid wondered if she did that often, given how tangled they appeared.

"What other ways?" Dylan's tone was laced with menace.

Malagant looked pointedly at Enid. "Ways that would make your human very uncomfortable."

Dylan shifted his position so that he was blocking Enid from Malagant's view. "I won't allow any harm to come to Enid. You have my word on that."

"And you have mine I won't hurt your human as long as you both cooperate," Malagant said. "Now, let us move on to more pleasant topics."

"How can my powers help you?" Dylan asked, ignoring Malagant's latest threat.

"The dragon prophesy mentioned your powers can put mine to sleep or trap them in this mountain. Don't you understand? Your powers must offset or be stronger than mine." Malagant's eyes kindled with excitement. "Besides my original abilities, I can also transfer powers. I've experimented successfully on many. After much trial and error, I discovered the only requirement for a full transfer of power is willing participation."

The bile rose in Enid's throat at this last bit of chilling information. How many beings had Malagant tested before finding willing participants? "Is this transfer permanent? What of the beings who lose their abilities? Do they suffer any ill effects?" Dylan leaned forward, and Enid was sure for the moment he forgot they were play-acting.

"For the willing, there were no ill effects, and to date, the transfers have all held." Malagant's eyes, direct as green lasers, shifted down and to the left. *Was she lying?*

"And for the unwilling?" Enid couldn't help herself, and her voice echoed her disgust as she pictured Aeddan's sister, Anna, wasting away in her cell when they found her. The tone of Enid's question elicited a green flash as Malagant studied Enid anew with narrowed eyes.

"For the unwilling, the survival rate was admittedly much lower, and the transfer effects were only temporary." Malagant addressed her answer to Dylan as if Enid hadn't spoken.

Malagant's words sent a chill down Enid's spine. She had suspected the Queen was ruthless, but she hadn't realized the true extent of her depravity. Enid could see now that they were dealing with a maniac, and she wasn't sure if they could find a way out of this alive.

"We appreciate your candid answers. You've given me much to consider. I should be able to give you my decision in a day or so." Dylan's tail again swished back and forth, the only outward sign of his nerves.

"I'm afraid I'm going to insist on your answer right now, not days from now. You know what you're going to do. I'm wondering if you have the guts to admit it?" Dark mist flowed from Malagant in increasing quantity.

Dylan's eyes gleamed with a glacial light. "You know my answer before it is given? You truly are magical if you can read my thoughts."

"Stop pretending. I can smell the humanity on that one from leagues away. Did you honestly think you would fool me?" Malagant sneered. "I'll admit you both surprised me by coming here instead of running far and fast. What happened to Ceridwen?"

Dylan glanced away for a moment, then met Malagant's steady glare. "Ceridwen attacked, and I had no choice."

At Dylan's admission, Enid wrestled with her rising panic. Now wasn't the time to have a meltdown.

"Poor Ceridwen. You cut her life of borrowed power tragically short. I wonder, my prince, how your friend Rhodri will react once he realizes you iced his twin? He is unpredictable, and might need to avenge himself on your human, perhaps? Will you regret your decision not to help me when this human screams in torment? I think you will." With her last word, Malagant erupted into a cyclone of dark tentacles. She seemed to be everywhere all at once, surrounding Dylan with her smoky, grasping appendages, just as in Enid's nightmares.

Chapter 28

QUEEN OF HEARTS

ENID RAN FOR COVER behind a column as she promised Dylan. Neither was sure the bargain that Malagant made would hold and protect her. Enid unsheathed her bow and waited, knowing there was no margin for error.

Both creatures seemed to dance in the air as they circled one another, looking for the best vantage point to strike. Dylan's wyvern form grew, and Malagant's tentacles strove to bite into his scales, but for now, found no purchase.

Dylan's golden scales emitted a blue light that Enid associated with his frozen fire. Malagant tried to hold Dylan, but he shielded himself. Malagant's tentacles tried to extinguish the light that Dylan emanated but failed to do so.

The two fae swam through the atmosphere as each strove for an advantage. There was an aura around Malagant as well, but instead of color, it appeared like a black hole.

Malagant's tentacles elongated and tried to cage Dylan's wyvern, but his serpentine form bent and twisted in amazing shapes to escape her clutches. Both fae tried to bite, scratch, and claw, seeming evenly matched.

Malagant's incisors elongated and bit into part of Dylan's neck. When Dylan roared in pain, Enid thought her heart would cease beating at the sound. Malagant's dark mist enveloped his golden form until Enid could no longer see Dylan's wyvern.

The room darkened and any warmth that was there got chased away by the lengthening shadows. She could see no trace of blue light. Enid's heart stopped cold in her chest.

At that moment, a shocking explosion of the brightest light ripped through the darkness right under the central dome where the two creatures grappled. Enid knew if she stared directly into the glow, it would be like staring into the sun, and she would be blinded. Enid heard a shout from Dylan. This was their signal.

Sure enough, his unearthly blue fire erupted and enveloped Malagant in its icy grasp. It continued to pour out from the wyvern endlessly. In the shadowy reflection, Enid saw both creatures touch down to the floor and step away from each other. The flames gradually went out.

Enid stepped out from behind the pillar and gave a nod to her childhood friend who had landed near the frozen mountain Queen. "Do you think that was it?" Enid asked as she trained her bow on the permafrost figure.

Dylan grimaced and shook his massive head. "I'm not sure."

Several seconds ticked by and they could hear no sound. It shocked Enid that the guards standing on the other side of the imposing doors hadn't stormed the chamber. Just when she was ready to lower her bow, a loud crack echoed through the chamber.

The ice chunks imprisoning the mountain Queen blew apart in every direction. The force of the blast launched ice particles that sliced into Enid's skin, but she held steady. After that explosion, Enid let a cursed arrow fly from Fail-Naught. It struck home, just as she intended, driving to the left of Malagant's breastbone and straight into the dark heart of the queen.

Malagant clutched at her chest and roared in pain as the arrow struck true. Blue blood seeped from the wound where the arrow protruded. Malagant gave a last gasp just before Dylan bombarded her with still more streams of frozen fire.

Is that it? Did we succeed? Enid inched closer to Dylan, but he motioned for her to stay put.

After several minutes, with no movement from Malagant's frozen figure, Enid made her way over to Dylan. Though he remained in dragon form, she gave him an unreserved hug. This was her best friend, and he had scored an unlikely victory against terrible odds. She wasn't sure, but she thought Dylan made a sound very much like trilling while they embraced.

As Enid and Dylan drew apart, a distant rumble echoed through the chamber, the sound growing to a terrible roar. Enid and Dylan looked at each other with wide-eyed disbelief. Had Malagant somehow survived traumatic blood loss after being shot through the heart?

A pillar of dark smoke enveloped the Unseelie Queen's figure where she stood with the cursed arrow suspended from one of her tentacles. In the blink of an eye, the arrow snapped into splinters and Malagant was across the room bellowing for her palace guards. A dozen entered and blocked the only exit. Enid and Dylan were trapped and outnumbered.

Enid tightly gripped her bow. There was no way they were going to give up now. They had come too far and fought too hard. Enid would defeat Malagant once and for all. She had to.

"So that was your ultimate plan? To freeze me? Pathetic. I thought the arrow through my heart was an especially nice touch, dear. At least there can be no doubt how you ultimately wanted this to end." Malagant tried to stare Enid down, but the girl met her glare for glare with zero remorse.

"Your rule will soon be over, Malagant. You have terrorized innocent people for far too long." Enid's voice sounded ice cold. "It's time for you to pay for your crimes."

Malagant laughed, a cold, cruel sound that sent shivers down Enid's spine. "And what exactly are you going to do to stop me?" she asked. "You are only a fragile, powerless human, after all."

Dylan stepped forward to stand beside Enid. "We won't let you hurt anyone else," he said.

Enid and Dylan turned back-to-back, facing their surrounding adversaries. Malignant shook her head in genuine regret.

The Unseelie Queen focused her attention on the Dragon Prince. "Dylan, it didn't have to end this way. We were meant to be joined. You are my match in power. This human does not deserve you. Even if you win the day, her regard will eventually change to revulsion. Humans are incapable of loyalty. They have always feared and hated what they can't control. It's not too late for us."

Dylan shook his magnificent head. "I'm afraid it is you who doesn't understand. I would never join forces with my parents' murderers and betray their memory."

"I have tried to tell you that my kingdom was not responsible for their deaths. Why can I do to convince you?" Malagant reached out a hand toward Dylan.

"Why would I place my trust in someone as unworthy as you? Someone who has stolen life from countless innocents." The fierce wyvern shook his head. "The core of who I am isn't a negotiation. I didn't doubt Enid. I only ever doubted myself. I didn't know where I belonged, but Enid came for me knowing and accepting everything. I could never ask for more loyalty than that."

"When my guards take her, you will change your mind. She will beg you to make the deal." Malagant's serrated teeth appeared menacing, still stained with Dylan's blood.

"I swore an oath to her I wouldn't bargain for her life. We will both die here before we let you win." Dylan extended his left wrist, illuminating the green script that glowed bright and clear.

"Oh, you poor fool." Malagant shook her head for a moment, realizing that a line was crossed, and any hope of Dylan's cooperation was long gone. When she popped her head back up, her wicked eyes blazed with green fire.

"Human. I blame you for all of this." Despite the bargain made less than one hour prior, Malagant sent a misty tendril of malevolent force aimed at Enid. Though constructed of vapor, it became solid as it traversed the distance between Malagant and Enid.

Without time to think through her actions, Enid let her instincts take over. She ducked and grabbed Aeddan's knife from her belt and brought it up to parry the appendage. When it collided with Aeddan's blade, Enid felt the jolt of the impact. Malagant grunted in pain as part of her tendril lay twitching at Enid's feet.

The grunt of pain became a shriek as the beautiful green script on Malagant's wrist glowed red like hot, burning coals. As quickly as it flashed, the glow faded to leave vivid, angry scars. "It burns." Malagant moaned between gasps, cradling her wrist.

"I told you I would never let you hurt Enid." Dylan's voice was fierce as he stepped between Enid and Malagant, shielding her with his body.

"And I told you that you would regret your decision." Malagant screamed in rage, her entire body shaking with the force of her fury.

The two friends shared a glance. The broken bargain had weakened the Mountain Queen, but would it be enough to give them a fighting chance?

Dylan's voice rang out over the massive throne room to reach the ears of all the guards who stood bristling, awaiting their

Queen's command. His tone caused Enid's silver ring to pulse with his words. "It's possible you disagree with your queen's actions. Please help us, or at least stay out of this fight."

Only one guard hesitated at Dylan's plea. He glanced left and right before laying down his weapon and turning to leave the chamber. In a blink, Malagant vanished and reappeared behind the unarmed guard. The Queen enveloped the man in her tentacles, and a shattering energy pulse reverberated through the floor.

"This is how betrayers are dealt with in my kingdom." When Malagant moved again, an empty husk of the defected guard lay discarded in her wake.

The remaining guards edged closer, their swords and spears quivering with deadly intent. Enemies surrounded the friends on all sides. Enid racked her brain for a winning strategy. "I'm going to shoot at anything that moves. Can you freeze these guys?" Enid knew how strange this all sounded. There was no way they would get out of this alive. Instead of focusing on their dismal odds, she readied her bow and tried to calculate how many shots she could take before being overrun.

"We need to take out as many as we can before they take us down." Dylan's words were grim, but his voice was steady.

They didn't stand a chance against the entire guard, but Enid refused to go down without a fight. She would somehow make Malagant pay for what she had done. Enid nocked an arrow, ready to let it fly.

"I have this, Enid. You should run." Dylan's voice cracked a little as he realized how outnumbered they were.

"I'm not leaving you to face this alone. We're getting out of this together." Dread twisted in Enid's stomach at the thought of what could happen if they failed.

Dylan turned towards her. His glowing eyes were lined with silver. "You have always been my greatest strength, Enid Davies. I love you so much."

"I love you too, Dylan. I always have. You're home for me, too." Any additional words were stuck behind the sudden lump forming in Enid's throat.

As the two friends struggled to say their last farewell, a loud thump came from the other side of the large brass doors that led into the throne room. The entrance glowed red before buckling with extreme heat, blowing inwards with a resounding clatter. There, on the threshold of Malagant's throne room, stood two large, angry dragons.

At the sight of them, Dylan's eyes flared, and his throat burned blue with suppressed icy fury, ready to defend Enid against the newcomers. Enid declared, "Dylan, I recognize one of those dragons. It's Aeddan. I think we just got reinforcements."

The guards burst into action, attacking the dragons as their Queen bellowed commands. The crimson firedrake, Aeddan, erupted with searing flames that took out another of Malagant's guards.

Vibrant, iridescent green scales covered the other dragon. The beast was a giant serpent with no limbs and long curved incisors. Enid expected to see molten fire or ice emerge from the new creature, but she soon realized the green wyrm depended on its teeth to subdue its prey. With the barest pressure of its physical weapons, each victim would fall motionless and stay down. *The green wyrm must be venomous.*

Dylan hurled icy blasts at another guard, and Enid got ready to fire at anyone who attacked him, though a better strategy would be to focus on attacking the Queen. Only after Malagant's defeat would the Gwyllion Kingdom surrender.

The Unseelie Queen had disappeared and reappeared several times during the fight but didn't appear to be an active combatant. Where was she going when she vanished? Enid suspected she was still in the throne room, but how to locate her? Malagant reappeared near the dragons each time. What was she planning?

A more chilling thought occurred to Enid. *Why hadn't the queen just appeared behind me to kill me?* But she was just a weak human to Malagant and easily killed after defeating the dragons. No, Malagant had bigger issues to tackle than one puny human. With that liberating thought in mind, Enid focused her attack on the queen.

Intent on tracking the Queen's whereabouts, Enid foolishly ignored her surroundings. A guard brandishing a sword appeared to her left. She yelped in surprise and fumbled with Aeddan's knife, certain she had waited too late and was about to meet her end. But before the guard could strike, the green wyrm appeared out of nowhere and clamped down on the guard's shoulder, lifting and shaking him with gusto. Upon release, the guard crumpled to the ground and Enid stared directly into Rhodri's deep brown eyes.

"Rhodri. Are you alright?" Enid's brow was knit with concern as she reached out gently to touch the four vivid scars marring his beautiful scales.

The green wyrm closed his eyes for a moment and inhaled deeply, then opened them and nodded in the affirmative. Enid was at a complete loss for what to say, so she settled on the only thing she could.

"I'm so sorry about Ceridwen. I wish there had been another way. Someday you'll find peace and joy again. Please know that my heart always heard you, and always will." Then Enid reached out to hug the creature with everything she had.

"I know, Enid. My heart recognized yours, too." Rhodri's dragon voice sounded gruffer than Enid expected.

Before they could say more, Rhodri's attention was drawn to Aeddan, who was in a rather tough spot, surrounded by jostling, stabbing guards. "Enid, you must be more cautious. I-I don't know what I'd do if I lost you too."

"I will and you be careful too," she said.

The green wyrm returned to the fray and the three dragons battled the remaining guards with quick, deadly efficiency. Her friends appeared to have the battle under control, so Enid crept to a vantage point where she could survey the battle without being seen.

Malagant came in and out of view many times as the Queen watched the dragons combat her forces. Did Malagant leave the room when she disappeared, or was she using camouflage? It was hard to say for sure, but after their encounter with the Dienw, Enid suspected camouflage. It would be foolish for Malagant to waste her energy using portals during a life-and-death struggle.

Was Malagant assessing which dragon would make the best ally? That thought alone almost froze Enid's heart in her chest. If Malagant won over Aeddan or Rhodri, all the realms would be in peril. Enid couldn't allow that to happen. She had to neutralize the Queen and put an end to this madness.

But how? Enid racked her brain for a solution but came up empty. *Wait—was the clue a false lead? The key lies within the hearts. Why didn't the arrow through the heart finish, Malagant?*

Enid glanced up at the elaborately decorated dome, which depicted an ultimate battle between fae giants. Enid noted it showed tentacles about to grab a wyvern. The sconces and the carving at the top of the Gwyllion throne had still more tentacles. The throne room was full of depictions of tentacles to honor the royal family.

Enid considered Malagant's tentacles. She knew they made Malagant a deadly foe. What did Enid know about tentacles in nature? Octopus? What had Enid learned about octopi? She knew the answer was there, dangling just beyond her reach, and then suddenly it came to her.

Malagant moved between the dragons like a moth fatally attracted to three flames. She appeared near Dylan's golden form first, then Aeddan's red firedrake, and then Rhodri's green wyrm. A pattern became obvious: Gold, Red, Green. Gold, Red, Green. Gold, Red... Enid aimed a cursed arrow toward the green dragon, closed her eyes, whispered a quick plea, and fired.

She opened her eyes and got rewarded with the sight of Malagant with a cursed arrow protruding from the right of her breastbone. Enid's bow hadn't failed her. She had hit Malagant's second heart, releasing another geyser of thick indigo blood.

"Cursed human." Malagant screeched. "You have insulted me for the last time."

As Enid expected, the Queen darted out with her tentacles and grabbed Enid with their punishing suckers. The freezing pain began as she pulled Enid closer. The fresh scars on Malagant's left wrist burned anew and multiplied, which only incensed the Gwyllion Queen further. Enid's life force drained away, and she struggled to remain conscious. Before Malagant could finish her, Enid raised her arm, the final cursed arrow was revealed clenched in her hand. With it, Enid stabbed through the center of the Mountain Queen's third and final heart.

The Queen coughed and abruptly released Enid, dropping her to the cold marble floor. "Curse you, hu..."

The Queen clutched at the arrow and crumple to the ground. *Was Malagant's body already becoming stone? Did the curse work?* Enid staggered several steps away and collapsed. Through a haze of pain, she picked up three separate voices, heatedly quarreling over her welfare. The last thing the girl remembered hearing was someone asking her to stay, but she was too weak to respond before disappearing into the blinding light.

Chapter 29

THE PEN AND THE SWORD

WHEN ENID BOLTED AWAKE, she was in her bed back in the human realm. The familiar shades of blue soothed her. Everything was right where she left things. Relief threaded through that she had made it back. Slowly her muscles unclenched, and she released her pent-up breath. She sat up with her pulse pounding at what seemed like a million miles an hour. *Oh, thank goodness my heart was still beating.* How close she had come to losing everything.

Dylan. What happened to Dylan? What about Rhodri and Aeddan? Are they safe? Is Malagant gone?

Enid's mind swirled with questions as she tried to make sense of what had just happened. She looked down at herself and she was wearing the same bloody clothes she had been wearing in the battle. Enid shuddered, remembering the terror and the chaos, and that last voice begging her to stay.

She pushed herself out of bed and went to the window, throwing it open and gulping in the fresh air. Enid leaned her head against the cool glass and tried to calm her racing thoughts. If her friends were safe, then where were they?

In the opposite corner of her room leaned Fail-Naught and her quiver with the remaining hawthorn arrows. Enid looked at her bedside table and saw the chrome flashlight. Enid was grateful for proof that the entire experience in the fae realm wasn't a hallucination.

She almost started crying when she detected movement downstairs. Tears fell when her father called upstairs, "Enid, are you ever coming down to eat breakfast?"

For a second, Enid's head throbbed. She'd been gone almost a week, and her dad hadn't noticed. But wait—Mr. Ambrose mentioned no one here would notice the passage of time. So, was it the morning after her party? Enid's head swam with all the implications. Her dad called out again.

Enid quickly ran to the door and opened it, her voice shaking as she tried to sound casual. "I'm coming, Dad. I just woke up a little late this morning."

Enid cleaned up, threw on fresh clothes, and flew down the stairs and into her father's waiting arms. He hugged her tight and Enid allowed herself to feel safe for the first time in she couldn't remember how long.

"What's all this about?" Enid's dad asked.

"I'm just relieved everything is back to normal, and that you've made me breakfast," Enid replied.

"Yes. I must admit I'm glad your party is behind us," Enid's dad said, misunderstanding what Enid meant.

"Definitely." Enid's laughter mingled with her dad's, but she was grateful he didn't know the danger she'd just been through.

The meal consisted of the best food Enid ever tasted. It was just sausage, eggs, and fried mushrooms, but to Enid, it was the first solid meal in days since entering the fae realm to find her friend. She skipped the cup of tea, though, deciding she may never drink the stuff again. Maybe coffee would become Enid's new morning beverage.

Her father then talked about the party and how much fun everyone had. The power outage was discussed, but no evil queens, fierce dragons, or friendly wizards were mentioned. Her father asked a question that almost stopped Enid's heart again. "Are you upset about Dylan?"

"W-What about Dylan?" Enid had a white-knuckled grip on the table edge in fear.

Did Dylan not make it? Is he hurt? Has he been discovered? The possibilities were so staggering, Enid almost burst into tears again.

"I think he is leaving with his cousin for the continent tomorrow. It's a shame they must leave just before the holiday. Didn't Dylan mention he would go abroad to spend a semester of school? What was the cousin's name again?" Enid's father hummed a little as he washed dishes, his back turned to face the sink, so he didn't see Enid's shoulders slump in relief.

"Aeddan, Dad. His cousin's name is Aeddan." Enid reached for another sausage.

"You didn't like the cousin much, did you?" Her father glanced over his shoulder at Enid and winked.

"Oh, I don't know. He grew on me during the party. He's not all bad." Enid remembered all the trials they had faced together. Enid hoped Aeddan's sister Anna was healing, but it would probably take some time.

"Oh. Another thing—I couldn't find Bendith this morning. Have you seen him?" Mr. Davies asked.

"No, but I'm sure he'll be just fine." Enid thought back to her last conversation with Rhodri, hoping it was true.

"I hope so." Enid's dad looked out the window and then Enid noted concern reflected in his eyes. "After what happened with your mother, I can't help but worry about everyone."

Enid stood and walked over to her dad, giving him a big hug. "I know, but I'm sure everything will be alright."

And Enid believed it. She had faced some of the biggest challenges of her life and come out the other side. If Enid could make it through that, she could make it through anything and hoped Rhodri could find his way as well.

"By the way, the boys mentioned they'd like to stop by later to see you before they leave on their trip, and we are invited to a send-off dinner tonight at the Roberts." Enid's father turned to dry his hands on a dish towel.

Oh no, another party, she thought.

Enid hurled herself at her father again and gave him the fiercest hug possible. "I love you so much, *Dadi.* Thanks for everything."

"I should feed you fried mushrooms more often, *cariad bach,*" her father said with a smile in his voice. He chuckled and returned his daughter's hug with a fierce one of his own.

Several hours later, Enid was busy hoovering the rugs in the dining room. It was hard to believe she had just been through a wild adventure in another realm, and now everything was back to the way it was before. Her hands shook a little when putting away the vacuum. *Not everything is the same*, a voice whispered. She wondered about Dylan and Aeddan. Would Rhodri show as well? After everything that happened in the other realm, it left her thinking, *what do I say to them?*

When she heard steps at the front door. Her father answered and Enid heard voices laughing and chatting about the weather and last night's party. After a few moments, her dad called her to the study where Dylan and Aeddan waited.

She needn't have worried about what they would say to each other. No words were necessary. All three friends gave each other a fierce hug.

When they finally let go, Aeddan spoke first in his typical snarky fashion. "Hello, little dragon, I am relieved to see you made it safely back to your realm. When you vanished like that, I thought Dylan was going to burst a blood vessel." Aeddan chuckled and clapped Dylan on the back.

Dylan blushed at Aeddan's comment. "I hate to admit it, but Aeddan is right. I was a mess. I'm glad you're safe."

"I'm glad to see you both. Is Rhodri here with you?" Enid's glance strayed to the study door, waiting for her other friend to enter.

The princes shared a look and Dylan said, "He disappeared right after you did, Enid, and no one has seen him since. I thought he might be here with you. We haven't spotted him in Ellyllon."

"Oh, no. I hope he will be okay." Enid's heart, bursting with happiness at the reunion, became much heavier with this news.

"Do not worry about Rho, little dragon. He is pretty tough. If we run into him, I will mention that you were anxious and would like to see him, right?" Aeddan offered.

"Yes, please do that. How is Anna? Is she alright? And what is up with the corny nickname?" Enid asked.

"Thankfully, your cursed arrows turned Malagant to stone. After that, the survivors regained their vitality. Anna was one of those few and she is getting stronger daily." Aeddan explained. "And 'little dragon' suits you much better than 'human', and it is true since you will always have a tiny drop of firedrake."

Dylan's head snapped to Enid, "A drop of firedrake?"

"Please don't ask," Enid said, shaking her head. "I'm glad Anna and the others are on the mend."

"They survived because of you," Aeddan said.

"No. It was because of all of us working together." Enid corrected.

"Well, I am grateful to you for helping Anna." Aeddan gave Enid another quick hug. "And I have something for you. Dylan mentioned humans exchange gifts at this time of year." He brought out a package wrapped in brown paper and tied it with string and handed it to Enid.

Enid took it from him and unwrapped it. Aeddan's knife that Enid had left behind in Afallon was revealed. "This blade now belongs to you," he offered. "It is a fitting sword for a fierce warrior."

"Thank you, Aeddan." It touched Enid that Aeddan had gifted her something so important to him, and her tears were close again. "I'll treasure it always."

Aeddan and Dylan took turns explaining what happened after Enid disappeared. Rhodri's brother, Prince Gwynn, arrived in time to help secure the Gwyllion palace and took over as a temporary advisor of the Mountain Kingdom.

Many in Afallon hailed Dylan as a hero. Dylan insisted Enid deserved the credit. At his last statement, Enid wrinkled her nose and said, "Again, group effort." She didn't want all that credit and responsibility. It made her feel anxious, somehow.

"Who concocted the 'semester abroad' tale?" Enid asked, changing topics.

"I did, because of my parents. Aeddan, would you mind giving us a moment?" Dylan asked.

"Sure thing, cousin. I might go to the kitchen to see if there are any leftovers. Your father is an excellent cook." Aeddan said and sauntered out.

After he left the room, the tension eased a bit and the two friends chuckled. "Honestly, Enid. I'm not sure how you traveled through Afallon without killing him."

"Your cousin takes some getting used to, but he has a good heart, and he's funny." Enid smiled, remembering their spats.

Dylan's smile faded a little. "I wanted to explain to you why I'm going back."

Enid reached for Dylan's hand. "No explanations are necessary, Dylan. Afallon is your home."

"Both Celliwig and Afallon are home to me now. I have my parents and friends here in this realm. And it turns out I have family in Annwyn too. I have an uncle, and I'd like to meet him. Aeddan has agreed to travel with me."

"Oh, Dylan. That is wonderful news, and I'm so happy for you. Wow. An uncle." Enid's face lit up with a genuine grin.

"I figure I will stay there until fall break and then come back here," Dylan said.

"That's a brilliant plan." Enid said.

"I want us to keep in touch while I'm gone, so I hope we can still write to each other." He said while rubbing his palms on his jeans. *Was he nervous?* she thought.

"Of course, we can write, but the postage rate might be expensive." She chuckled.

"I obtained something special that should assist us to keep in touch. It's not as lethal as Aedan's gift but can be used to defend yourself." Aeddan handed Enid a box wrapped in silver paper.

When she opened it, a beautiful midnight blue pen with a sharp gold tip was revealed. "Oh, Dylan. I love it."

"And the bonus is that it will never run out of ink. Tonight, you'll get the matching stationery, so you can see my replies. But

I wanted you to have the pen now, so you can get hold of me, day, or night." Dylan blushed.

"This is perfect, Dylan. Thanks. How will you keep in touch with your parents?"

"I've planned for postcards to be sent, and I will give new meaning to the term long-distance phone calls," Dylan said.

"Good. Because I know they'll miss you terribly." Enid thought, *I'll miss you, too.*

"I'm a little nervous about meeting my uncle. Do you think he'll like me?" Dylan sounded uncertain.

"How could he not like you? I'm so glad to hear you have a family there too. It's fantastic news," she said.

"I keep telling myself it's like going away to school, but I'm going to miss everybody, especially you." Dylan's lips pulled down as he studied his hands.

Enid reached out for one and squeezed. "I will miss you, too. I'm glad you're traveling with Aeddan. You need to keep each other safe."

Dylan looked down at their joined hands, and then back at Enid. He slowly leaned closer until their breaths mingled. "Enid..."

The study door banged open, and Aeddan appeared with a plate full of fluffy pastries. Enid wouldn't get to hear what Dylan was going to say next. "Uh, sorry, but Mr. Davies sent me in with snacks."

Dylan and Enid sprung apart, both blushing furiously. "Did I interrupt something?" Aeddan asked.

Enid stammered a negative reply, and Dylan a positive one.

Dylan's glance lingered on Enid as he mumbled they had to get back to the Roberts to help set up for the dinner party.

"Humans have a lot of parties. See you tonight, little dragon." Aeddan winked at Enid.

Enid hugged both her friend's goodbye but gave Dylan an extra squeeze. "Be careful." She whispered in his ear.

Chapter 30

PREMONITIONS

SEVERAL WEEKS PASSED SINCE Enid's fateful sixteenth birthday when her understanding of the world changed. She had time to process her experiences in Afallon, though she still was in shock.

One day, she had an unexpected visitor at the cottage. "Hello, Enid. How are you? No ill effects, I take it?" The illustrious wizard gave her a wink.

"Thanks for asking, Mr. Ambrose. I'm just fine." Enid set aside the furniture polish and dust rags and took a seat by the fire. Mr. Ambrose nabbed the other chair.

The shopkeeper looked resplendent in a crushed blue velvet coat, bright red breeches, and a yellow waistcoat. On his head was a red-striped stocking cap like one of Santa's elves would wear. "Enid, I must tell you how impressed I am with your loyalty and bravery. I don't think your friend Dylan would have made it through his trial without you."

Enid's cheeks heated at the compliment.

"Oh, I don't know about that." Enid looked down at her hands. "But I had a question for you about your dragon prince prophesies because it required more than just Dylan's powers to defeat Malagant."

"Yes, but the dragon prince's kidnapping incited Malagant's ultimate downfall, didn't it? Sometimes prophecies are tricky and can have multiple interpretations." Mr. Ambrose's eyes twinkled with amusement.

Enid turned serious for a moment. "I met Viviane, Mr. Ambrose. She gave me your message, and she wanted me to tell you she was glad you were free and that she was sorry."

Mr. Ambrose blinked away the sudden moisture in his eyes. "I was very sorry, too."

"She also mentioned that she had met my mother. Do you know anything about that?" Enid asked.

"Met your mother?" Mr. Ambrose looked lost in thought for a moment and then repeated the question. "I'm sorry, dear. I lost a lot during my imprisonment."

"I understand, Mr. Ambrose. But it was worth a shot to ask. My mother travelled to Afallon at least once," Enid said.

He looked Enid in the eye. "Your mother must have been very special. You are a true credit to her, and I am so grateful to you for everything you have done."

Enid gave him a warm smile. "That's alright. I'm just glad I could help."

Mr. Ambrose nodded and said, "You are a courageous young person."

Enid beamed at the compliment. "But tell me, Enid, what do you plan to do now that your adventure is over?" Mr. Ambrose asked.

"I'm going to finish school, of course, and then I'm going to travel." Enid replied. "There's so much out there, and I'm determined to see and learn as much as I can."

"An excellent plan," Mr. Ambrose said with a smile. He leaned back in his chair and looked at Enid. "I wonder if those plans include a return trip to Afallon. After all, you have friends there and are hailed a hero. How did you come up with the plan to defeat the queen?"

Mr. Ambrose appeared wide-eyed with curiosity when Enid explained that she'd remembered a strange fact from a long-ago school trip to the aquarium. She learned octopi have three hearts instead of one like most creatures, and she put that together with his clue.

Mr. Ambrose nodded and said, "I knew you were a bright young person. All knowledge is magic."

Enid cleared her throat. "None of us would have made it without the others. I'd say all of us are heroes."

"Oh, you are so humble. I know it would gratify your ancestors to know they made the perfect selection for the ring." Mr. Ambrose clapped his hands as if satisfied with solving a complex puzzle.

"Ancestors? What do they have to do with my ring? Who are you talking about?" Enid leaned forward with a face scrunched in confusion.

What is Mr. Ambrose suggesting?

"Well, Enid, I would have thought the answer was perfectly obvious. I'm talking about Sir Cai and Lady Sulis, your distant great-grandparents. They wanted you to have that ring." Mr. Ambrose nodded and pointed at the silver ring named the Ring of Dispel that hadn't left Enid's hand since she picked it out at his shop on her birthday. "And they were right."

Enid's eyes bulged at the implications. "What?"

Mr. Ambrose continued his story. "You are directly descended from Sir Cai, Arthur's foster brother, and Lady Sulis, a powerful witch, from your mother's side of the family."

"Sir Cai and a witch? But how?" Enid leaned forward in her chair.

"Well, Sir Cai met a woman warrior on his travels with Arthur. She belonged to a coven of nine witches. He fell hopelessly in love with Sulis, their champion. She returned his regard but declared he must defeat her in a battle to test him. Sir Cai trained relentlessly to achieve his actual goal. Not to get the object of power, as the legends claimed, but to gain the hand of the woman who had stolen his heart. Luckily for you, things went in Sir Cai's favor."

"What you're saying is incredible, but why was the ring hidden away? Why wasn't it just passed down through the family from my mother to me?" Enid unconsciously rubbed the ring that still hadn't left her finger.

"That ring holds powerful magic. After Arthur's rule ended, the ring was hidden so someone could never misuse it. Sulis knew where I was trapped by Viviane." He paused there a moment and his words trailed off.

Enid couldn't blame him if he couldn't finish this part. After all, Merlin had been cruelly betrayed by love, stripped of his spells, and imprisoned for centuries. He continued, "Unfortunately, Sulis could not free me, yet she tied the Ring of Dispel's protection to my magic."

When Mr. Ambrose paused again, Enid asked, "Why did she do that?"

He cleared his throat and took up the tale. "They prophesied no one would discover the ring until someone from Sulis' line inherited her magic. I don't believe it was supposed to take so many centuries. The ring chose you, and the tree freed me."

"It freed you..." The pieces clicked into place for Enid.

"Yes, though I'm not entirely sure how that happened." Mr. Ambrose said.

Enid shook her head in wonder at the tale. "Everything you're telling me sounds like the stuff of legends." It was everything she'd ever imagined in all the stories she and Dylan had play-acted through the years, come to life.

"It is all true, Enid. And now it's time for you to write the next chapter." Mr. Ambrose nodded and leaned back in his chair with a twinkle in his eye. "I believe great things are in store for you."

Mr. Ambrose claimed Enid had inherited some abilities from Sulis, through her mother, and she needed to train. That very day in her father's study, Mr. Ambrose offered her a job as his shop assistant and apprentice, where she would learn the ways of magic. Enid had to train her mind, power, and sword. She would learn how to harness her powers. She hoped her mother would be proud of her decision.

Dear Enid,

Hi. I miss you. Your last note was a little shocking. Magic lessons with Mr. Ambrose must be tough, but I'm sure you'll master them. Don't turn yourself into an owl or anything, because he might forget how to change you back.

Everybody here is doing fine. Aeddan is always getting into something, but you were right about his good intentions. When he's not trying to show off, he can be fun (but a little infuriating). And before you ask, yes, he is still calling you a little dragon. I'm fine with it, if I don't have to call him big dragon (ha, ha).

I'd forgotten how beautiful Annwyn was. It reminds me a little of Llandudno, but more medieval in style. The beaches are amazing, and I can't get enough of being in the water. Unfortunately, Aeddan swims, so no break on that one, and there is no such thing as pirates here. Can you imagine that? Yet knights are literally everywhere. You'd love it.

My uncle is impressive. He is my father's brother, and he's been telling me what it was like for them to grow up together. I guess my dad was a prankster when they were younger.

You were right. It's awesome to hear all the stories, even if our loved ones are gone. I feel closer to my dad when my uncle talks about him, which is a lot.

It's been exciting to get to know everybody here, but I miss my mom's cooking. The food here is different, and I prefer the human realm's cuisine.

It's funny, but sometimes I think I see you skulking around when we go into the village. I guess I miss you more than I thought, right? It is weird, though, because I swear, I can smell you as well. Possibly, I'm getting a little homesick.

The countdown for a human realm visit has begun, and I can't wait. My uncle has been teaching me to cast a portal, which will make traveling easier.

Write back soon, and give me some details about your recent adventures, please? I need some distractions.

Yours,

Dylan

DYLAN MADE NO MENTION at all of Rhodri's fate. Enid inquired about her missing friend in her notes, of course, but Dylan had no new information. She was concerned and had many sleepless nights and haunting night terrors from worrying about Rhodri. Her dreams were full of feral growling, slashing claws, and danger. Enid tried not to dwell on them too much.

Deep down, she realized Rhodri needed time to recover from the loss of his twin. She hoped he surrounded himself with his family, sharing in their grief and healing.

Enid wrote Dylan as well, describing her magic lessons, which were challenging but fun. She told Dylan about her and Zoe's plans to study at Shrewsbury College for their A-level exams.

Enid was careful not to mention the lingering after-effects of their adventure. She easily startled now and always on guard for danger, expecting the worst. She barely slept anymore, and those final indelible moments with Malagant haunted her at the oddest moments. Enid decided not to burden Dylan with all of that. He would feel responsible.

Working at Mr. Ambrose's shop part-time helped and added excitement to her afternoons. One day Tommy Brighton, the bully who threw rocks at her all those years ago, entered the shop. Enid expected him to be nasty toward her, but he wasn't. He treated her just like anyone else. She supposed since she had grown through her experiences, maybe Tommy had too. Enid hadn't realized it, but she needed that closure. She didn't have to hate those bullies anymore. She could move past all that.

Mr. Ambrose had become a welcome fixture in her extended family circle. He and her father had grown close. Why, just last week, Mr. Ambrose had surprised Enid's family with movie tickets. Enid also invited Zoe, who always loved to see a movie.

Zoe declared that Mr. Ambrose was hilarious, and his unique views on history fascinated Enid's father so much that Mr. Davies considered having them published in a book.

It was Sunday, and Mr. Ambrose had given Enid a rare day off from training and working at the shop. The free time was so unusual, she almost was at a loss about what to do with herself. But then she came upon the perfect plan for the day. Enid stole a tart from the kitchen and rode her bike to the lake on the neighboring property. When she missed her friends, she often visited this spot. Somehow, she felt closer to them there. However, today the lake didn't have its usual soothing effect.

After a few hours of trying to concentrate on reading one of her dad's latest books, Enid gave up and headed home. The sun would set soon, and she intended to help prepare supper.

As Enid pedaled her bike out of the trees on the path from the lake, she spotted a tall figure standing by the spot where the fairy circle had been. Distracted by the sight, Enid's bike hit a large rock, and she swerved and tumbled.

Enid winced from the cut on her knee, but as she stood up, she noticed the tall, dark-haired figure was still there by her house. *Did it have tendrils?* Enid's pulse pounded in her throat, and she ran.

But the figure ran too, and Enid could hear breathing as it caught up to her. Enid screamed as something grabbed her arm and spun her around. *Isn't this the ending I'd always expected?* But then she saw a face.

"Dylan. You scared me half to death. What are you doing here?" Enid asked.

"Sorry for the surprise visit, Enid. I didn't mean to startle you. I just really wanted to see you," Dylan said.

Enid's pulse still raced, but she smiled at Dylan's boyish grin.

"I've missed you, Enid," Dylan admitted.

Enid's heart melted, and she threw her arms around his neck and clung tightly.

"I've missed you too, Dylan," Enid said.

They moved a little apart to take in the sight of each other. Dylan slowly closed the distance between them again. He gave Enid ample time to pull away. She didn't. Dylan traced her lips with his, and Enid's knees grew weak. She couldn't help herself. Her lips parted, and every thought flew from her head. Her heart was beating so fast, she wondered if it would burst. Dylan's lips felt so right as he finally kissed her.

Enid's eyes fluttered shut, and she surrendered to the moment.

When Enid came up for air, Dylan was resting his forehead against hers.

"Wow," he said. "I didn't expect that."

"Me neither," Enid admitted. She was still trying to catch her breath and calm her racing heart.

Dylan took Enid's hand and led her to sit on the front steps of the cottage. They sat in silence for a few moments, just looking at each other and smiling.

"So, does this mean we can go on a date now?" Dylan asked with a grin.

Enid blushed and nodded. "Yes, we can go on a date."

Dylan leaned in and kissed Enid again, and, for that moment at least, everything was just right.

"It's good to be home." Dylan sighed in her ear.

As he placed his arm around her and held her close, she knew there was nothing more perfect than a tale of sleeping dragons and the girl who woke them up.

ACKNOWLEDGEMENTS

WRITING ANY NOVEL IS a lot like embarking on a long strange journey. You definitely want trustworthy companions for such a Herculean task.

Luckily, I have the best family. My patient husband, lovable daughter, genius siblings, and supportive mom were all there for me when it counted, at the beginning when fragile dreams can be so easily crushed. My wonderful group of friends of over twenty years (the Unicorns) also cheered me every step of the way. You guys rock.

I also had the privilege of working with extremely talented professional collaborators who helped me tell this story. This is a shout out to the Girl with the Red Pen, Wgoulart, the Literary Consultancy, and editors from both Fiverr and Reedsy. I really appreciate all of your efforts.

I'd like to give a special thank you to Melissa Stevens who designed this beautiful cover.

Finally, I have to thank you, the reader, for spending your time with Enid, Dylan, Rhodri, and Malagant. You inspired me to make this possible. If you would consider leaving a review and letting me know what worked and what didn't, I'd appreciate it. Cheers.

Continue reading for a sneak peek of S. Ramsey's upcoming sequel to *Tales of Witches and Wyverns*.

Epilogue: A Crack in Reality

Dusk settled in over the quaint cottage by the edge of the forest. The day had been especially warm, but now a cooling breeze flowed through the trees. The sun made a fiery spectacle as the rays dipped below the western horizon.

Fireflies started their light show by dancing cautiously around a form paused just inside the tree line and hidden from view. The shape shifted, revealing piercing golden eyes that studied the cottage with an unwavering intensity.

The crickets began their evening song, as the figure tensed while witnessing another passionate embrace and the young couple entering the cottage. The sight left the shadow shaking with a suppressed emotion. An all-too-familiar agony pierced through the heart, and, if not carefully contained, might devastate everything. The wounds left by recent discoveries still bled.

The silhouette focused on the task at hand. They couldn't afford distractions when the stakes were so high. Everyone sacrificed so much already.

No matter the cost, Enid must be warned.

The form released a long-held sigh and shook its head. In the end, everyone assumed their adventures were well behind them. However, the shape appreciated better than anyone that things were far from resolved. Their first adventure only scratched the surface.

How to inform the others? The figure considered its options after witnessing Dylan leave, and the cottage lights dim. Everyone appeared safe for now, but how long would it last?

When Enid looked so happy, was it even right to take away her newfound joy?

The silhouette almost admitted everything to the girl. All day long, it shadowed Enid and witnessed as she pined for her absent friends. The girl looked so sad that the figure almost revealed itself.

She would only get pain from the truth. The shape stayed in the shadows, waiting. Soon, action would be necessary, and Enid would understand everything.

The dragon prince was not the only one with debts to pay.

Before the girl went into the cottage, she glanced back into the forest right at the spot where the form waited. Did she sense who waited there? Did she mark the shadowy presence? For a moment, the silhouette recognized a look from the girl as Enid peered through the darkness. The old knowledge shone through and appeared locked away inside the girl.

The power would come out. But when?

The shadow remained until the last cottage lights winked out for the night, and then it too slipped away into the trees. The silhouette melted back into the darkness and waited for morning. Things were about to get interesting. After all, their adventures had only just begun...

Enid would have to be told soon. The time for secrets had long passed.

ENID'S GRIN HADN'T LEFT her face since Dylan's return, but something was wrong. Something about him seemed different like he was hiding something.

The night Dylan came home was the first night in months that Enid experienced her 'Dylan' dream. How could she forget his haunted face? The light and love that made his eyes shine earlier today appeared non-existent in her nightmare. He appeared an embittered shell of his current self.

This time, Enid tried to ask him questions about this dream. How best to help him? She desperately needed to know the answer.

In response, Dylan studied her with eyes containing no spark. To her insistent pleas, he said, "You stabbed the hearts, but has Malagant gone?" He opened his mouth, and a river of ice flowed from his lips.

The crystals built up and took on a shape. Enid watched helplessly as a form emerged. She knew if it completed the transformation that it would be the end of everything she loved most.

Enid reached out to Dylan to shatter the ice. Instead, Malagant's smoky tendrils enveloped her. *Wasn't Malagant gone?* Enid's heartbeat thundered in her ears, and she was certain it would burst. This dreamscape suddenly seemed too real.

Enid cried out for Bendith, but no help came. Pain welled up from inside her. The dream-Dylan's eyes filled with horror as he gazed at her. Something was... *wrong.*

Thankfully, she jolted awake. The dream left Enid shaking. *What was all that about?* She suspected Dylan was still in danger. She tried to convince herself it was only a dream, but a familiar sense of dread had resettled in the pit of her stomach. Enid had to warn Dylan, but about what, exactly.

Enid spent the rest of the night in a daze, her mind racing with old questions and fears. *What did the return of that nightmare mean? Was Dylan still in danger?* And if so, could she help? *Was Malagant somehow back?* This question alone made her tremble.

The next morning, Enid planned to tell Dylan everything. Even if he didn't believe her, or thought the dreams meant nothing, she still had to try.

Enid found Dylan in the forest where they had arranged to meet. He perched casually on a fallen log, looking lost in thought. The sun dappled through the gaps in the canopy and bathed him in a flickering glow. When he saw her, his eyes lit up from within, and he smiled. For a split second, Enid forgot all about the nightmare. Any concern chased out of her head with a single smile. Seeing Dylan this happy made her happy, too.

But then reality returned, and her exuberance dimmed.

"Hey," she sat down next to him. "I need to talk to you." She brushed her shoulder affectionately against his.

Dylan's smile faded a little, and he turned to gaze at her with a troubled expression. "What is it? Is something wrong?"

Enid tried to talk to Dylan about what's been going on. "I feel as if there is something you're not telling me. I sense danger. This isn't like before. If we want a deeper relationship, you need to trust me."

Dylan insisted everything was fine. "Enid, if something is going on, I'm not aware of it. I won't hold back from you again. It's probably just my sudden surprise appearance. I'm sorry I scared you yesterday."

Enid took a deep breath before she began her story. "It's not just fear. I get these strange dreams that warn me of danger. Last night, I had another one, and I haven't dreamed like that for weeks. You still might be in danger."

Enid lowered her gaze, clearly embarrassed.

She seldom told anyone of her dreams, and she wasn't sure what to expect.

Dylan was quiet for a moment, deep in thought. Finally, he spoke. "I think I know what this is about Enid. There is something I should have told you earlier, but I wasn't really certain of it myself, and I didn't want to sound paranoid." Enid looked up at Dylan, her eyes wide with anticipation.

"I've had a sense I was being followed, since the day I left for Annwyn." He trailed off as Enid gasped.

"I'm not sure who it could be, or what their intentions are." Dylan placed his arm around Enid's shoulders comfortingly.

Enid now knew there was at least some truth behind her nightmares, and although it scared her to face such danger head-on, she felt relieved to have finally told Dylan. And he listened to her, instead of deflecting the conversation. *That was progress, right?*

So focused on each other, the couple didn't hear the footsteps behind them until it was too late.

"I've been waiting for you," a voice said from the darkness. Dylan's eyes flared with icy fire in response as Enid turned to spy a familiar figure lurking in the shadows of the forest. "We need to talk." Rhodri stepped into the clearing.

It overjoyed Enid to see her lost friend and relieved her that at least his outward scars were healing. So absorbed by his sudden appearance, she almost missed his next comment. "Something is wrong... *off*. It's hard for me to explain. Can't you both sense it? And Enid, it's complicated but I believe I've seen your mother."

Made in the USA
Columbia, SC
18 December 2023

28901435R00157